❖❖❖

I . was puzzled that Malcolm asked me to marry him," Valerie said carefully.

"Oh, that," said Reggie. "We tossed dice, you know."

"Dice, of course. I understand," she said, not really knowing what he was referring to.

"Thought you would understand," said Reggie cheerfully. "Well, when your brother died, it was the only thing to do. We all knew you were left alone. Couldn't leave you like that, so we tossed dice over you. See which would look after you. Malcolm lost."

❖❖❖

Amethyst Love

Rebecca Danton

A FAWCETT CREST BOOK

Fawcett Books, Greenwich, Connecticut

AMETHYST LOVE

A Fawcett Crest Original

© 1977 by Rebecca Danton

All Rights Reserved

ISBN: 0-449-23400-2

Printed in the United States of America

10   9   8   7   6   5   4   3   2   1

Amethyst Love

"Miss Gray, there be a young gentleman in *uniform* to see you!" The young maid was bobbing and beaming with excitement. Nothing much happened from day to day but work and more work. This was something to talk about!

Valerie Gray sprang from the rocking chair, still clutching the baby, the youngest Bloomer child, a fat drooling infant who invariably cried much of the night. "A gentleman—who—is it my brother, Clarence? Did he say Clarence Gray?"

She had grown even more pale with hope. Could it be? Could her brother have returned from the wars on the Peninsula and dashed to her rescue? She had written, telling him of her situation. She had had to sell Gray Court, even the furniture, to meet the debts of her dead father. And then Clarence's debts.

Oh, how she had prayed every night that Clarence might return and require her for his new household. That he might be miraculously cured of gambling, settled down, more calm. Cured of his reckless rakehell ways, of his wild companions. And needing her! Needing her to come and live with him.

"I couldn't say, miss. He do have some grand braid about his shoulders," said the maid hopefully. Who could work up much delight in the sight of a mere brother? But a young gentleman friend, that was more like!

Valerie turned over the baby to the maid, brushed down her apron over the snuff-brown dress, and without waiting to push back the brown curls under the unbecoming gray mobcap, she walked out of the nursery. She was trembling. An officer to see her, perhaps Clarence, perhaps one of his fellow officers with word of his safety . . . Her heart beat wildly as she made her way down the long stairs to the second floor, then to the first.

Mrs. Job Bloomer was waiting her in the hallway. A plump middle-aged matron, shrewd, cold, jealous of Valerie for her youth and the fact that she had once been mistress of the grand Gray Court, she had taken Valerie in, as a distant relative must, but made her understand she must work for her living. "I'll have no idlers here, miss," she had said. And she kept her word. Valerie worked with all six of the children, tutoring the older, caring for the younger.

Valerie was a bit dizzy this morning. She had not slept well, she had been up much of the night with the baby, who was teething. And she was thinner than ever, overworked, undernourished.

"There be a gentleman for you, Valerie," said her cousin, with intense disapproval. "I was going to forbid him to enter. You know I do not approve of gentleman callers, especially during working hours. But he would see you and said he had a-come a distance for it and would not turn back."

"Is it—my brother?" Valerie asked hopefully. "Clarence?"

"No. A Major Villiers, he said."

Valerie's shoulders drooped. Hope died a little. He might have word of Clarence, but Malcolm Villiers was no substitute for the beloved brother she had hoped to see.

"Half an hour, then, no longer, then back to work!" said Mrs. Bloomer, and retreated.

Valerie nodded with resignation and went to the small

back sitting room. She opened the door and found the room cold on that January day of 1809. No fire was in the fireplace. The gentleman in the mud-splashed uniform was striding up and down vigorously, trying to keep warm by swinging his arms.

He turned at once as she entered. She managed a pale smile. "Major Villiers you are welcome, sir. How good of you to come all this distance."

She searched his handsome face anxiously. He seemed tired, stern, the light amusement and teasing gone from it. As he came toward her, he was limping heavily.

"Miss Gray, it is good of you to receive me." Their hands clasped. Even in the cold room his was vigorous and warm. Hers felt chilled.

"Pray be seated. I am given a half hour to speak with you, sir. My brother—you have news of him?" She could not keep from asking him at once.

His handsome full mouth tightened to a hard line. He gestured to a chair, she sat down. He lowered himself carefully to a chair opposite her. He grimaced as he noted her look at his right leg. "Bullet in it, invalided home for a short time," he said briefly.

"I am so sorry, sir," she said politely, on edge for news of Clarence. Her chapped, reddened hands clasped and twisted in the apron.

"I am 'mazed to see you in these circumstances," he said, finally. "Clarence said you had to sell Gray Court. Would you mind telling me what has happened? You have the money from it?"

She wondered wildly if Clarence were in debt to this officer. If he had come for money from her, he was completely out of luck. "I regret, sir, that it was necessary to sell Gray Court," she said, with forced composure. "After my father's death, his debtors pressed me until I had to sell the house. I wrote Clarence about it, he wrote back only to tell me to pay also some debts of his. I was forced to sell everything, furniture—even the—family portraits."

Her voice choked, she composed herself again with a great effort. The experience had been intensely humiliating as well as personally agonizing.

"I am sorry. Very sorry to hear it." He bit his lip, stared at the floor. "I am sure Clarence did not realize the extent of the debts. He kept on—I mean . . ."

"Gambling? I regret, sir, if he owes you aught. I have nothing at all with which to pay you. Nothing. I work for my food and room, that is all." And now the bitterness did reveal itself in her voice and face. She swallowed. "What—what news of him? I pray you, sir—" She glanced anxiously at the door. She would not be surprised if Mrs. Bloomer should come in and order her back to work at any moment.

Still the officer did not answer her directly. He studied her face with a frown, he glanced at her red hands, her thin waist. "You are so changed from a year ago, Miss Gray," he said, finally. "I should not have known you. That dress, it is dreadful!"

She smiled faintly. Malcolm Villiers had been as blunt as herself, she had liked him for that, so different from the fawning compliments of others intent on getting their way with the wild Clarence's sister. She had felt more secure with this younger son of the Earl of Arundel. He was an all right, as her brother had said.

"I must wear it for my work, Mrs. Bloomer insists," she said, in a low tone. In spite of her frightful appearance, Mr. Job Bloomer had not been averse to pinching and touching her whenever his formidable wife was not about. Valerie had hated his touch and hid from him in the nursery. But he had pursued her, and the older children knew it and taunted her about it.

"You cannot remain here," said Major Villiers abruptly.

"I cannot do anything else, I am not trained," she said, thinking of the wasted education of her brother, the money spent on tutors, while she, hungry for knowledge, was denied even a governess. Women did not need learning, it spoiled them, said her father, and that was that. She had managed to sneak into the library while her brother was being tutored. She listened, memorized, read avidly in English, French and German, teaching herself much of the time.

Malcolm Villiers seemed to be thinking deeply. Finally he cleared his throat, straightened out the leg which pained him, and began again, "Miss Gray! I regret very much that it is my—duty, my responsibility, my pledge— to inform you—that I—well—" He finally faltered, meeting her clear, anxious brown eyes.

"Sir?" She was holding her breath. "Clarence—he is— wounded?"

"He was wounded, yes." Villiers flinched from the look on her face, half turned from her, but finally finished what he had to say, like a man. "I regret so much, Miss Gray, to be the bearer of such sad news. Your—esteemed—loved brother—Clarence—has died—in battle."

The silence in the room was intense. She was still staring at him, willing the words to be changed, to be taken back, to be removed from her consciousness. It could not be. The death of her only close relative, her reckless, laughing, loving brother . . . his death . . . leaving her alone in the world, with only cold, distant relatives who cared not a fig for her . . . no one to care what happened to her. Her hopes were dead as his body . . .

"No," she whispered. "No . . . no . . . no . . ."

"I regret so much . . . so much . . ."

She put her hands to her face, fighting against a cry of despair and anguish. She was trembling with the shock, the horrible feeling of being so alone. What would she do? And poor Clarence, so full of life, so eager for experiences.

Malcolm came over to stand beside her, to take her hands, to chafe them in his own big warm hands. "I regret so much," he said more strongly. "That I should have to tell you—this horrible news . . . You must be brave and strong, Miss Gray. He died in a most valorous way, saving the life of the Colonel. The action was fierce, he jumped up and ran forward, into the path of the bullets. He died instantly, he could have felt no pain. . . ." His voice went on and on, but she scarcely heard what he said.

"Poor Clarence," she finally said in a dull voice, her hands still in those of the major. "He enjoyed life so much. And he was but twenty-three. So young, so brave, so splendid . . ."

"He was all that. And all honored and loved him. I—I brought back his body with me, Miss Gray," said Major Villiers very gently. "It is to be buried at Arundel. I promised him before—well, when I heard about Gray Court, and he was concerned—if aught should happen to him. . . ."

"That was good of you, so good and kind and—and fine." She managed to choke it out. "When . . . when . . ."

"As soon as we return," he said. "Oh, yes," he said, to her surprised look. "I shall take you back to Arundel with me. You will wish to see him properly buried, I regret you cannot see him. He is—sealed in—in his coffin. His uniform was brushed and fine, we put flowers in with him before . . ." He was stammering, but she pressed his hands tightly with hers.

"Thank you. Thank you." She whispered it, her eyes tight shut against the tears.

She released one hand, groped for a handkerchief but found only her apron. She raised it to her eyes, found a fine white lawn handkerchief pressed hastily into her hand by Malcolm. She held it to her face. It smelled of a faint masculine scent, somehow reassuring. She wiped her eyes, gulped back a sob. Men hated tears, Clarence had always flung out of the house when her mother cried.

She managed to say, "Thank you—very much. I should like to return—for the—funeral—but Mrs. Bloomer . . ."

"Valerie," Malcolm took her hands tightly in his again, speaking urgently. "You can't stay on here. Surely you can see it is impossible. That dreadful woman! Sorry . . . she *is* your cousin! But she is horrible! You must come back with me to Aurndel and let us look after you. Matter of fact . . . I promised I would take care of you. Promised," he repeated impressively.

She shook her head drearily. "You owe me nothing— but thank you. I shall—take care of myself. . . ."

"You can't," he said bluntly. "Listen, Valerie. I know I'm the younger son, no prospects. Good old Eustace is the heir, and all that, don't begrudge it to him. I'm no farmer! Let him look after the lands. But we could have a good time of it, when I get home again. Want you to marry me now."

She blinked, her long lashes wet with tears, her brown eyes dazed. Was he mad? He seemed sober, not drunk. His hazel eyes were close to hers, he was studying her intently. He was slim, vibrant, medium height, like Clarence. But somehow full of intensity, seriousness.

"You see, I promised solemnly that I would take care of you, Valerie," he said, as she did not speak. "Promised! Sacred word. And I'm not old enough to be your father, and you're not young enough to be anyone's child. I'm sort of a guardian to you, word of honor. But how can I look after a young lady like you, unless I marry you? So it's got to be marriage, Valerie."

She did not follow his reasoning. It seemed wild to her. She kept shaking her brown head, the long bobbing curls escaping from her gray mobcap. "No, no, I cannot, Major Villiers. Thank you—I'm sure. But I shall manage. . . ."

"You can't manage, Valerie. You're a woman! For women, there ain't anything to do but teach or marry. And I'd hate to see you wasted on other women's children," he said.

Poignantly, his words struck home. Other women's children. Sometimes, nights, when she had rocked the unattractive, spoiled, Bloomer baby, she had longed for a little one of her own, sweet and cuddly, her own child. Not one with the red round face of Job Bloomer, and the fretful nature of his wife.

She sighed deeply and kept shaking her head. There had to be some other answer.

The brief knock on the door did not wait their reply. Mrs. Bloomer opened the door and stepped in. "It's long past half an hour, Miss Gray," she said, sternly disapproving. "The gentleman must go now." Her small eyes showed her curiosity. "Bad news?" she asked eagerly.

Valerie put the large white handkerchief to her eyes. She felt dizzy and overcome. It was all too much. The thought of going back upstairs and taking care of the baby, the older ones . . . their lessons and the monotonous routine of the drills . . .

Malcolm Villiers spoke for her. "I regret to inform you, madam, that Miss Gray's brother has been killed in action on the Peninsula. He died bravely, honorably, saving his Colonel's life. I have come to take her back to Arundel with me. The funeral will be held as soon as we arrive."

Mrs. Bloomer's thin mouth gaped in surprise. "Dead, is he? Well, I'm not surprised. A more reckless, thoughtless, young man I have yet to meet!"

Valerie gave a stifled sob. This cruelty, on top of all . . .

Major Villiers said, very coldly, "That is not how his country looked on him, Mrs. Bloomer. His Majesty has sent a personal letter of regret and a wreath of flowers and laurel. Now, time is growing short. I propose to take Miss Gray back with me, yet today. We can make it by late evening if we start at once."

"Take her away? Indeed, you will not," said Mrs. Bloomer, indignantly. "She works for me, sir! She'll not absent herself, not without making a peck of trouble for herself! I'll get Mr. Bloomer to speak to you, I will!"

"Miss Gray is now under my protection, Mrs. Bloomer!" Major Villiers drew himself up, so he appeared more than his height. "She returns to Arundel with me. My parents are anxious to greet and console her, as her brother's friends are also."

"She don't need to go nowhere," said Mrs. Bloomer flatly. "He's dead. No need to go into such a fussy dither about it. She stays. Besides, her beau is coming this evening. Mr. Bloomer is going to give his permission to wed. The squire is quite a catch, he is."

Valerie gasped aloud. She jumped up. "The squire? Oh, no, I have not said I would . . . oh, Mrs. Bloomer . . . you know my feelings on the matter! I have said I would not receive him again!"

The squire, Phineas Kastner, was a widower of some forty years, with four husky young demons, as the villagers said. He had had his eye on Valerie since she had arrived, just the one to take his four in hand, he said, beaming and looking her up and down like a prize cow.

"Nonsense, you cannot remain here while a fine young man like the squire is asking for you and needing you." Mrs. Bloomer's cold eyes belied her friendly manner. Valerie realized the woman had seen some of the pinching and touching of her husband, and she was not about to allow him his little pleasures. She shuddered. Between Job Bloomer and Phineas Kastner there was not much choice. She detested them both—and feared them.

"Madam, you have the situation completely wrong," said Malcolm, stepping between them easily. "Valerie Gray is promised to me. She is to marry me, so that I might offer her my protection, now that her brother is deceased. I propose to take her to my mother at once. Our marriage shall follow shortly."

Mrs. Bloomer gulped, so did Valerie. What choice did she have? She hated it here. Perhaps if she went with Malcolm, he might be able to find her another more acceptable post, or his mother would be sympathetic with her longing to work in a more congenial place.

So she remained silent, as Malcolm took the situation in hand.

"You will go and pack at once, everything you have, Valerie," he said, in a tone his men usually obeyed immediately. "I shall send up my footmen to bring down your trunks. Ask a maid to assist you; I wish to be upon my way practically at once. The carriage is standing, and the horses will be chilled."

Valerie looked at Mrs. Bloomer, aghast, puffed with fury, baffled, arrogantly sure of her right to rule. She looked at Malcolm Villiers, strong, straight in spite of his injured leg, the keen look of his eye, the clean-cut face.

"I'll go—pack at once. I shan't be long," she said. She raced from the room as though demons were at her heels. She ran up the stairs, to the third floor where the back room was hers.

Cold, chill, barren, but for the two small trunks and the valise which she had brought with her. She did not glance again at the room until the maid had helped her pack her few garments, her pitifully few possessions from her old home. When all was in the trunks, they were closed and strapped. The valise was shut, she put on her worn cloak, and then she took one last look about.

The grayish white bedroom, with the wind whipping around the beddrapes so that they rustled constantly. The tiny mirror, cracked along the side. The white-painted night stand with the small jar for hot water, the china basin. It had been a bleak home for a year, but now no more.

The maid's face was beaming with excitement. All the gossip she would have to relate tonight! Even the butler and the cook would be quiet while she talked, thought the girl. They would want to know every detail.

"Where would you be a-going, Miss Gray?" she ventured.

"To Arundel," said Valerie Gray. "My brother is dead, I must see him buried. Then—I'll see—"

The footmen came up, carried down her trunks easily between them. Valerie followed with her valise, the maid watched until she had turned the bend in the stairs.

Malcolm waited in the hallway, his face stern, his hat on his arm. His cloak was folded about him, he was obviously ready to go.

Valerie paused at Mrs. Bloomer's side. "I wish to thank you for taking me in, when I needed . . ." she said, steadily. "I am—most grateful to you and to Mr. Bloomer."

Mrs. Bloomer's red face expressed her exasperation. "You don't show it, walking out like this! Let me tell you, cousin or no cousin, you won't be coming back here! There'll be no welcome this time! You left us in a bad way, with no one to look after the little ones, no notice and all!"

"I regret that," Valerie began. Malcolm interrupted.

"Her friends may wish to send their condolences," he said, seeing to loom tall in that small hallway. "You may tell them to address Miss Gray in care of my father, the Earl of Arundel, at Arundel, Kent."

"The Earl—of—Arundel?" whispered Mrs. Bloomer, suddenly pale.

Malcolm bowed, and took Valerie's valise from her. "Come, Valerie. We must be on our way at once."

Mrs. Bloomer trotted after them, toward the front door. "But—but you didn't say—Earl of—Arundel. . . ." She was crying piteously after them. She was probably thinking of the small dark sitting room, the unlit fires, her manner toward Malcolm.

In the coach, Valerie sat back with a shudder of weariness. Malcolm, unstrapping his valise, said, "You must wear a heavier cloak. I have one here, of Scottish plaid." So saying, he took out a thick crimson cloak and draped it tenderly about her. It was so thick, so warm—like a blessing folded around her sore, aching heart.

"You're—very—kind. . . ." She shivered into the cloak,

cuddling under its warmth with pleasure. She leaned back against the velvet squabs. It was such a comfortable coach, tight against the January cold, rolling along on well-sprung wheels. She roused enough to say wearily, "But I cannot marry you, you know."

"Yes, you will," he said positively and leaned back to rub his thigh. "Deuced leg. It'll take a couple months to come right. Mother scolded me for coming after you like this, but she'll say I'm right. Miserable house, horrible female! How did you stand it, Valerie?"

"When you have to, you must," she said.

"Right you are. Found that out in Portugal," he said reflectively. He sighed, stretching out the leg. "I'll talk, if you don't mind. Gets my mind off the beastly leg."

"Oh, please do go on. I'm so sorry about your leg. Is there anything I can do—I mean, I do have some experience with nursing the children. . . ."

"One of the footmen takes care of it each night," he said. "Pours on stuff, stings like the devil, but eases it. I'll be all right. Oh, we change horses at Waterton, get a bite to eat, then on. Should be home by late evening. All right with you? Or we could break the journey somewhere, stay overnight. Mother said no, though," he added dubiously. "Your reputation and all."

"She sounds—most considerate," said Valerie. "Tell me about her."

It was like a dream, this journey, with the handsome young man drawling along about his family, his ambitions, the battles.

He told her about the family first. "Mater is fidgety, always fussing. But she's good and has sense under the flutters. Father is always off about the estate. He loves to putter in the garden too, grows some prize roses, you should see them. You *will* see them," he added with a smile down at her, huddled under the crimson cloak.

He told her about Arundel.

"It ain't one of your big drafty castles. It's a smaller

place, we like it immensely, been in the family about four hundred years. Too small to catch the eye of a king, so we kept it," he added with a small laugh. "Comfortable, too, you won't have the wind catching your ankles every turn of the hall. We'll have the suite in the west wing, I like it best."

She opened her mouth to protest that, but he went on cheerfully about his family.

"Eustace is a good sort, moody, and not too well sometimes, but a fine chap. Rides to hounds like the best, stands up in quadrilles every dance. Engaged to Lady Deidre Ramsey. Now *she* is a beauty." There was unmistakable admiration in his tone.

She listened and memorized all he said. Eustace Villiers, the Viscount Grenville, the heir to the Earl of Arundel, was about three years older than Malcolm, then about twenty-nine, Valerie figured. He was serious, too, took his duties well, said Malcolm. Rode about the estate when he wasn't in London.

Deidre was a beauty, blonde hair, blue eyes, stunning in any color she chose to wear. She was now living with them, as they had announced their engagement. Hannah, Countess of Arundel, was schooling her in her duties. Besides, they all liked having her about.

The more Valerie heard about the charms of Lady Deidre, the more her own feelings sank. She could never compete with such a nonpareil. No, best to attend the funeral of poor Clarence, then be off on another position, hopefully a better one than before.

Malcolm reached into his pocket, drew out a small box. "Brought this along. Mother let me poke about the family treasures before I left," he said. "I recalled how you looked in a violet gown one night—remember the party when Clarence had his twentieth birthday? You wore violet." He flicked open the lid, took out a ring. It was a huge heart-shaped amethyst, deep purple in hue, glowing in the dim light of the coach.

He took her hand, pulled off the worn glove, and shoved the ring awkwardly on her finger. It was a little loose, but not a poor fit. "Oh, but you should not—you told your mother?" gasped Valerie.

"Yes, she remembered you, she'll approve," said Malcolm confidently. "There's more of the amethysts. You'll like them—a necklace, and a bracelet, and some drops for your ears, and a pretty little tiara with diamonds in it. Later I'll get you some other stuff, but I always liked this—you know what it means. It's steadiness, and that sort. . . ."

Valerie did know, she had read all kinds of books before her father's library was sold. Amethysts meant steadfastness in love and friendship. Perhaps that was ironic, she thought. Perhaps . . . perhaps it was a hope for their future. She leaned back with a sigh, admiring the beautiful ring on her rough red hand. Was it so crazy then, to think of marrying Malcolm? He was so sure, so strong. It would be pleasant to lean on his strength . . . if only . . . if only . . .

She did not know where her thoughts were leading her. She fell asleep against the velvet squabs, worn out by her work and by the emotions of the day.

Chapter Two

Valerie spent the next few days in such a turmoil of emotions that she felt quite drained. The funeral of Clarence had taken place at once. He had been buried in the family crypt of the Arundel home, and she was intensely grateful to all of the Arundels for their kindness and extreme courtesy to her.

The countess had taken her firmly in hand. The west suite was already prepared for her when she arrived, exhausted, at midnight. A maid had been assigned—Glenda, fiftyish, severe, devoted to the Arundels. She had unpacked swiftly, settled Valerie in the immense canopy-covered bed, and left her to sleep. In the morning, she had appeared again, with a teatray of silver, cups of the finest china in blue and gold, with the Arundel crest on them.

As for the Earl of Arundel, he was a very pet, thought Valerie, with a sigh. He was graying, heavy-set, bluff, kindly, with twinkling brown eyes. He escaped family discussions and dissension by disappearing into his precious gardens, roaming about in more disreputable tweeds than the head gardener, poking carefully about the roots of his precious roses, or tying up vines, or digging in the vegetable beds.

Eustace had been so kind, he might have been her brother, transformed into a thoughtful, serious, grave young man. It was to Eustace that Valerie finally confessed her doubts.

"You see, Malcolm takes it for granted that I shall marry him. But indeed, I can make a living for myself. I can be a governess. Though I have no formal schooling, I can prove myself in French and Latin and German. I can watercolor and paint, I draw commendably, and spell . . ."

Eustace had listened to the end, drawing on his pipe, studying her vivid, eager face. He had not cut her off nor told her not to be foolish.

He nodded when she reached the end. "That's your side of it, Valerie," he said, in his calm tones. "Now, maybe I should present our side of it. Malcolm's, if you wish."

"His side?" Valerie was frankly puzzled. They were seated in the earl's study, where Eustace also had a desk. The earl's secretary, quiet capable Mr. Louis Kenyon, was across the room, scratching away at the accounts. She thought he heard what they said. But everyone trusted Mr. Kenyon, everyone knew he was devoted to the family. He was a distant cousin of the earl, with one foot shorter than the other, so that he limped heavily. The earl had taken him in when he was a lad and trained him to the work. "What side has Malcolm? He cares nothing for me, he loves to fight, and lives only to return to the Peninsula. He told me so himself."

"That is just exactly the problem." Eustace puffed on his pipe, smiled an apology, and laid it aside carefully in a large ashtray with the family device on it. "The mater has worried over him for years. Thinks he'll end up in some battlefield, or a gaming hell, or worse, with a mistress who'll sink her claws into him. She likes you, so do we all."

"You mean, if he marries me, he might settle down." It was a discomforting thought, rather humiliating, thought Valerie, to be married for such a reason! Yet . . . yet if she could help the sweet, fluttery countess, or the blundering, gruff, likeable earl, who would like to do so. They had been kindness itself to her.

"Exactly. You are a good girl, of good family. Oh, I know you have no money, but we have plenty," said Eustace comfortably, disposing of that problem with a wave of his slim, graceful hand. "Mater likes you. Father thinks you understand gardening, and there could be no greater compliment! Seriously, I am often in London, as my fiancée enjoys the delights of it. If you and Malcolm were about, I could go with an easier conscience. Together, we can all run the place, with less work for father. If only Malcolm would sell out . . ." Eustace frowned down at the desk, his face suddenly in older lines.

"But surely there are more acceptable ladies . . . I mean, he must have met dozens of females, some with titles . . ."

Eustace nodded ruefully. "Oh, yes, dozens. Hundreds. But never has he expressed a wish to marry any of them! We thought he would never marry! But suddenly he comes home, and says he will marry you, and no other! We are vastly astonished, but so relieved. Mater prays every night that you may persuade Malcolm to sell out and remain home," he added simply.

The countess said much the same thing, her vague brown eyes peering at Valerie hopefully over her sewing. "If only, Valerie dear, you might tell Malcolm that you wish him to remain, he might listen to you. He has never listened to us," she told her plaintively.

Valerie hesitated, torn between duty and independence, and also a longing to be coddled and cared for as she had never been. Her recent years had been nightmares of nursing her mother, then her father, worrying about Clarence, trying to think what to sell next to meet the debts of the gambling father and brother. Then the horrors of life as a servant in her cousin's household. And the squire shoved at her . . . She shuddered.

"I have so longed to have a daughter," said the countess. "I wanted a little girl so much, and I had two big burly sons! No one to dress in pretty muslins and bows. Do you like colors, dear? I do wish we did not have to dress in black. . . ." She sighed.

Valerie glanced down at her pale violet muslin with the black ribbons on it. She had refused to let them buy gowns for her, only a black bonnet for the funeral, and she had borrowed a black velvet cloak of the countess. "Clarence would not like it," she said gently. "He detested black for mourning. And he liked to see me in pretty colors."

The countess smiled, and patted Valerie's hand with her own fragile, slim, white one, alight with diamonds. "What a dear boy Clarence was, to be sure. I quite liked him the best of Malcolm's friends," she said gently.

And Malcolm himself . . . He was just calmly sure she would marry him. "Of course, Valerie," he said. "There's nothing else quite so suitable. Mater is looking forward to chattering with you all day, and father is sure you will help him with the estate. Of course, I shall return to the Peninsula as soon as my leg is well again. . . ."

His hazel eyes lit up, as they did when he mentioned the battles there. Valerie looked at him worriedly. He did remind her of Clarence, so reckless, so gallant, so courageous. And so foolish. He would dash into danger, just like Clarence, and get himself killed. And what good would it do? Just so old Bonaparte should not have Spain and Portugal! What kind of good would that do anyone in the world, thought Valerie, with a recklessness that would make a British general shudder.

Lady Deidre Ramsey had departed for a visit to her own home for a month. Valerie was glad of that, she felt ill at ease with those sure, cool blue eyes studying her. Lady Deidre had been presented at court three years before, and had torn a swathe through the ranks of the gallant beaux, said the countess proudly. She was the catch of any season, and Eustace, quiet though he was, had caught her and had his ring on her slim finger.

How Lady Deidre would smile if she saw Valerie's uncertainty! She detested anyone with a pretense of learning, she had drawled, gazing significantly at Valerie. She had met real scholars in the drawing rooms of London, brilliant men who guided our country's destiny. Any young mouse like Valerie would scamper for cover, said Deidre, with a gay laugh, at being caught in an argument with one of the real wits!

No, Deidre was not one of Valerie's favorite persons. And the thought of living in the same mansion with her, huge though it was, was enough to dampen her spirits further.

She sighed again. Malcolm, lounging at ease in the sitting room of the west suite, looked at her thoughtfully. "Why the wind blowing?" he teased her gently. "You cannot endure the thought of settling down to domestic bliss with me?"

"I don't want to marry at all," said Valerie bluntly. "Oh, we have been honest with each other, Malcolm. I don't think you want to marry any more than I do! So why not let it be! I can search for another living, perhaps your mother can recommend a position to me. I am sure I can become a governess, and not have to work so hard as I did with Mrs. Bloomer's children. I should enjoy teaching, it is a noble profession. And I could read all the books I choose—"

"Arundel has an excellent library," said Malcolm. "Besides, I ain't about to let you become a bluestocking. Ruin you, it would. Come on now, say yes. Mater is anxious to arrange the wedding. It will be a quiet one—in the family chapel. But she wants to invite half the county—"

"I don't want to marry," said Valerie, setting her mouth.

"You cannot manage on your own," said Malcolm,

equally stubborn, his firm mouth set in even harder lines. "Come on, now, Valerie, give in, do!"

He sounded so like Clarence coaxing her, that tears filled her eyes. He quickly took advantage of that, patted her hands, kissed her cheek, and coaxed her, until she had agreed to his plan.

The wedding was held in the chapel in a week's time. The countess gave in to Valerie's request for a very quiet wedding, and invited only some twenty-five persons. The local squire and his family, the parson and his family, several cousins, with Eustace to stand up beside his brother, and the earl to give her away. They were all so kind, so jolly. And Valerie had been lonely and afraid.

Perhaps they were right, she could not manage by herself. And it was terrifying to think what might happen, should she become ill from overwork, from eating poor food. What if she landed in another such family as the Bloomers? She might die in a few years. She was young and hopeful, she did not want to fade and die.

The dressmaker in the village had taken the cloth that the countess had given her and had come up in record time with a lovely wedding dress of white silk covered with fragile white lace like a spider's web, with small lace flowers caught in it. The veil matched it, and the small train swirled about Valerie's white slippers. The mirror showed her with great dark eyes, brown curls to her shoulders, and the hair in back caught up in a Psyche knot. Real pearls were at her throat and in her ears.

Malcolm wore his splendid uniform and limped scarcely at all. He met her at the altar, gave her a grave smile, spoiled it with a quick wink, and altogether behaved as though it were a great lark to get married. He was the life of the reception, teasing Valerie, teasing his mother who wanted him to get married so his wife could look after his buttons, teasing his brother that he should get married soon, or Malcolm would have more children than Eustace.

The earl was gravely pleased, patting Valerie's hand, telling her he had been sure she was a right one for Malcolm. Only Lady Deidre, hastily returning, seemed to disapprove of the whole proceedings. She looked more grand than the bride, in a stunning new-fashioned blue silk gown, cut low at the neck, like the French, covered with a blue velvet cloak, with blue sapphires at her throat and ears. Valerie felt demure as a mouse beside the grandness of Lady Deidre's shining blonde curls and brilliant blue eyes, and elegant conversation.

The reception was over by midnight. Valerie retired to her bedroom, grateful for peace and quiet. Glenda came to help her remove the fragile gown and veil, the little white slippers, to rub her feet that felt so cold and tired.

She helped Valerie into the white negligee and nightrobe of white silk and lace, a present from the countess.

"My lady, the countess, says as how she is sending for new dresses for you from London," said Glenda, a little chattily, for now Valerie was one of Them, married to Mr. Malcolm.

"Oh, dear, I told her not to," said Valerie, yawning. "She has given me so much—"

"But you must be properly dressed for teas and such, ma'am," reproved Glenda. "And they'll be giving balls. You'll be going up to London, and may be presented at court."

Valerie stared at her. In all their arguments about her marrying, this had not come up. They had one and all spoken of how much she could help with the estate, assist the countess, perhaps divert Malcolm from going back to war. Balls? Being presented at court? She had never considered that! She sat on the edge of the bed, thinking, worrying. Because of their poverty, the Grays had not partaken of London's hospitality and grandeur. She had lived a quiet life, and now she much preferred books and a stroll in the garden.

"There, now, if you'll just slip into bed, I'll blow out some candles," said Glenda, beaming down at her, as Valerie obediently slipped into bed like a child. She drew up the covers under Valerie's chin. "I'll just keep a couple alight for Himself," she said, and blew out the candles in the stand near the wardrobe.

Valerie was closing her eyes as the door closed behind Glenda. All of a sudden, the words sank home. For Himself? For whom? For Malcolm? But he couldn't come in here . . . he could not . . . They had never discussed it, but Valerie had thought they would gradually become acquainted . . . but he had scarcely kissed her! He had scarcely touched her, except to help her up the steps, or into a coach, or in a dance!

The door opened softly, and her eyes popped open. Malcolm came in quietly, setting his boots down near the door. He was staggering a little. His leg, or too much drink? She sat bolt upright in bed, holding the covers to her.

"Don't come in here!" she ordered firmly.

"Now, don't be silly, Valerie," he said, and struggled out of his jacket, cussing it a little. "Damn buttons. I should have had my valet unfasten me first. Get that button, will you, Valerie?"

And he sat down on the side of the bed and offered his sleeve to her. The fine white lacy cuff had become entangled in the buttons. Her fingers trembled as she unfastened it. He took out the fine diamond studs and laid them carelessly on the night table.

"Nice wedding," he said, getting up, and shrugging out of his shirt. "Not a big-fussy one . . . can't stand fusses . . . just friends about. You looked pretty, Valerie, quite pretty. I like you in white. Mean to get you some more dresses from London, the mater reminded me."

"I d–don't need more—" she began, still sitting rigidly up in bed, staring at him in the dimness. "M–Malcolm, what—what are you doing?" The words were a squeal, as he unfastened his trousers and began to push them down.

"Doing? Getting undressed, Valerie," he said practically, but a little devilish grin quirked his large mouth. "You don't think I'm so uncivilized as to go to bed with my spurs and boots on, do you? Though there was a fellow in Portugal, just got married, and he—"

"Malcolm!"

"All right, all right," he said, with a laugh. "You're not used to my stories yet." He reached for his long nightgown and she closed her eyes, and turned her face away.

"Malcolm, please. We did not plan this—I mean, I did not think you would take advantage—I mean, we scarcely know each other, and—"

He did not answer. She cautiously opened her eyes, to find him blowing out the last candles, and then coming toward the huge bed. He closed the large canopies against the night cold, and slid his length into the long bed. Then he reached for her.

"M—Malcolm! Please, don't!"

His mouth on hers smothered the words, his long arms were unexpectedly hard and tight about her. He drew her to him, and his hands were smoothing over her shoulders, her arm, down to her waist. She felt one hand on her young breast, so rounded, so soft—and he caressed it with his fingers until the nipple stood up against his palm.

She made one more weak protest, then was silent. It was no use, he had her mouth closed, his hands seemed everywhere at once. He was kissing her with violence, passion, yet tenderness, and she had never felt such a storm of emotion breaking over her.

His mouth pressed against her bared shoulder, then roamed over to her throat, where the pulse beat madly. "Soft, sweet," he said, in a sort of groan. "Oh, Valerie—" And his lips nibbled at her breast in a kind of savage worship. "You're such a pretty thing."

A pretty thing! She felt outraged and flattered all at

once. She had prided herself on her sharp mind, her quick memory. Malcolm laughed at her longing for more knowledge, he scoffed and took a book out of her hands when she tried to read. And he just wanted her body, she thought bitterly.

But she could not think coherently after a while. His kisses, his embraces were rousing emotions in her she had never felt before. And when he leaned to her and took her completely, she was shocked, shaken, overwhelmed.

He slept, later, his arm flung across her in careless hard possession. She was longer getting to sleep, her brain a—whirl with new thoughts. So this was what happened when married people went to bed. And no one had ever told her! Would she have a baby at once? Or—what else went on? Her skin felt on fire from his caresses, she knew her body would show bruises in the morning. His hands had been so tight on her thighs, pulling her to him.

When she wakened, the curtains were pushed back. She stirred, lazily, felt a hard leg against hers.

"Ouch," said Malcolm, plaintively. "Love, that's my bad leg. Do you want some tea? It's almost cold."

She turned about, shocked, to stare up at his hazel eyes. He was sitting up against the pillows, the white nightshirt casually opened at his brown throat, drinking from a teacup. The tray was beside him on a night stand.

She felt one wild blush of embarrassment. To be in bed with a man! She sat up primly, drawing the covers with her, to her throat. He laughed down at her, his gaze on her bare arm.

He bent, and kissed the arm nearest him.

"Don't," she said automatically.

"You're sweet in bed," he said. She gave him a helpless look, then turned away. She did not want to remember the wild night they had had, the fight, then the surrender of herself.

"You shouldn't talk about it," she scolded feebly.

"Why not? We're married," he said. He leaned over,

poured out the cup of tea for her. "It's warm," he said, and handed it over. She sipped slowly, to make it last. She could not, could not get out of bed before his eyes.

Malcolm finished his cup, set it down, got out of bed. He grimaced as he came to his feet, his hand went automatically to rub his thigh. "Damn leg," he grumbled. "Excuse me, Valerie. Mater said I should stop cussing while I'm home."

"Could I—I mean, could I—fix your leg for you?" she asked timidly.

"Oh, it's a mess, you don't want to see it," he said.

He was obviously in pain. She reached for the white negligee, managed to get into it before getting out of bed. "Where is the medicine?" she asked.

"I'll get my valet to bring it, and some hot water," he said. "You sure you want to do this? It looks horrible," and he seemed downcast about that.

"I'll do it," she said. When the valet had brought the medicine and a pitcher of hot water, Malcolm sat down on the edge of the elegant bathtub in the bathroom, and exposed his thigh. She stifled a gasp of sheer horror.

It was a real mess, the bullet had torn a jagged hole in his thigh, and ugly purplish flesh had bunched up around it. Malcolm watched her face as she bent to examine it. "Don't—if it makes you sick," he said quietly.

"It must hurt you badly," she managed to say. She poured some of the medicine into a bowl, added hot water, and began to sponge the wound. He flinched, she paused. "Oh, I'm hurting you more!" she cried in distress.

"It has to heal," he said, philosophically. "And your touch is easier than my valet's."

She forced herself to continue, bathing until the water was cool. Then she applied salve, and a fresh bandage over the wound.

He thanked her. Somehow that little service to him made her feel easier. He called his valet, who was setting out his clothes in the smaller bedroom beside hers. He gave him orders, about his clothes, an event that evening.

Valerie rang for her maid, and the door closed between their rooms. Valerie sat down, hugging herself against the cold. She felt as though she had grown up overnight. Her wedding night, the way Malcolm had embraced her, and now this morning, she had tended to his wound.

She was a married woman, a wife.

Glenda brought a request from the countess. "She would be pleased to receive you at eleven this morning, if you will, ma'am," she said.

Valerie nodded. She dressed in a white muslin, tied the lilac ribbons below her breasts in the new high fashion, and sat down to eat her breakfast from the tray the maid brought. Malcolm came in to join her, sitting easily across from her, splendid in his tweed coat and riding breeches.

"Do you ride, Valerie?" he asked easily.

She shook her head, "No." They had not been able to afford a stable of riding stock, only two horses for the carriage.

"I'll teach you. There's a mare that should do well for you," he said. "What about this morning?"

"Not today," she said, flushing a little. She felt sore and bruised. He only nodded.

"Maybe tomorrow," he said. He rose, finished his coffee standing up, then strode from the room.

She went to the countess, who greeted her with a cool kiss of the cheek, and a gentle smile of approval. "I thought we might talk for a time, dear Valerie," she said.

What she wanted to talk about, Valerie soon discovered. The countess must have had her orders to school Valerie in the ways of society. Valerie hid her humiliation, and listened quietly as the countess talked of titles, how to address certain ranks, the duties she would perform.

"Does Lady Deidre also do these things?" asked Valerie presently.

"Oh, yes, at her home. Here, she is a guest. One day, she will take over as Countess," said Hannah Villiers, a shadow flitting across her plump serene face. "But she will know how to act. She was presented three years ago. You have not had her experience."

Valerie left the session with a secret rebellion in her heart. She did not want to be schooled in the ways of society. She wanted to read, to study, to prepare herself for teaching. She was not at all sure she would be happy here in this great manor house, or in London, a timid mouse in the midst of butterflies like Lady Deidre who looked at her with cold eyes.

She sought out the earl's library, gave Mr. Kenyon a timid smile. "I thought I might read for a time, Mr. Kenyon."

"Of course, Mrs. Villiers. May I recommend this chair near the window? The light is much better here." And the graying man limped over to the chair, tugged it into place beside the window.

She thanked him, chose a book, and sat down, to lose herself in it until luncheon. Malcolm sought her out, a scowl on his handsome face.

"Reading again? I told mater to inform you about some of your duties and give you some idea of what is expected of you," he said angrily. "And she was to make up a list of gowns for us to order from London. Have you done that?"

Valerie stiffened. "No, I told her I needed none," she said, frigidly.

"Nonsense! You need dozens of gowns, and some cloaks, and boots, a riding habit. I looked through your wardrobe. Why, Deidre has a hundred times what you have!"

"I'm sure she can afford them," said Valerie, with offended dignity.

"Pooh. Mater and Eustace order them all, and father pays the bills. Deidre's family don't have a cent," said

Malcolm, with crude frankness. "She's a doll to dress, says Mater. And you don't hear her going all wildcat over the matter, either!"

Valerie bit her lips, to refrain from saying that Lady Deidre did not have her pride and independence, either.

Within a week they had a visitor. One of the officers of the same regiment as Clarence and Malcolm came to call.

He was Captain Reginald Darlington—Reggie to his friends—and all the world was his friend. He was young, handsome, with fine blond curls, vivid blue eyes, a gentle nature. One confided in him, as in a brother. He had been badly injured and after recovering, his aged aunt had persuaded him to sell out and remain in London with her. He escorted her about and had gay stories to tell of London.

He walked with Valerie in the gardens while Malcolm was out riding over the estate with Eustace. "I say, I am sorry about Clarence," he said with sympathy. "Was there at the time, you know. Dashing fellow, we all loved him."

"Thank you, Reggie. I shall miss him sorely," she said. She had quarreled often with Malcolm this week, her heart hurt her. She was bewildered, scarcely knowing where to turn. Malcolm wanted to groom her into a lady of quality, present her to society. She was timid and unsure of herself, therefore the more belligerent about remaining with books. Malcolm had finally made up a list of clothes without her approval and sent off for the items. They had fought over that, and he had not been in her bed for two nights.

Presently Reggie said, "I wish I had been the one to come after you, Valerie. We might have made a match of it, instead."

She stiffened, his tone was odd. She said, carefully, "I was puzzled that Malcolm came for me. I did not think he and Clarence were so close, though you were all friends."

"Oh, that," said Reggie, who had had a bit too much

wine for luncheon, and whose tongue was usually loose anyway. "We tossed dice, you know."

"Dice, of course. I understand," said Valerie, thinking he spoke of some gambling during the night camps.

"Thought you would understand," said Reggie cheerfully. "Well, when Clarence died, it was the only thing to do. We all knew you were left alone, and your last letter to Clarence was read aloud. Couldn't leave you with that horrid lot, so we tossed dice over it. See which would look after you. Malcolm lost."

She froze. It was an intense effort to continue walking in the cold February weather, across the wintry garden, her cloak closely about her. Carefully casual, she said, "Malcolm . . . lost . . . the toss of the dice. And so . . . came home . . . and after me?"

"Yes. He did tell you, didn't he? Wounded home, anyway. So was I, and four others. We all tossed for you. He lost," persisted Reggie, earnestly. "Could have cussed when he saw the way it turned out. Never wanted to marry, he said. But you're a pretty girl. I shouldn't have minded losing. Time I settled down myself."

Alternately burning and chilling, Valerie did not trust her tongue to say anything. In silence, they walked back to the manor. She excused herself and fled to her bedroom. She paced the floor, rehearsed burning speeches, pictured herself fleeing forever from the hated marriage.

She had never felt so humiliated, so bitter. The officers had tossed dice over her—over *her*, who hated gambling with a wild passion. Gambling had brought her to servitude, then to a loveless marriage. Dice! Malcolm had *lost* at dice, over her! And he had come home, come to her, proposed marriage, taken her to bed—all without saying one word about it!

Oh, how she hated him! He had been paying a "debt of honor," a gambling debt. They had tossed dice over her! And Malcolm had *lost*!

She caught sight of the ring on her finger, paused to

stare at it. The heart-shaped amethyst shone there, deeply purple against her slim hand, now losing the redness and soreness of the long year of labor. Amethysts. She thought of the matched set which had been her engagement present. Amethysts. Symbol of steadfastness in *love*. And Malcolm had dared to give them to her—for her engagement! How ironic, how bitter!

She raged up and down the room, pounding one fist in the other hand. What could she do? She would leave at once. She would go—but where? She must prepare herself, look for a position as governess. Once she had it, she could not escape rapidly enough from this humiliation! How Lady Deidre would laugh and mock her! A bride at the toss of a pair of dice!

Would she face Malcolm with it? How horrible to do that! And he would face Reggie and bawl him out, perhaps challenge him to a duel. He would not like to have the facts brought to light.

Valerie flung herself into a chair, stared into space. The light rose silk of the chair under her fingers reminded her of the care his whole family had extended to her, their gentleness, their sympathy. A poor way to repay that.

She gazed about the room vaguely, at the rose-hung canopy, the draperies about the huge mahogany bed. At the mammoth mahogany wardrobe with the mirrored doors. The clothes that gathered inside, mute evidence of the countess and her thoughtfulness. The jewelbox on the dresser, full of gifts from Malcolm, the countess—even the earl, who had awkwardly given her a ring of garnets and pearls that his mother had once cherished. No, she could not hurt them like that.

But she could not remain, she thought. Her mind went around and around frantically, considering the possibilities. Malcolm would probably return to the Peninsula, he was already exercising his leg, writing to his commander, reading the gazettes anxiously. She could not prevent him from leaving. Once he was gone, she herself would leave, to become a governess, use her brain, use her learning. She would not endure to remain the unloved wife of a man who had won her—not at cards even—but at the dice!

✦✦✦✦✦✦✦✦ Chapter Three ✦✦✦✦✦✦✦✦

The countess fluttered over the slim white pieces of card. Then she laid down the last ones carefully. "There," she said, pleased. "Imagine, if you will, Valerie," she nodded encouragingly to the girl beside her on the blue silk sofa. "Imagine that this is a dinner table, and you have set everyone about the table. Is this arrangement correct? If no, change it," and she leaned back with a sigh of satisfaction.

Valerie bent to her task. It was all the same to her, whether an earl was seated beside a countess, or a knight beside an honorable. But she struggled with the cards, changed them about, studied them, her finger to her lip, puzzled, until she was satisfied.

"Oh, very good, very good," said the countess, much pleased. "Quite right. Well, that ends our study for today. You have the little book of etiquette? Yes, yes, do study that, a dozen more pages, and we shall quiz you on that tomorrow."

Valerie bowed to her as she left the room, practicing her curtsy. The countess solemnly returned it, then smiled, and waved her away with a flutter of her white hands. She was trying her best to teach Valerie to be a lady. She would be presented next year probably, after the mourning period for Clarence was over.

Lady Deidre passed Valerie, and Valerie held the door for her as she glanced down at the book in Valerie's hand. "Studying hard, my dear?" she asked, with a little mocking laugh. "You have much to learn, I understand!"

Valerie's mouth compressed against her quick anger. She watched Lady Deidre enter the countess's drawing room, heard her mother-in-law say, "Lady Deidre, come in, my dear! We shall have a good coze this morning!"

"I have had a letter from papa," said Deidre, in the little-girlish tone she used with her future "maman" as she called her. "I wanted to consult you about it, dearest!"

Valerie shut the door and went on, her heart bitter. Malcolm's mother obviously preferred Deidre and, of course, Eustace, as the elder, was her favorite. Valerie would probably never be able to do anything right in their eyes! They had held a dinner party for Reggie, and Valerie had been conscious of them all watching her anxiously, to see what she might do wrong! It had made her so stiff and self-conscious that she had spilled her wine on the white lace tablecloth.

She went down to the library, chose a book, and set aside the etiquette book rebelliously. Mr. Kenyon watched her with a slight though understanding smile and came over to her.

"Shall I go over your lesson with you, Miss Valerie?" he asked gently. "Perhaps to speak of it will be easier than just reading."

Reluctantly she laid down the slim volume of Shakespeare's poetry, and took up the etiquette book again. "I should not take your time, Mr. Kenyon," she began.

"Not at all. I am happy to be of service to you. You see, I have the setting of tables for the countess as well as other little duties to perform, which have made them familiar to me over the years. Now, what are you to study this morning?"

She showed him the pages, and he moved his lips silently as he looked over them. "You have read them?"

"Yes, but they are so full of whenevers and whereases and if insteads, that I cannot endure it!"

He smiled and told her what it meant. They went over the pages together for an hour, and he nodded and said she learned amazingly rapidly. That was balm for her sore heart.

The earl came in as they finished. "What, mulling over that dry stuff?" he snorted. "Come on, Valerie, come away with me. Get your bonnet and cloak and some mitts, and we'll be off!"

She smiled at him. "Oh, sir, where are we going?"

"Off!" he said mysteriously. "Louis, tell them we are gone about our duties today and shall return in time for tea—if circumstances do not prevent us!" And he chuckled like a boy, for all his gray hairs.

It was almost twelve. Malcolm would be angry that she ran off without telling him. However, he was off with Eustace somewhere. She gathered up her cloak and mitts, set the bonnet on her head, and fastened the ribbons under her chin. The lilac ribbons and cream straw suited her pretty complexion, so much better for the good food and sleep she had had recently.

She ran down the stairs again and met the earl in the hallway. Furtively, he guided her to the side door, where a groom and carriage awaited them on the graveled road. He helped her in, and they were off.

She giggled like a child. "Do tell me where we go, papa," she said. He had asked her to call him that, and she did when they were alone. He was so sweet and kind to her, more like the father she had longed for than her own handsome, reckless parent. He patted her hands.

"We are going to see my bailiff, then off to the fields," he said contentedly. "I like a clear blue day like this, when I can go and look at the fields, wintry though they are, and plan against the springtime."

She agreed happily and settled back against the comfortable cushions. He talked on amiably about his plans for the summer. He would sow that field in clover, that one in wheat, the other in corn. She looked, agreed, enjoyed the wintry scene. The air was chill, and the wind whipped about, but in the carriage it was comfortable, with the rug about her lap, and her purple velvet cloak about her.

Presently, he said, apropos of nothing, "You must not mind the lessons in etiquette, my dear one. Mother means no insult to your fine mind. She is anxious only that you shall learn so much that you may move gracefully in society. When you learn to know her, you will love her as we do."

Valerie turned her face away abruptly. "I know that, sir," she said, in a smothered voice. "But Malcolm—and I do not wish to be presented to society! We have quarreled over that, I—I don't know what to do. He keeps pushing me to learn more of household management—"

The earl grrumphed and hawed uneasily. "Well, well, I don't mean to interfere," he said finally. "Not my field, no, not at all. But we do long for Malcolm to settle down. Have you talked to him about selling out?"

She shook her head. "He would not listen to me," she said, positively. "He—he longs for the day to return to battle. He and Reggie talk of nothing but battles, and maneuvers, and one general and another. He is just like Clarence, longing for excitement and dangers. And he cares nothing for me," she burst out, her bitterness leading her on.

"Oh, my dear, but he married you," said the earl gently. "He must care deeply for you. Only he is a wild reckless fellow just now. It is up to you to lead him to domestic bliss, and once you have a child, I am sure he will give up all these extravagant adventures."

She shook her head violently, and tears spilled over. She took out her handkerchief and wiped them away, then blew her nose. "He will not," she said. For, she thought, she would never have his child. He did not care for her, he thought only to school her to his way of life, then forget her.

She would not endure it. She would be off about her own adventures, she decided fiercely. She would have adventures of the mind! She would read, study, think, become a governess, maybe a learned bluestocking! A woman should be able to earn her own living in a reputable fashion, gracefully, without leaning on any man!

"Well, well, we'll speak no more of it," said the earl unhappily, and the carriage stopped just then before the bailiff's pleasant stone house. "Here we are, there is Rodger to greet us. There you are, there you are," he said in relief, as the bailiff, grayed and plump, came up to the carriage with a broad grin on his pleasant face. "We came to luncheon," said the Earl, "and your good wife is most kind to invite us."

Rodger Parker helped Valerie down. "You honor us, sir, and Mrs. Villiers. Yes, sir, we've been looking forward to this. You'll not mind all the young ones about, sir? Mother has the care of them while the women are quilting."

Mrs. Parker, tall and lean as her husband was short and plump, stood in the doorway to greet them, a baby clinging to her neck. Valerie came toward her up the path, between rows of fragrant flowers and herbs. The girl drew a deep breath. "Oh, how beautiful it is here!" she cried, in genuine pleasure.

Mrs. Parker smiled at her, pleased. "There now, Mrs. Villiers, you like flowers? You shall have a carriage full to take home with you."

"No, I shall not rob you of these!" declared Valerie. "But how fragrant they are—and what is this?" She stooped to touch a tall blue flower poised on its stalk.

Mrs. Parker named it, then pointed out the pinks and roses, the lilies and stock, all cut back against the winter. "They will bloom in the spring, you shall come then," she declared. "Only my herbs and the strong ones are a–blooming now. But I have flowers the year around in my Shakespeare garden."

Valerie came on into the house, delighted with the pleasant hallway scrubbed clean, the sturdy oak chest and bench, the formal sitting room with flowered chintz covering the maple sofa and chairs. "Shakespeare garden?" she asked. "And what is that?"

"Did you never hear of that?" asked Mrs. Parker. "Well, my mother had one, and her mother before her. When I come to live here, I said to Rodger, I must have my garden, and he fixed it up against the house in the most sheltered place against the winds. All these years, I've had my Shakespeare garden. It's all the flowers and herbs and such that the man mentioned in his plays. One of my sons, he writes down what each is, and where the flower is mentioned in the plays."

The conversation lasted them comfortably through the pleasant meal that followed. Mrs. Parker had felt awkward, having the earl and the new daughter-in-law in her home. But she soon found, as she said afterwards to her best friend, "They was as common as grass, and that easy to talk to. Not that the earl, he was never difficult, you see. But she has no airs about her, and she did hold the baby and dandled him like she knew how."

The earl was quite pleased with the success of his little thought. Valerie had seemed more at ease than in his own home. And later in the carriage, as they drove to the home of one of his tenants, he said, "And how should you like to help me make a Shakespeare garden, Valerie? Eh? Wouldn't that be a project, though? I've got roses, and pinks, and such, but never took it on, to try to put out all the herbs and flowers that he writes about."

"Oh, I should like that immensely," she said, clasping

her hands eagerly. "Just think of all we could put in! Beds of little pansies, and poppies, mint and balm, rue and columbine, and cowslip—oh, let me see—"

"You could look them up in the Shakespeare books," he said encouragingly, watching her eager face as they drove on in the wintry landscape. "Give us something to plan for this winter. We could make starts in the greenhouse, ready to transplant in the spring. We could draw plans—"

In the spring. With a start, Valerie realized she would probably not be here in the spring. She would go away, as soon as Malcolm left.

Her face shadowed. "Or would it be too much work?" asked the earl, quick to see, and sensitive that he might be pushing too much on her.

She shook her head. "I—I would love to do it," she said softly. "If only—" She broke off, and repeated softly,

" 'I know a bank where the wild thyme blows,
Where oxlips and the nodding violet grows,
Quite over-canopied with luscious woodbine,
With sweet musk-roses and with eglantine.
There sleeps Titania sometimes of the night,
Lull'd in these flowers with dances and delight—' "

"Charming, charming!" declared the earl, delighted. He hated to see shadows in the great, wistful, brown eyes of his new daughter. How those eyes changed, as the sun drifted across them, as the huge oak trees shadowed them, and they came out into the sunlit fields again. They showed her moods, her uncertainty. He felt that she was not happy, rumors of her quarreling with Malcolm had come to him through his valet. Cuss the boy, he did not know how to handle such a sensitive girl, thought his father. He cared little for Deidre, she was hard, he thought shrewdly. Behind her cute little ways, she had managed to get quite a sum of money from them, through her engagement to Eustace. And they had bought all her clothes this past year, plus jewelry.

And this girl, married to Malcolm, was too proud to accept hardly anything.

"Well," he said briskly, "you shall help me in my project. Not a word to the others, it shall be our secret. You shall hunt out more sweet verses for us, and we shall enlist the gardeners. What kind of plot shall we make? A square, or a circle, and how much room?"

The discussion kept them through the afternoon, along with a visit to a tenant, a shrewd look over the fields near his cottage, and finally tea with another tenant who had some grievances about his neighbor's cows in his pasture.

It was past five when they left the second tenant. Valerie said thoughtfully, "Did you know, papa, that she has refused to send her children to school? She said that the schoolmaster is cruel to the children, hits them often with his ruler, and forces them to stand out in the cold air when they do not know their lessons. I do like a good master, papa. It does not sound as if he is one. Do you know much of him?"

"He is new this year, the other moved on to a better-paying post," said the earl, scowling. "So—he is being cruel, is he? I'll see about that! I shall have no such complaints! If he will not mend his ways, he leaves!"

They were speaking of it as they entered the great hall of Arundel, cheeks ruddy from the wintry cold, voices eager from their conversation. Malcolm came out from the drawing room, frowning. "Here you are, here you are at last," he said, jealously. "And what has kept you all this day, Valerie?"

She put up her chin. The earl said quickly, "I enlisted her help, Malcolm. She has been riding about with me to the tenants. Good ideas, she has, which we can discuss later. Is there any tea left for us, eh?" And he rubbed his hands briskly, and gave his thick cloak to the butler, as Valerie gave hers to the footman.

Deidre was sitting cosily near the fire as they entered the drawing room. Her dainty blue slippers were up on a hassock, her cold blue eyes studied them as they entered.

"I should not dream of interfering with the tenants," she said, in her little-girlish high voice, smiling demurely at the earl. "I am sure *your* judgment is infallible!"

"You would be wrong," he said bluntly, sitting down near the countess. "I am human, I can be wrong, so can anyone." He smiled at his wife blandly. "May I have some more tea, my dear? It was a long, cold ride."

"It was too cold for you to be out," said Malcolm in a low angry tone to Valerie as she held out her red hands to the blaze. "And you did not tell me where you were going, nor ask my permission."

"You were not about," she said, her head turned from him.

"I encouraged her to come with me," said the earl quickly. "I needed her advice. After you are married to Eustace, my dear Deidre, you will need to learn much about the estate."

Her pretty face was a study at his open rebuke. Eustace gazed thoughtfully at his father and said nothing.

"I hope Mrs. Parker is well?" said the countess gently. She smoothly turned the talk to Mrs. Parker, her children and grandchildren, and the heated atmosphere cooled somewhat.

When they were alone, however, Malcolm did not hesitate to rebuke Valerie again. "You should not have gone off like that. We had guests for luncheon. They thought it very rude of you to be gone."

She sat bolt upright in the huge bed, automatically pulled up the covers to her chin, and glared at him. "Your father asked me to go with him! I am honored whenever he requests me to help him, it is a great compliment! And he has much work to do on the estate!"

"You think more of him than you do of me," said Malcolm sulkily, sitting down in his nightshirt on the edge of the bed. "If I asked you to go riding in the carriage, you would have some excuse! Yet you go off with my father when he beckons—"

Her voice wavered. "He is like my own father—he is so kind, so gentle. Even more thoughtful than my father. And he—he—" To her fury and dismay she began to cry, tears dripping down her face.

Malcolm melted at once. "Oh, darling, don't cry! I can't endure it." He climbed into bed and snatched her into his arms, pressing her head against his broad chest. "Don't cry, love. I keep forgetting you have just lost all your family—don't cry. Of course, they are all your family now, mother and father. I even provided a big brother for you, wasn't I thoughtful?"

He coaxed and teased her until the tears ceased, and they lay together under the covers, and he began to caress her. His big hands were so clever at rousing her emotions, and his kisses nibbled gently over her chin, her cheek, down to her shoulder. He brushed aside the nightdress to kiss her soft skin, over her shoulder, down to her breasts.

He was more gentle with her tonight than he had been for a time. His fingers played with her, he whispered to her how lovely she was, how soft and silky. "A pretty thing, my love, a pretty thing, with your hair so loose and perfumed. I love your hair, I could play all night with it," and he kissed the soft strands, burying his face in them.

Something softened in her, she sighed, and put her arms about his body, drawing him down to her. In silence, they embraced, and she answered his kisses shyly, then more boldly. He had a way of pressing against her lips coaxingly until her mouth opened, then he would thrust his tongue inside, and tease her, until she felt on fire. Sometimes she could forget completely the abominable reason he had married her—over dice!—and relax and yield to his desires.

His hands went over and over her body, down to her thighs, moving up the nightdress so he could caress her silky limbs. A fire seemed to burn in her, and she wriggled and pressed herself to him. He muttered something, deep in his throat, and his kisses became more ardent, until he was pressed to her, and their bodies joined in a wild quest for fulfillment.

But only two days later, they were quarreling again. She had been assigned by the countess to plan the meals for a week. She had fussed and worried over it, going over and over cookbooks, menus, changing and changing yet again, with the patient cook helping her.

"What in the world is this?" asked Deidre one evening, wrinkling her nose over the fish course.

"There's a new sauce," said Valerie, defensively. "I found it in a cookbook—"

"Ugh," said Deidre. "I am sorry, my dear, but I do wish you would refrain from experimenting! I cannot eat this, take it away," and she waved the dish from her.

Valerie looked hopefully at Malcolm, who tasted curiously. He made a face. "Too much vinegar, I think. Tastes like some peculiar thing I had in Portugal." And he too set down his spoon.

The countess set her lips, disapprovingly. "It is not a bad effort, Valerie," she said, with restraint. "Next time, will you consult with me before changing the sauces."

A mild rebuke, from her it was devastating. Valerie felt like crying, especially when even the earl, to please her, could not bring himslf to eat the fish with the sauce. In a strained silence, the guests laid down their forks, the course was hastily removed, and the beef brought in.

After the dinner, Valerie fled to the library, instead of joining the company for coffee. She buried herself in a book of Shakespeare. She would not be with them, she hated them all! She had not wanted to become a housekeeper for Malcolm Villiers, she had not asked to be made a lady he would be proud of. She sniffed, fought back tears, she felt very weepy recently. She wiped her face, thrust the handkerchief away, and strove to find pleasure again in *Midsummer Night's Dream*.

"I say, do you mind if I come in?" It was Reggie Darlington, at the opened door, peering in hopefully.

"If you wish," she said curtly, sniffing back another tear. She wiped her face furtively again, but he saw the gesture and entering, shut the door and came over to the sofa.

"I say, that was too bad this evening, in front of everyone. I should have eaten it right down, and said never a word," he said gallantly.

"You're very kind. But they are all perfect here," she said bitterly, extravagantly. "I'll never fit in, never!"

He patted her hand. "You're a grand girl, Valerie, they just don't appreciate you. If I'd only known," he sighed.

"Reggie, do you return to London next week?" she asked.

He nodded. "Back to Aunt Darlington," he said. "She's a dear, but gets a bit cross—her legs, you know. Crippled up. A regular bluestocking, gruff as can be, but good as gold. Aunt Seraphine is in her seventies, but you'd think twenty years younger, she is so bright and keen."

"I wonder—if you would do me a favor."

"Anything! Are you coming up for the season? Deidre wants another bang-up season before she settles down to marriage and hum-drum," said Reggie eagerly. "I'll show you about if Malcolm ain't here—"

"No," she said slowly. "I shan't go up for the season. I have no wish to be presented at Court and dance around. I am not Deidre! And I do want something else—"

Reggie was looking at her in amazement. "Don't want to be presented? But you'll get a whole new wardrobe, gowns, jewels, the lot. What do you want, Valerie?"

"To earn my own living," she said and could have laughed at the frank shock of his earnest face. "I wonder, Reggie, if you would be so good as to scan the gazettes for me and clip out any offers of positions as a governess?

I never see the London gazettes here, and I want to remove myself—oh, far away!" and her slim arms in the violet gown swung wide.

"Good gracious," he said, simply. "Governess? What will Malcolm say?"

"He won't be here," she said. "I want this to be a secret, where I am going. He doesn't really want me here—besides, I shall never make a lady! So would you listen, or your aunt—"

"Of course. And I'll ask Aunt to listen about for someone nice," said Reggie, recovering from his amazement. "She knows the whole world, does Aunt Darlington. I'll write to you, shall I? Send you clips, and advice from Aunt. She's a shrewd thing."

"I would appreciate it very much," she said, smiling at him. He was so naive, so good-hearted, such a friend.

Malcolm snapped behind them, "So there you are! Is it too much to ask you to join us? Mater wants you!" He was glaring at them both. Valerie wondered how much he had heard.

"Of course," said Valerie, coolly. She had recovered her self-possession and her determination to quit this place. No matter what happened, she would leave. He did not want a wife, and she would never endure to stay where she was not wanted.

Reggie left the following week. Malcolm was restless, talking of rejoining his regiment. The fighting had grown bitter. There was a ship he could get at the end of March, taking reinforcements down to the Peninsula. The earl was distressed, the countess tearful, but Malcolm was all eagerness to be with his beloved troops. So much for her ability to keep him here at her side, thought Valerie, with growing anger.

Malcolm had found her with a book in her lap, note paper at hand, writing down some Shakespeare quotations she had found for the garden. "Writing and reading, reading and writing," he jeered, furiously. "I thought you were trying on your gowns for the season! You'll never be ready to be presented!"

"I am not going to London, Malcolm," she said, laying aside the book. She turned a little pale, but she was resolute.

"Not going! Nonsense, of course you are. Mater is going to present you. You shall write me all about it. Not afraid because I shan't be at your side, are you?" he asked, with a side glance at her.

"Not a bit of it," she said stoutly. "I am going to apply for a position as governess. Our marriage was a bad mistake, Malcolm. After we are parted for a decent interval, you may apply for a—a divorce," she ended in a whisper. So few people got divorces, they were thought to be a disgrace.

Malcolm went pale under his ruddy tan. "Divorce?" he echoed blankly. "Are you mad? Our marriage is for a lifetime! You don't think I shall give you up—"

"Yes, I think so," she said dully, looking down at the book, remembering the bitterness of learning he had diced for her—and *lost*—and felt himself obliged to marry her. "I think you will adjust very well. And I—I shall devote myself to a life of books and thought, teaching and—"

"A bluestocking!" he scoffed furiously. "You will not! You are married to me, and you'll do what I say!"

"You have never admitted that I am a person," she said, thinking of the books she had read recently, by some bluestockings, on the positions of females in English society. "I value my mind, I value my soul, I shall develop them as I choose!"

"Along with dear Reggie to help you?" he jeered angrily. "Do you plan to join him in London?"

"No, I am applying for a position as governess, as far away from here as possible!"

He drew a deep breath, his fists clenched behind his back. "So that is how you feel," he said, finally, in an unnaturally soft tone. "You cannot wait to leave us! Well, just wait. The fighting is furious at this time, and you may soon be a happy widow! Then you can do as you please!"

He turned and strode out of the room.

They scarcely spoke together more than a few polite words before he departed. He was furious with her and slept alone in his small bedroom. The earl looked anxiously from one to the other, Deidre smiled complacently, and nodded her understanding.

Malcolm sailed at the end of March for the Peninsula wars, leaving the household tearful, desolate, fearful for his safety.

Chapter Four

After Malcolm had left, Valerie applied herself seriously to her books. She refused to be fitted for more gowns, she refused to learn any more etiquette.

The countess was dismayed, her small hands fluttered about. "But my dear child, I promised Malcolm I would do my best to fit you for society! And you are to be presented in two months!"

"No, madam, I thank you, but no," said Valerie firmly. She turned her head from the anxious look of her mother-in-law. She would soon console herself with lovely Deidre! Deidre was a beautiful woman, a girl to be proud of, a girl to show off to society. "I plan to leave as soon as I obtain a position as a governess."

"But whatever will Malcolm say?"

"I told him before he left, he did not believe me." Valerie shrugged. "That is his problem, he never believes what I say. He shall see! I can earn my own living and need not depend on him."

"But you are married!"

"He may get a divorce and marry someone more suitable."

The countess clutched at her breast, and looked faint. Valerie rang for her maid, then left the room. She would not be deterred by fainting nor arguments.

She read and studied hard. She reviewed her grammar books, wrote small compositions, practiced handwriting, practiced the little piano lessons she had studied, muttered over her French and German. She walked back and forth, reciting multiplication tables. The earl found her doing this and studied her gravely.

"My dear Valerie," he said finally. "I cannot believe you mean to leave us like this."

He looked concerned and worried, and she wanted to weep a little. But she stiffened her spine. They would all forget her when she left.

"I am sorry, sir," she said stiffly. "I have enjoyed your company, and you have been very good to me. But I cannot remain married to Malcolm."

"Some silly fuss you had before he left," he said, troubled.

"We are not suited to each other," she said firmly. "He wishes excitement and danger, then to fly about gambling and dancing. I have a more serious nature, I wish to read and study and teach." She put a bold front to it, not expressing the fears that haunted her at night, the fear of living alone, of starving. . . .

A woman had two choices. She could marry, or she could teach. That was all. Valerie must be strong and brave and firm, she thought. Independence cost much, but she would find it worthwhile.

As fate would have it, Lady Seraphine Darlington wrote to Valerie within two weeks. She had a fine up-standing handwriting, very black and firm on the pages, although a tremor here and there betrayed her age and state of health.

She had an offer of a position for Valerie. Her god-daughter was a Mrs. Thomas Fitzhugh, in the Cotswolds. Her husband had recently become the squire on the death of his uncle. Wrote Lady Darlington:

> *They have a small but adequate home in a good-sized town. Bess is troubled by the many occasions when she must play the Lady Bountiful for the country-side. Also she possesses four lively children, with Thomas, Junior, giving her the most trouble. Eliza, at fifteen, is a sensible and serious girl. Jeanette is given to brooding and much reading. Marianne is but six.*
>
> *My Reginald has informed me that you are of a so-ber and good nature, much accustomed to managing a household. I am sure the Countess of Arundel has also given you instruction. If you could see your way clear to becoming governess and companion to the young Fitzhugh household, I for one should be immensely grateful. The pay to begin would be three hundred pounds a year.*

Three hundred pounds a year. Little enough to the Arundels, but a fortune to the thankful Valerie. Not just her room and food, but money besides to set aside against a school of her own one day.

She wrote quickly to the address, informing the earl be-cause she needed a frank for the letter. He stamped it for her, with a grave look.

"And if she will have you, shall you go soon?" he asked wistfully. "And what of our Shakespeare garden?"

"Oh, sir, you know you will manage right well without me," but tears filled her large brown eyes. He pinched her cheek affectionately.

"Now, no tears, but you must promise to write often and give us news of you. What Malcolm will say, I have no doubt! He will blame us all for letting you go. Well, well, when he returns you will make up your difficulties and differences—all marriages have them," he said with more cheer.

Mrs. Fitzhugh answered so promptly that Valerie suspected Lady Darlington had already written to her. She implored Valerie to come, assured her she would have every consideration, and they were longing to make her acquaintance.

So all there was to do was to pack and be off. It was April now, and a letter from Malcolm saying that he had arrived in the Peninsula was expected soon. The fighting, according to the gazettes, would be joined shortly. Sir Arthur Wellesley had arrived in port and would be leaving for Lisbon at once. Then, predicted the gazettes, with intense satisfaction, they would soon learn, those Frenchies, what a British general could do! And Malcolm also, thought Valerie, with a sigh. If she knew him, he would be in the thick of it. Since Moore's death, all England had waited to see what would happen there.

When the countess heard that Valerie was actually packing to leave, that she had a position far away in the Cotswolds, she was much distressed and dismayed.

"But my dear child, I cannot believe you are serious! We mean to take you to London in two weeks!"

"No, madam, I cannot go. I regret so much that I must disobey your wishes."

"I will speak to my husband. He is so fond of you, he will persuade you to accompany us. Eustace also will speak, he loves you like a sister."

But the future wife of Eustace did not love her, thought Valerie. Deidre would be all too glad to have Valerie out of the way. She would have all the more clothes and jewels to herself.

When they were convinced that she would leave, the

earl said, "Then Eustace must accompany you, it is a long and dangerous journey."

Eustace had barely recovered from a bad bout of the flu and still a heavy cold hung on. Valerie shook her head.

"It would be bad for him," she told the earl simply. "No, please, I can take the coach."

"Never, never! My daughter-in-law in a public coach! Never!" And he commanded the heavy imposing barouche with the family crest on it, and two coachmen who were middle-aged and long in their service to accompany her.

Valerie was surprised on her last evening to have the countess come to her sitting room. She welcomed her, fussed over her, made sure the lady was seated in a warm place near the fire, as the April night was chill.

"But my dear child," said the countess plaintively. "Your maid tells me you are not taking her with you!"

Valerie smiled, a quick grin that lit up her brown eyes and her rather serious little face. "I cannot see arriving at my new position in a barouche with a crest on it, maman," she said impulsively. "And if I should take my own maid—oh, no, they would think I was too high in the instep as it was!"

The countess sighed, looked about. "You do not take your lovely evening dresses, your velvet cloaks," she commented. "And your jewels, I wanted to give you some diamonds of your own. Malcolm spoke to me of it before he left."

Valerie suppressed the hot words, spoke gently. The countess looked old and weary tonight, and in the firelight there were unaccustomed lines about her eyes and mouth.

"It would not be appropriate to my position. I shall take a few modest gowns, and I thank you for your kindness in giving them to me. But I do not expect to be much in the social swim."

"It seems such a waste," the countess murmured. "The

right wife for Malcolm—oh, dear, I do wish he had not gone. I am sure he is not safe—oh, I have the most terrible dreams at night—" Her voice trailed off, her hands fluttered and were still, clasped tightly to each other.

Valerie soothed her, turned her thoughts to the subject of the tenants, and the new apple orchard, to the times they would have in London.

"May I charge you with a message for Lady Darlington? I am most grateful to her for her trouble in assisting me with the position," Valerie requested.

With unusual pettishness, her mother-in-law replied, "I am not grateful to her, not at all! Without her interference, you should still remain with us. I shall tell her I am most displeased!"

Valerie's heart warmed somewhat at this, yet she felt that her mother-in-law would be quite satisfied with the presence of Eustace and Deidre.

The next morning, she started out early. The trunks were strapped into the coach, she was made comfortable with more rugs than she needed, cushions against the chill, several more warnings to the grooms that they must have every care of her.

Eustace came down in his silk and velvet dressing gown to bid her farewell. He remained in the warm drawing room, with their warnings ringing in his ears, but he insisted on kissing Valerie on both cheeks.

"And my dear, you will write often, and tell us how you do. We are not strangers, but your family, you know," he said sweetly, with an anxious look on his handsome drawn face.

"And you will come home as soon as you can," added the countess wistfully.

Valerie opened her mouth to say she did not intend to return. She caught the warning eye of Mr. Louis Kenyon, and his slight shake of the head.

"I shall miss you, maman," she whispered in the countess's ear, and the lady kissed her farewell.

Then Valerie turned to the earl. "I shall see you into the carriage," he said gruffly. He had a sad, gloomy look to his face, he seemed older this morning.

He took her to the coach, lingered to cover her with rugs, admonish her to write often, ask her for the tenth time if she had sufficient funds with her.

"You must write when you need more, my dear!"

She forebore to tell him again that she would be earning a salary for her duties, and leaned forward to kiss his whiskery cheek with great affection.

"You have all been so good to me, too good. You must forget—" But she choked on the words. The groom took away the steps, the door was banged shut and fastened, and the horses whipped up. She turned about for one last look at the earl and the great hall, but the sight was blurred by her tears.

It was a long dreary journey of two days, made worse by a light incessant rain that dripped onto the barouche top, chilled the horses, and wet the grooms through. They stopped for luncheon and a change of horses, went on, through the afternoon into the evening. At the inn the earl had recommended, they spent the night.

Valerie ate a light supper, drank thirstily of the hot tea, and fell into the strange bed, to weep into her pillow for sadness and sheer exhaustion.

The next day was like the first. The rain continued, the April day was gloomy and dark. They entered the Cotswold region in late afternoon, and she sat up to peer out with interest at the golden stone of the hills, the creamy gold of the cottages, the thatched roofs, the early roses that twined about every hedge and cot.

About seven of the evening, they reached the village of the Fitzhugh family. The coachmen opened the door for Valerie, helped her out. She was stiff with weariness. A light blazed from the good-sized manor house, a maid, a butler, and a plump graying lady came hurrying out to greet her, with an awed look at the splendid barouche.

"Here you are, here you are, Mrs. Villiers!" exclaimed Mrs. Bess Fitzhugh, with kindly accent. "There now, what a long journey you have had, to be sure! You shall be made comfortable at once!" And she directed the butler to tell the coachmen where they would spend the night.

Valerie thought she was being treated more like a guest than a governess. For she was shown to a pretty rose-decorated sitting room, with its own bedroom and bath, on the second floor. A silver tray of tea and cakes was brought up, a maid helped her unpack.

Mrs. Fitzhugh fussed about her in a manner that reminded Valerie of the countess. She fluttered, she fretted, she showed her kind thoughtfulness in a hundred ways.

"We have guests this evening, I wish you to meet them, unless you are too weary—"

Valerie assured her she would be glad to attend dinner in an hour, or at least to take coffee with them. The children were waved away, they could be introduced tomorrow.

"Although they are vastly curious to meet you," smiled Bess Fitzhugh comfortably. "How good is Aunt Darlington! I have longed for someone of your quality to come, and despaired of finding anyone. And she but waves her stick, and produces you!"

Her look was curious, but her manners and gentleness too ladylike to ask questions. Valerie thought she must one day explain to her why she had left the comfortable nest of the Arundel estate to make her own living.

For the evening, Valerie put on her violet silk dress, brushed her hair up severely into a coronet, then added the beautiful amethyst necklace and ring that Malcolm had given to her. She felt that was hers, that she could not yet part with it, though it had been an engagement present from a husband she was determined to divorce.

The guests were kindly, curious, attentive. Some nice likable young people and middle-aged ones from the village, all deference to the new squire, yet familiar as one who liked him. Thomas Fitzhugh was a man of almost forty, a lively, busy man with a twinkle to his eyes and a briskness to his manner that Valerie liked at once.

She had fallen soft, she thought thankfully that night, as she went to her four-poster bed. She drew the rose-sprinkled curtains about the bed and nestled down.

Then, unaccountably, she thought of Malcolm. Where was he tonight? In some comfortable officer's billet, or bedding down preparing for battle, in some straw-filled stable, as he had told her he often did? Or was he already in some battle? Were guns booming about him? Did he crouch, musket in hand, listening for the approach of the enemy? She tossed and turned, too weary and stiff from the journey to sleep. And finally she found relief again in tears, until sleep came to blot out the memory and the worries.

The next day, she met her new charges. Eliza was sober and serious, even for fifteen. Jeanette eyed her with aloof curiosity, probably waiting for her to show her knowledge or ignorance. Little Marianne clung to her with instant affection and demanded a story. Thomas was nine, and would continue at the village school which was an excellent one, said his father.

She set up a routine for their studies, after talking with each of the girls about her progress and her wishes. For Eliza, there were lessons in deportment (for which Valerie was relieved that she had put in one of her trunks the despised etiquette book). Also she must have lessons in piano, drawing, penmanship, polite letter writing, a little history and geography.

For Jeanette, at twelve, there were lessons in arithmetic, spelling, reading, geography, history, drawing, and singing. Marianne was just beginning her lessons, and was a cheerful learner, so long as she was entertained in the doing.

So Valerie settled into her new routine, grateful for the goodness of her composed but timid mistress. She found herself advising Bess Fitzhugh on her dresses, her manners, the setting of her table, the disposition of her guests around the table.

As she wrote to the countess, now in London:

> *I am most grateful to you, madam, for teaching me, for now I can instruct dear Mrs. Fitzhugh in matters she longs to learn. If you should see in one of the London book shops another even more detailed book of etiquette and polite manners, I should be most grateful if you would purchase it and dispatch it to me. Also, if you might find a little book of geography, with some maps of England—*

She found herself writing often to the countess, who replied promptly with kindly thought for her. The books were sent, at once, with others which the countess thought would be of interest. Some were chosen by the earl, some by Eustace, all with her fondly in mind, as they said.

She missed them more than she could have thought. How good they had been to her, and continued to be, all through her obstinate decision to be parted from them. Never a word of reproach did they voice in their courteous letters to her. She was Malcolm's wife, a girl whom they loved, and she would return to them one day, every letter breathed this message.

She found she was free and independent about two hours a day, with time to read and think. Also on Sundays, in the afternoon after church, she was free to walk about and do as she wished. Yet when one earns her living, thought Valerie ruefully, one was never really free. When Marianne begged to walk with her, Valerie had not the heart to refuse the child. When Eliza, growing older, slipped into Valerie's sitting room, and curled up to confide her doubts and fears about the future, Valerie gave her a ready sympathy and attention.

Jeanette became gradually won over, and then she also wished her share of attention, confiding her wish to become a great poet. She showed her shyly some of her efforts, and Valerie praised them sincerely. They were indeed advanced and excellent for her age.

Bess Fitzhugh needed her most of all. The woman felt overwhelmed with her new duties. "Indeed, I never dreamed that Mr. Fitzhugh's uncle should die and leave no heirs but my husband," she said, pressing her hand to her cheek in a shy sweet way. "How awkward it is! And most distressing. His cousins all dying in the war, not a male cousin left to inherit. It all devolves on Thomas, and he was not trained for this either."

"He is fitting the position gallantly," said Valerie, reassuringly. "Indeed, Pastor Martin informed me that never has a squire in his memory come to the post with such ease of manner, such sympathy for others, yet such justice at his command, that all are satisfied eventually with his decisions. If he was not trained, then surely God has given him the talents which are his that suit him as squire."

"You are good to say so." Bess Fitzhugh's eyes lit up, she was silently adoring of her handsome, charming husband, and wondered often what he had seen in her, plump, gentle, shy, when he might have had any girl in the county.

Valerie had little time to think, then, about her own affairs. They had courteously not pressed her as to her motives. No one asked why the daughter-in-law of the Earl of Arundel chose to make her living as a governess. They knew that Malcolm Villiers was in the Peninsula, and small Thomas would ask eager questions about the battles, and indeed showed more knowledge than Valerie had of the action there.

Only at night, as she lay down to sleep, did she have

time to think, to muse, to ponder. Had she done right? She had forced herself to leave the comfortable nest, as Eustace called it. She must not stay where she was not wanted, where her husband had married her only because he had lost at dice! They did not understand her pride and her independence that pressed her to leave and make her own way.

Sometimes, absently, she pressed the amethyst heart-shaped ring to her lips, and recalled how Malcolm had awkwardly put it on her finger. If only he had done it in liking for her, a growing love! Then she might have accepted the position in which she had found herself.

However, with nothing between them but a sexual desire on his part and a pride on hers, parting had been inevitable. And she must make the best of it, she would think, and turn over to try to woo sleep again.

Chapter Five

Malcolm's first letter to her was forwarded from Arundel. He wrote briefly of the action, in a hurried scrawl that told more eloquently than his words how busy he was. He apologized for their leave-taking.

> *I regret so much that we parted in anger. Forgive me, Valerie, for my harsh words. You have tried to adjust to the part you were given to play. I beg you to forget what I said, to write to me often with news of you, and pray for me often.*

He was very gracious. Valerie wrote at once, assured him he was nightly in her prayers, told him of her new life. His next letter was furious!

> How could you dare to leave Arundel? I am most angry. I have written at once to Eustace and to my father, to go to you and return you to your rightful home! To leave behind my back in such manner! It is most ungracious! You are as impulsive as Clarence was! I might have known you had more of his nature than I had considered! What a gamble you have taken on, to be sure! He was all for the chance and laughing at the outcome! I cannot have you live apart like this! You must! must! must! return at once to my parents' home! They are presently in London. I have given instruction that you are to have more fine dresses. Eustace is to escort you about, just as he does Deidre. You must learn to take your place in society, much though you dread it. Mater will continue to instruct you. You might take lessons from Deidre as well, she is a fine lady, conversant with all the proper manners required of a lady—

Take lessons from Deidre! Valerie had to lay down the letter and fume a bit before she could continue to peruse the scrawled pages, much torn about and the ink sometimes dimmed, as though water or rain had fallen upon the pages.

There was a break in the letter. Malcolm had drawn a heavy line. Then he continued.

> I continue this letter two days after the earlier part was written. I beg you to return to the protection of my parents' home. The action is fierce. I cannot tell you details. We prepare for another battle, sometimes I am out, gathering intelligence. I am so weary tonight my head will not make sense. Someone has promised to take this letter to Lisbon for sending on to you by the next ship. Therefore, will I close with haste—
> Pray for me. We live constantly with the fear of—

The next words were hastily marked out, with heavy black ink. Then he went on,

> *One of my best friends, Lord Reston, is dead today. He was out with me, I saw him shot from his horse. I have the direction of his wife, will you write as from us both, and give her my condolences. He was a fine fellow, brave as anyone—*
> *Must finish. God bless you, Valerie. Write to me.*
>
>   *Your loving husband,*
>
>   *Malcolm.*

Valerie had sought the sanctuary of her pretty rose-colored sitting room to read the letter in private. She was glad that she had, for at the close of his letter, she must set it down, and let the tears come. He was in danger, he was weary, the shaken hand told her he had written perhaps late at night, after the turmoil and deadly work he had been about. And his best friend dead! At the bottom of the letter he had added hastily the name and address of Lady Reston. Valerie remembered Malcolm speaking affectionately of his friend, how they had gone to school together, how they fought, and tried to remain near to each other in battle.

She looked again at the date. Malcolm might have gone into battle again—he might be dead now! Tears flooded her eyes, rolled down her cheeks. She wiped them away with determination. She must return to the schoolroom and give a lesson.

A light tap at the door, and Mrs. Bess Fitzhugh peered around the edge of the door, her plump face concerned.

"My dear? I would not disturb you, but I was troubled—is there bad news?"

Valerie wiped her eyes again. "He is in danger, his best friend killed. Oh, dear, I must compose myself—" Her voice broke. Mrs. Fitzhugh came to her at once, took her in her motherly arms, and petted her until Valerie wept again.

Thomas Fitzhugh was much concerned, and offered to take her himself to the home of her husband's parents in London. Valerie had herself in hand by that time and shook her head firmly.

"No, I must remain. I am determined to be independent. I do not wish to leave, though I thank you most kindly." She attempted a smile. "I wonder, have you a map of the Peninsula? I wish to trace where he is."

"But of course," and Mr. Fitzhugh took her and his son to the study, and they traced out on a large map in an atlas he had, where Malcolm would be, the location of Lisbon and several other landmarks of which Malcolm had spoken.

They remained concerned and interested in him, and whenever a fresh letter arrived, she would read parts aloud to the family. They treated her like a daughter, she thought, and told Malcolm so. Young Thomas was especially keen to hear about the battles, though Malcolm spoke little of that.

The squire applied to a friend and had the London gazettes sent down regularly. Then they all read eagerly of the battles, sometimes hearing of them before a letter arrived from Malcolm. Wellesley was on the Douro. Marshal Soult of the French armies had arrayed his forces against him. What could Wellesley do? They read breathlessly of the battle that followed, how the French were surprised by the clever crossing of the Douro River by the large wine-barges, with the men crossing, and some cannon, taking occupation of a seminary. The building was fortified, the French routed when they had no idea that Wellesley's troops were even crossing the river.

Wellesley ate the luncheon prepared for Soult! How they laughed over that. The French Marshal had to leave in such haste that he had not time to eat, and Wellesley marched into town so quickly that he was able at four in the afternoon to sit down to Marshal Soult's meal!

Portugal was clear of the French. But soon worse news came. The leopard, spoken of contemptuously by the French Napoleon, had come in and driven the eagles back into the mountains of Spain. Wellesley met with the Spanish General Cuesta to plan their next step. A worse battle would be the outcome.

Malcolm's intelligence work increased. His scrawled letters were almost unreadable, but with patience, Valerie deciphered them. The French were pouring troops into the Peninsula.

The countess wrote—of the pleasures of London. Deidre had been so charming last evening, in a new gown of pale blue silk covered with golden gauze. How lovely she had been! How often she had danced. How they had all wished that Valerie had come. The Countess had located a beautiful piece of rose silk, and wished to make a gown for Valerie of the same kind as Deidre, covered with golden gauze. She would look charming in it.

The earl wrote a different tune.

> *London is full of dancing, whist, and the chatter of empty-headed fools. I passed a market-barrow on the street yesterday, it was full of white and red roses. I was at once struck with a sickness for my own roses, and a hunger for Arundel. If only you were here with us, to laugh with me over these foolishnesses. Or we might return to Arundel, to the peace of our Shakespeare garden. Once you left, I had not the heart to continue it. Do you stay long in the Cotswolds? Are you not weary of teaching yet? We hear from Malcolm, his mother weeps, and I have tears which I must hide. If only the reckless boy would return, how happy we should be.*

Valerie smiled and sighed over their letters. She wrote weekly to Malcolm, on Sunday afternoons, after her du-

ties were done. She wrote at length, for he welcomed her
letters, and thanked her eagerly for them.

She told him of her work.

> *I am succeeding in teaching arithmetic to Jeanette.
> She would do nothing but read romantic novels, should
> I allow her. But she is becoming a charming little lady,
> and I have persuaded her that a lady should know a
> little something of everything in the world. We all look
> at the maps to see where you are. Geography goes
> swimmingly this way! We also study the French maps,
> to see where Mr. Napoleon is about—I refuse to call
> him Emperor. He is not of the stuff of greatness!*

Another time, she wrote:

> *I worry about your health. Have you recovered from
> the heavy cold? Do keep your clothing as dry as pos-
> sible, especially your stockings. That is important, I al-
> ways told my father so. Does it rain so much now?
> Here the weather has been dry and warm, the sunshine
> is so welcome. We had our lessons in the garden today,
> and the roses and honeysuckle teased our noses with
> their fragrance.*
>
> *I attended a dance on Saturday with the Fitzhughs.
> They insisted on it, and Mrs. Fitzhugh said I must tell
> you what I wore as you are interested that I have suffi-
> cient gowns to look smart. My dress was the lavender
> tulle with the two rows of flounces. I wore with it a
> gauze scarf about my shoulders, of deeper lavender.
> Also my amethysts, which I brought with me. The
> necklace and bracelet are much admired, and the ring
> on my finger brought several remarks. It is so large and
> unusual a purple stone, said one older gentleman, who
> seemed to know much about gems. One lady teased me
> that amethysts mean faithfulness in love and asked
> about you.*

Valerie paused, and nibbled at her finger. Should she
write that to Malcolm? Her heart ached strangely sometimes, as though she really missed him, much as they had

quarreled and disagreed. Oh, well, he might see nothing
in the remark. She sighed, and went on:

> *Eustace has been ill, but is better now. I suppose you
> have heard from your mother about this. I think his
> chest is not strong, and the London air is heavy with
> dust, your father wrote.*

She wrote again:

> *How good the Fitzhughs are to me. Whenever a let-
> ter arrives from you, it is brought at once to me in the
> schoolroom. The postman brings it from the coach, and
> says, "Here is another from the gentleman in the fight-
> ing, and best wishes to him." Mrs. Fitzhugh often
> brings up the letter to me herself and lingers to make
> sure the news is good. All the children are eager to
> hear your news. It is as though you were their own
> brother, they are so anxious over you. I have mailed a
> package of four pairs of warm socks, a new pair of
> boots, and a thick sweater of my own knitting. I do
> hope all fits you and suits you as to the coloring. I
> thought the beige color would not stand out as you ride
> of a night, much as that worries me. Would you rather
> have black? I remember your dislike of black. Shall
> your next sweater be gray?*

Malcolm wrote, but often their letters were weeks and
months in crossing. He would answer a letter of hers,
written five weeks before. She managed to keep all in
mind, and no matter what her intentions as to her own future, she tried to write cheerfully and not distress him by
insisting that she would divorce him. She did not wish him
upset and made moody, as could so easily be done,
Thomas Fitzhugh assured her gravely.

Thomas Fitzhugh had seen action and sold out, just before his marriage. He said, "A man in battle wants a free
cheerful mind, to give his best to the action. If his mind is
divided, it could be fatal for him. I beg you, Mrs. Villiers,
to write of nonsense rather than to worry him."

The countess wrote that they heard little of Malcolm now, and would dear Valerie send her some news from his letters? London increased with news, but much of it was of little value and proved false.

> *The season is most amusing, there are many here, and some gallants in uniform. I feel tears in my eyes when I see one of the coloring of dear Malcolm. I almost feel he is there, I am about to call out to him, then I see it is not Malcolm at all. Dear me! You will think me foolish. But indeed I am so concerned about our dear foolish boy. How reckless and gallant he is. I do wish he would sell out.*

The earl wrote,

> *How much I miss you in London. Would you had come with us to relieve the tedium. I have no one to talk to, as Eustace must dance attendance on Deidre, who goes out from noon to midnight, then sleeps all the morning for her beauty! She has ordered a hundred gowns, and dressmakers clutter up the parlor much of the afternoon. I wish they were married, perhaps Eustace would have more sleep! She flutters after one idea and another, she will have a tea, and a ball, and entertain fifty guests to dinner. I think they plan now to wed at Christmas. I shall be glad when that is all over. What a turmoil it will be, to be sure!*

Valerie read between the lines on that one. The earl disapproved of Deidre more and more, but would say nothing to hurt the feelings of his elder son. But surely Deidre would settle down after marriage and be a comfort to them all. She was Eustace's choice for a wife, she must have sense and worthiness. But Valerie, remembering the cold blue eyes, the high baby-voice, had her doubts. Did she marry to have a soft nest for herself, and think to give little but her body in return? That was not marriage, that was like a doxy, thought Valerie immorally. She had heard of the females who sold their favors in return for clothes and jewels and the rent of their fine houses.

In August came the news, more grave this time. Marshal Victor of France had joined forces with General Sebastiani and King Joseph, brother of Napoleon. At the end of July the battle had begun, and the engagement at Talavera had brought horrible casualties. The news came out by degrees. Valerie formed the habit of being in the downstairs hallway when the postman came, to seize the letters anxiously, also the gazettes.

Mrs. Fitzhugh would come out from her parlor. "What news of Talavera? Any news of your dear husband?"

Finally in mid-August, they heard the news. The battles had been heavy with casualties, but Wellesley had won. What casualties? Valerie's heart was heavy with dread, and some ominous cloud seemed to hang over her, until finally she had the welcome letter from Malcolm. He was alive. He had been injured, but slightly, compared with others.

In relief, fear, and exasperation she shot off a letter to her husband.

> *My dearest Malcolm,*
>
> *Should you be close, I should not be able to refrain from shaking you! What injuries have you? Of what extent? What are you doing for them? Have you a comfortable billet? Are you in Lisbon? Have you a doctor close? Pray you, write at once, and relieve my mind! For I am most upset and fretful about your scanty news. I realize you have more important things to do than to write to an errant wife! But I beg you—Malcolm, do write at once, and let me know the extent of your injuries, if you might come home—*

The pen slackened and paused. Come home? But that would force her to a decision, whether to return to Arundel or the London town house, or to remain with the Fitzhughs and admit an open break in her marriage.

Reluctantly, she conceded to herself that she did not

wish to break the marriage. If he did not love her, she would remain away. But if he loved and needed her, she would return. Her attachment and concern for Malcolm were stronger than she had thought possible. She closed her eyes, rested her chin on a weary hand, and thought. Then she wrote again, with more composure.

> *I hear often from your dear father and mother. They miss you immensely. I would beg you for their sakes to sell out and return home. They worry about you, and at their ages, the worry is not good for their health. Do consider your family, Malcolm, and think what is best for all of you.*

She continued then, with news of the Fitzhugh family, in whom he had taken an affectionate interest, though he had never met them save through her letters. Then she concluded, "Your anxious wife, Valerie."

She franked it, and sent it off before she could regret or take back any wording. He wrote again and again before she knew he could have received this letter. About his injuries, he said nothing. His billet was in a comfortable home of a fine Portuguese gentleman, who treated him like a son. Three of his brother officers were with him, and he spoke of their pranks and efforts to find good food in the ravished countryside. And so she had another worry—did he eat enough? And well? She doubted it very much. Malcolm was not one to be picky about his food. If he found nothing much to eat, it was for lack of the supply of food.

She read proudly in the gazettes about the elevation to the peerage of Sir Arthur Wellesley. There had been no time to consult him about a possible title, his brother had been consulted instead, and William decided on the name "Wellington." So all the gazettes were full of the new Viscount Wellington of Talavera. Valerie basked in the many-times reflected glory, that her husband was off serving for the new viscount.

The earl wrote wistfully again from London, demanding what news she had of his son. She wrote to him faithfully every week, indeed most of Sunday was spent composing letters to her husband, her father-in-law, and mother-in-law.

She gave him the news she knew he longed for, then continued:

> *You speak, sir, of my being quiet in the country. Indeed, we are not so quiet. In the past month, I have attended no less than four grand dinners, a ball in the town hall, no end of teas, and Mrs. Fitzhugh has given a dinner for above twenty-five guests. I assisted her in the planning of the latter. You may tell the countess that her invaluable assistance was evident in the correctness of the seating, the planning of the menu which was praised by all, and the manners of sweet Eliza who made us all proud of her as she entertained us at the piano after dinner.*
>
> *I think of you all often. How does Eustace? I do hope he has recovered well from his coughing. Is London so chill yet? I had supposed September would be sunny and bright as it is here in the Cotswolds. You must all come to see me one day, for you will find it an exceeding pretty country. The blue hills of the Malverns are so fine on a sunny day, and even on a rainy day they brood in purple above us. The stone for the cottages is all local, and turns a soft creamy yellow with age. Covered over with roses, honeysuckle, morning-glories of blue and purple, and clematis, and bordered with columbine, daisies, poppies, each in her season, the Cotswolds are fine indeed. I love going for walks with young Marianne, she is so appreciative of the joys of the country. We pull on men's boots, and go trudging about in fair weather or foul, in rain or shine, and come home with ruddy cheeks and fond memories of the sights we have seen.*

The earl answered promptly. Valerie suspected that he wrote so often because he was intensely bored in London and longed to be back at Arundel.

My dearest daughter,

Your welcome letter has me longing for Arundel, or for your fine Cotswolds. I sighed over your pictures of roses and honeysuckle, the pretty cots with flowery vines trailing over them. I fear my roses are neglected this year, the news from Arundel is indifferent. If only we had been home—all cozy together, and puttering about.

I have attempted a garden here in London. You may imagine the dismay of my good wife. However, I assured her that in my worn tweeds and disreputable hat, everyone will think I am the gardener, and so it has proved. Ladies pass me with never a nod, noses in the air at the smell of good black earth.

However, London has contrived to defeat me in my efforts. My roses are puny and show few buds. Black dust inhabits my green hedges. Not a rabbit have I seen. I poke about daily, encouraging the little buds, speaking softly to the few flowers which dare to come up. Poor things, they should be in the country, as should I.

Eustace was ill again above a week, and Deidre was much annoyed that he could not accompany her to an event at which His Majesty was to be present. We satisfied her with a distant cousin as escort, grand in uniform, so she was well pleased and tells us she danced every dance.

Valerie laughed and sighed over the letter and finally showed it to Mrs. Fitzhugh. "Is he not a dear? It breathes in every line," said Valerie affectionately.

"He is, indeed. Thank you for showing it to me, dear Valerie. Do you not wish—" She hesitated, flushing. "Do you not want to give in to their wishes and return to them? I think he at least needs the comfort of your presence."

Valerie shook her head. "I do not wish to go to London," she evaded, her brown eyes turning serious. "I am determined to make my own living."

"I confess I do not understand you," said Bess Fitzhugh. "It is not my affair, yet I am concerned for you.

You have helped us so much, it will wrench our hearts when you leave. Yet—when your husband returns . . ."

Valerie hung her head. Mrs. Fitzhugh tactfully changed the conversation. Valerie was thinking that when Malcolm returned, then she must take action. She would be twenty-one if he lingered much longer on the Peninsula. Then she would go ahead in her action for a divorce. He must be free to choose someone more suitable for a wife, if indeed he wished to marry at all.

Before his marriage, and the wars, he had been a gay rake, enjoying the attentions of light ladies, gaming, plays in London. He might be all too relieved to return to this, unencumbered by a wife.

A disgraceful incident momentarily pushed the Peninsular war from the headlines of the gazettes. Canning and Castlereagh fought a duel on Putney Heath on the twenty-first of September. Canning was wounded in the thigh. Castlereagh lost a button off his coat. All England was scandalized. Two Cabinet Ministers, to act in such a manner!

The Tory government might fall over it. All wondered and conjectured. Instead there was a new Tory government, with a lawyer, Spencer Perceval, at the head. Canning and Castlereagh were both out.

Valerie could not care much. They could all be dismissed, for all she cared. If only the war would end, and Malcolm would come home! She admitted secretly to herself, that was all she could hope for—that he would come home, safe and sound, teasing her, deviling her, even wounding her with his indifference—just so he might be safe and sound.

Chapter Six

The October days were cold and rainy. Valerie had felt a black cloud over her spirits for many days now. She had not heard from Malcolm for four weeks, then all at once, four letters together. Yet still she continued to brood, as she confessed to Bess Fitzhugh.

"Something is wrong, I feel it," said Mrs. Fitzhugh, troubled. "I would not upset you, my dear. However, there is something in me that whispers of trouble. Oh, dear, I should not have spoken. Thomas will be angry with me."

Valerie passed her thin hand over her face. She had not been able to eat much lately, she felt so troubled herself. "Do you have the second sight, then?" she asked in an attempt to cheer.

Mrs. Fitzhugh nodded soberly. "Yes, I think so. I felt it before my mother died, and then again when my brother was killed in action. Oh, I pray nightly for your husband and yourself, my dear."

"How good and kind you are!" Valerie thanked her and returned to the lessons, trying to thrust her worries from her. The weather was so dark and gloomy, it was depressing all their spirits. She would soon have another letter from Malcolm, and all would be well, she told herself.

But the next afternoon, a grand barouche drew up in

front of the manor house of the Fitzhughs, and Mr. Louis Kenyon stepped out. He was limping heavily, his face gray and lined with fatigue.

He came in at once, and the butler showed him into the cosy sitting room and went himself for Valerie.

In the schoolroom, puffing a little, the butler stammered, "Mrs. Villiers, there is a gentleman here to see you, Mr. Louis Kenyon. Shall I tell Mrs. Fitzhugh?"

Valerie had gone white as a lily, and her hands went to her face. "Mr. Kenyon?" she asked. "Oh, it must be bad news—oh, my God in heaven—"

She could not compose herself, until she saw how she was frightening the girls. She stiffened her spine, set them to a lesson and descended the stairs to the first floor.

Mrs. Fitzhugh reached the sitting room as soon as Valerie and put her arm about the girl's waist as they went inside. Mr. Kenyon got up painfully from his chair and bowed to Valerie.

"I will reassure you at once, we have had no bad news from Malcolm," he said when he saw her pale face.

"Oh, thank God," she said faintly and sat down heavily on the nearest chair. Finally she recovered her manners, introduced Louis Kenyon to Mrs. Fitzhugh. "He is the dear cousin of my father-in-law, and helps him immensely about the estate."

"Mrs. Villiers has been such an aid and comfort to us," said Mrs. Fitzhugh. "I do hope you have not come to take her away."

Mr. Kenyon smiled slightly, but his eyes were suffering. "I fear I must. I have a letter here from the Earl of Arundel," and he put it into Valerie's hand. "Pray, do not read it yet," he said quickly. "I must tell you first—"

"There is bad news!" whispered Valerie, clutching the letter to her.

"Yes, there is. I fear the news is most shattering to us all," said Mr. Kenyon. "There is no easy way to tell you, my dear Mrs. Villiers. Eustace Villiers, Viscount Grenville, has died of a fever in London."

Valerie stared at him. "Eustace?" she whispered, remembering the grave courtesy, the kindness, and sympathy of her brother-in-law. "No, he could not—oh, no "

Mr. Kenyon, still standing, made her a deep bow. "It is my honor to inform you that you are now the Right Honorable the Viscountess Grenville."

The silence in the room was profound. Eustace dead. And Malcolm heir to the title! It was incredible. Valerie shook her head automatically, her hand went to her face, her fingers over her eyes, as though she would deny what had happened.

Mr. Kenyon continued, gravely. "Lady Grenville, I beg you to make haste and return with me to Arundel. The family has returned home with—the body of young Eustace. The funeral is in two days, if you can return with me. Needless to say, the earl and the countess are so grief-stricken that they scarce know which way to turn. The last thing the Earl said to me was, 'Bring Valerie home, my dear Louis, bring her home, for I cannot endure much more.' And so I have come, to ask you to return at once with me."

Valerie seemed incapable of speech, sitting there numbly with the folded letter in her hand.

Mrs. Fitzhugh said, tremulously, "I will send a maid to pack for you, dear Mrs.—I mean, Lady Grenville. Let me send also for Thomas. You will remain overnight with us, Mr. Kenyon?"

He nodded, and she slipped away to make the plans.

"Oh, Mr. Kenyon," Valerie whispered at last. "Tell me it is not true. Not dear Eustace, dead—how did it happen?"

His face turned bitter, he half turned his body from her, groping for the mantelpiece. "My Lady, I fear I cannot control my anger. I have prayed for myself, to keep control. But Lady Deidre would go out night after night, in fair weather or foul, and dragging poor Lord Grenville with her, sick though he was. Nothing we said could turn her from enjoying amusements. 'I must be gay, I must be gay until my marriage,' she cried to us all. And now, oh, God, there is no marriage."

Valerie bit her lips against equally angry words. Mr. Kenyon had dropped his face on his hands at the mantel. He seemed years older, and she thought of how devoted he was to his cousin's family, who had been closer than his own.

"Dear Mr. Kenyon," she said finally. "We cannot judge or condemn. It is an act of God. But oh, how bitter it is, how bitter it is." She thought of the cold blue eyes of Lady Deidre, her haughty manners, the frantic search for pleasure, for more beautiful dresses, one more season in London while she was still a girl, unmarried.

Mr. Kenyon raised his head, nodded, unashamedly wiped the tears from his eyes. "Forgive me, I should not have burst out. It is not my place. But my heart aches for the earl, my cousin. How he grieves! If only he can manage to get Malcolm home, it may ease the pain."

"He has written?"

"At once. And also to His Majesty, begging him to release Malcolm from service immediately. His Majesty's secretary wrote, saying His Majesty was ill and could not reply, but action would be taken and letters sent. That is all we know for the present."

Mrs. Fitzhugh came in, the butler following, with a silver tray of hot tea and sandwiches. Mr. Kenyon was thankful to sit down and eat, talking in a low tone of the grief they all felt, of the situation in London during the final illness of Eustace.

Mr. Kenyon was then shown to his room. The two grooms were cared for, as were the horses. Mr. Fitzhugh had come home and expressed his grief for them, and his offer to do anything at all to help.

Valerie retired to her room. The maid had packed for

her, and all her small trunks and valises were ready, except for the final garments in the morning. It was then that she opened the letter from the earl. Expecting to have a long, emotionally exhausting letter to read, she stared at the few lines.

> *My dearest Valerie, I beg you to come home. We must have you here. Our hearts are breaking. Come home and remain with us. Your loving papa.*

Tears rained down her cheeks. They needed her desperately, and she must go to them. No matter what her relations with Malcolm, she must go to them.

And so she left the kindly home of the Fitzhughs the next morning, with all her possessions. She begged them to come and visit her at Arundel.

"For I could not bear to leave you, thinking I should never see you again," she told Mrs. Fitzhugh, Mr. Fitzhugh, and the four children. "How dear you all are to me, and how kindly you have treated me."

She kissed them all. Mr. Kenyon added his thanks and the earl's for their goodness to Valerie.

Mrs. Fitzhugh begged her to write upon her return and assure them of her safe arrival. "And write us about Malcolm, and how he does!" cried small Thomas, as the huge barouche pulled away.

The trip home was physically and emotionally exhausting. Mr. Kenyon did all he could to make matters easy for her, yet he also was weary, limping heavily, with grave lines of pain on his cheeks.

She was unutterably thankful to arrive home, as the great barouche rolled heavily up the last hill to the open gates of Arundel. The rain still poured down, the October day was short, and it had turned pitch dark before they came to the lighted doorway.

She went inside, to be greeted in the hallway by the

earl himself, enveloping her in a bear hug of relief. "You have come, my dear, you have come!"

"Oh, dear papa," she said, overcome and bursting into tears again. She hugged him and kissed his cheeks, noted with pain the grief in his face and eyes. He seemed older by years.

"We dine alone," he said presently. "My wife is prostrate, and Deidre has taken to her room, to weep alone."

"Let us eat then in the sitting room, with Mr. Kenyon to keep us company," she said, trying to be more cheerful, wiping away her tears. "You cannot imagine how kind and good he was to me on the journey, whiling away the hours by telling me more of the family history."

"You are a good soul, Louis, I cannot thank you enough." The earl pressed his cousin's shoulder. After Valerie had bathed her face and washed her hands, she went down to join them in the drawing room with the fire lit, and a cheerful table of food before it.

They talked a little. The earl told again and again of the sad last days in London. "If only he had not gone out, I told him not to, the doctor told him not to. But he would go out," he said with a great sigh.

Louis Kenyon looked significantly at Valerie, she nodded. She would not reveal his outburst against Lady Deidre.

"I think you said he had been ill much of the summer," she said. "And his chest was not strong."

"No, he was never a strong lad, though he forced himself to many activities. He took after his mother, delicate and sensitive of nature. Now Malcolm, he is more like me. Strong as a horse and lively as a cricket." The earl's face brightened. "You have heard from him lately?"

"Four good letters. They are here in my small valise, I brought them down to show to you." Valerie took them out, and on his eager invitation, she read him parts of the letters.

"Oh, that he would come home now," said the earl. "I

hope to have results from my letters soon. Louis, who else can be applied to? Shall we ask the new prime minister? What about Viscount Wellington himself?"

They discussed it seriously. Valerie persuaded them to wait until they heard from Malcolm.

The funeral of Eustace, Viscount Grenville, was held the next morning in the family chapel. He was then buried near to Valerie's brother Clarence in the small graveyard, which held the remains of Arundels for more than four hundred years.

The Countess appeared, heavily veiled in black, leaning on her husband's arm. Lady Deidre was in black also, but a dainty black chiffon, with black velvet cloak over her. Her bonnet was a huge fashionable black bonnet with long black streamers.

Valerie stood with them, in a gray dress, with a dark cloak over it, her small gray bonnet newly hung with black ribbons. She looked her last at the peaceful face of Eustace and saw him put into the wet ground. Poor Eustace, how gentle and how good he had been. Too good, too gentle, she thought.

Across the grave, she lifted her gaze and glanced at Lady Deidre. Tears streamed down the pretty blonde face, the blue eyes lifted. And hate gleamed from the blue eyes toward Valerie. Hate, furious and hot. There was no mistaking it.

Hate, for me? thought Valerie over and over. Why hate? What have I done? But she shrank from the self-possessed girl, who hung about the skirts of the countess, and wept on the shoulder of the grief-stricken older woman.

She could not help feeling that Deidre was acting. If she was upset, it was because Eustace had died before their marriage. Now she was nothing, one could not be fiancée to a dead man.

How she must despise herself, how she must berate herself for the lost opportunity! Valerie thought she had the key to the puzzle. Lady Deidre hated her because Valerie had married in haste, and was safely one of the Arundels, no matter what happened to Malcolm. But Deidre had put off the wedding, until she had somewhat satisfied her love for gaiety. And now she had nothing.

Mr. Kenyon said privately to Valerie, "And now the Lady Deidre must look about again for a husband. Her mother is furious with her! Risking her opportunities like this. They were engaged for three years. She might have married him, had a son of him, and the succession tied to her."

Valerie nodded soberly. "I think she is very angry with herself."

"By rights she should be," said Mr. Kenyon curtly. "She is a selfish piece and led Eustace a sorry chase. Oh, well, that is over and done with."

But it was not. Deidre lingered on. She would return home to her parents for a time, then return, charming and desolate in black silk, black chiffon, black velvet, to weep over the countess and recount her grief all over again. Valerie thought she was more sorry for herself than for them.

Malcolm did not come home. He was deeply involved in the fighting. He wrote hastily, of his grief and surprise, begged Valerie to put flowers daily on the grave of Eustace for him. "However, I cannot quit now. They depend on my intelligence, I have some sources among the Portuguese peasants. We ride out often, they trust me. I cannot come home at this time. Beg my father to be patient with me. I long to come to him, but not until my duty is done."

It was a sad Christmas and holiday time. Lady Deidre had returned to some friends in Scotland, and they were alone—thankfully, said Louis Kenyon with unusual spite. He would never forgive Lady Deidre, thought Valerie, for being the cause of the death of Eustace.

Valerie was pleased to have a gift from the earl that

suited her immensely, a new edition in four volumes of the complete works of William Shakespeare.

"How beautiful, nothing could please me more!" she cried, turning over the thin beautiful linen pages with great delight. "I shall go over and over them, and search out lines for our garden."

The earl smiled affectionately at her. "I hoped you would say that. I have set aside some plots for us to start a garden in the spring. Shall we not plan it? It would give us something to think about this winter."

"And what is that?" asked the countess, brightening up a little at their pleasure. She was in drab black, her face white against the black veil. Her face had lined more heavily, her hair was a snowy white now. "My dear Valerie, what have you there?"

Valerie brought the book over to show her, the first volume of the series. "We are going to start a Shakespeare garden, mama," she said with as much cheer as she could command. "You see, one finds the passages in Shakespeare which mention a flower or herb, then one can plant that in the garden."

"What a charming thought, my dear," and she roused slightly from her gloom. "Have you opened my little present, my dear?"

"Yes, it was immensely good of you. But little? That is not the right word!" Valerie tried to laugh, thinking of the immense box which the countess had presented to her.

On opening, the box had revealed a dozen silk dresses, in rose, blue, violet, lilac, and some with silver or gold gauze overskirts in the newest styles. Valerie was not in mourning dress, she disliked black as Malcolm did, and wore a black band on her sleeve only. The mourning for Eustace was in her heart, deeply, at the loss of a dear brother.

"I had great pleasure in ordering the gowns for you in London. If only you had joined us there," sighed the

Countess, pleating her black skirt nervously in her thin fingers.

"We shall go another time," said the earl. "When Malcolm returns—"

Christmas and the holidays over, Valerie turned once more to work. She had many projects she wanted to achieve. The mothers in the village were more dissatisfied than ever with the hard schoolmaster. She asked the earl to dismiss him, then she herself taught for some months until a new one was hired. They managed to find a keen, intellectual young man, just down from university, who understood the nature of children and enjoyed them.

From her experiences in teaching, Valerie decided to write an article about dealing with young minds, and teaching with love and concern, rather than with a rod.

The article was accepted by a magazine for young ladies, and the editor, a female of some years, wrote to her,

> *I have rarely read anything so well expressed. I can scarce believe it is by another female. I beg you to write again for us. Have you anything on the subject of the education of a girl of about sixteen? So many are frivolous and think only of marriage. They do not think ahead to the days when they will have children and must train them in the way they must go.*

Delighted, Valerie wrote another article and sent it off. After receiving some suggestions for revisions, she made some changes and it was printed before the spring in the same magazine. The earl read it aloud to them all, with many a harrumph of pleasure.

"There, now, what a sensible girl you are, Valerie! I am proud of you! Such common sense and good thought in this! Do you not think she is a smart girl, mother?" he asked the countess.

"I always did think so, my dear," said the countess, smiling at Valerie. "Lady Deidre always said she was most intellectual. And so I think. I only wish she cared more for dancing and frivolities!"

Valerie bit her tongue and managed to say nothing. She spent more and more of her time with the earl, their minds were in tune with each other. She spent long hours in his library as he and Louis Kenyon worked. At her own table in the corner by the window, she would read and study, and finally write down her thoughts, and form them into articles.

It was the earl who suggested that she might write little moral stories of fiction for the magazines. "For indeed, I think you have more talent than a dozen of these females who write for them," he said, indicating the pile of magazines she was reading. "Why not write something as for young Eliza Fitzhugh? A story that would delight her romantic heart, and at the same time teach a moral lesson?"

Mr. Kenyon agreed heartily that she could do this. So with some trepidation and concern, she began to write stories also. She sent one out, had the pain of having it returned. But on sending it to another magazine, she was stunned to have it accepted and a payment of five pounds for it!

"Good heavens, they have paid you for it," said the countess. "Dear me, how clever you are, Valerie!"

The rest of Valerie's time was spent in the greenhouse and potting shed. She and the earl were seriously planning their Shakespeare garden. She was growing a number of herbs, thyme and balm, camomile and fennel, mints and saffron, and all she could find in the plays. The earl and she had many flower projects. Of course, his beloved roses would be prominent in the garden. Also they would have peonies and pinks, violets and carnations, columbine, daffodils, lavender and lilies.

She rode out often with the earl, learning to ride sidesaddle, and also to drive his light carriage. She delighted in this, and they returned laughing, with cheeks glowing scarlet from the brisk air.

They visited Mrs. Parker and received good advice on their garden. Valerie enjoyed these visits, for often in addition to talk of flowers, there was discussion of children and babies. One, two or more of the grandchildren were often with her, and Valerie could pick up one and hold the child in her arms. She loved doing this and gradually grew more confident of the care of children, absorbing the good woman's suggestions on their care.

On returning home one day, the earl said, "You shall be most expert when you have a child of your own, Valerie! I am delighted with your interest. Your son shall one day be Viscount Grenville, you realize."

She started violently and almost lost control of her gentle mare. She knew she had gone crimson, her face felt so hot. A child of her own! A son to be heir to the title! It had not struck her like this. She had worried about Malcolm, wondered what would happen when he returned home.

But the earl was thinking ahead with satisfaction to their children, his grandchildren!

She scarcely knew which way to look. But the earl was humming happily to himself an old song from his childhood, and was gazing into the distance where his fields lay rich with black earth as the plowmen dug deep. March, and then April, and they could set out their garden, he was thinking.

"Growing things, and young people, Valerie. They keep a man feeling young and strong," he said happily. "One cannot look back to what might have been. One must look forward, to the future. When Malcolm returns, we shall make more plans. He must settle down now, he is the future Earl of Arundel. He must be more sensible. You shall help us, eh? He has paid little attention to the estate. However, you understand the needs here, and he shall learn. Yes, it shall all be well, it shall go brightly now."

And she could not hurt him by saying she wished to

leave. She sighed, stifled the sound, and urged the mare around a small clump of trees. They had been so good to her, they treated her like a daughter. Yet sometimes she felt rebellious and hurt, that Malcolm had married her because of a dice play.

Was this all that a woman was worth? A play at dice? A toss of the game? She longed for something more and scarcely knew what it was. To be valued for herself, her body and mind as one, not just for sexual desire, or because with her strength she could produce a strong young heir to the title and the estates.

She loved the earl more than her own father now. Yet the countess was still distant, enjoying the visits of Deidre, weeping with her again and again over the death of Eustace. Deidre was what the countess wanted in the way of a daughter. Someone frivolous as herself, longing for balls and dancing, parties and pleasure. A girl who loved to be dressed like a doll, admired, and flirted with.

Valerie could not endure a life like that, she thought. If Malcolm became like his father, she could live with that, but Malcolm thought only of fighting battles, racing, gambling. Without love, without mutual esteem, without mutual interests, how could their marriage endure?

✦✦✦✦✦✦✦✦✦ *Chapter Seven* ✦✦✦✦✦✦✦✦✦

The fighting in Spain was fierce at times, they learned from the gazettes. A small skirmish here, then action there, and fresh English troops were sent óut. The rumor was that the Emperor Napoleon had now turned his full attention to the Peninsula, and experienced French troops were increasing the forces there, some said up to 350,000 men.

Malcolm wrote more irregularly, and his writing was scrawled and scratched—like hen-tracks, sighed the countess. Valerie worked over the letters, figured them out, wrote out fair copies for the others to read.

Then the letters stopped altogether. At first, when two weeks went by without a letter, she was a little concerned. Then it was three weeks, then a month.

"I shall hear all at once, with a grand array of letters," she reassured the earl and Louis Kenyon in May. But still no letters came.

She watched anxiously for the postman, secretly at first, then boldly standing in the hall, then in the front court-yard waiting for his horse to appear on the slopes of the hill below the castle.

"Sure, I'm sorry, nothing today from Viscount Gren-ville," the village postman would apologize, handing her whatever he had, a bundle of gazettes, a letter from Mrs. Fitzhugh.

May departed, in sunshine, with carnations, columbine, and early roses appearing in their beautiful Shakespeare garden. They had fashioned a wheel, with a sundial in the center, and all about it triangular plots of earth, each with its flowers, and borders of herbs and low fragrant bushes.

Digging in the earth, cutting carefully of the new bushes, bringing in proudly some of the young flowers, gave Valerie some satisfaction. Only by working hard out in the fresh air and sunshine could she become weary enough to sleep at night. Otherwise, she would lie awake worrying, her heart aching.

For herself as well as the earl, she knew. She worried about Malcolm, longed to hear from him. He must be ill, or wounded. Surely they must let her know soon. No word might be good. No news was good. Only the finality of death . . . But she turned abruptly from that thought, keeping up her spirits as well as those of Malcolm's parents as well as she could.

Deidre came less, she had retired to a country home with her mother, where there was a promising squire, said Louis Kenyon. But he had not a title, nor as much money as the Arundel fortune she had lost. Still she wrote, and reminded the countess constantly how much she missed her and Eustace.

June came, and the roses bloomed in white, pink, rose, deep crimson, and beautiful yellow. The yellow tea roses were so lovely that Valerie was one morning cutting some for the table, choosing the finest opened flowers.

She was working in the Shakespeare garden at the side of the manor, some distance from the roadway. The sundial pointed to about ten o'clock, and she was thinking she would soon go to the road and watch for the postman.

Then she heard a shout. She glanced up, and saw the sedate butler, Forrester, in his fifties, grayed and serene, running toward her, his face a ghastly white.

The roses dropped from her hands, she began to run toward him. She felt blood draining from her head and heart, she was dizzy. It was bad news—it must be. . . .

"My lady," panted Forrester, reaching her. "He has come, he has come. Come—my lord says come—"

She said one word. "Alive?" she asked, numbly.

At his nod, she came alive once more. She raced around the wall to the front, there to find a great carriage, closed, with dark panels, and a crest on them. And two footmen, with the earl directing them, were carefully lifting out a litter.

Malcolm on it, white of face, bearded, a blood-stained bandage on his forehead.

Reggie Darlington caught Valerie's arm as she would have gone right to him. "My lady, keep clear. They will have him out in moments. He must be taken up to his room. He is exhausted."

"What—what happened?" she stammered. Her brain seemed fuzzy, she could not think. She could only stare as Malcolm was carried past her, his eyes closed, as though in death. "He—looks—so—oh, God, he is not—"

"No, he lives. But the journey has wearied him, he is feverish, and knows not what he says," said Reggie hurriedly. Now that Valerie looked at him, she found their gay light-hearted friend also haggard, unshaven, his garments pulled every which way, his hands stained with dirt and blood.

Something dreadful had happened. Silently she followed the little procession into the house.

Someone was sent to keep the countess away until Malcolm could be cleaned up so as not to shock her so much. Someone else was sent hastily for the doctor.

Valerie followed them up to the small room where Malcolm would sleep. His valet, faithful Ralph, graying, tall, and thin, had with his usual efficiency prepared the bed for his master. They laid him down, and began cutting away his clothes, thick with dirt, encrusted with salt and blood.

They would have sent her away. "Not a sight for you, my dear," said the earl, and Louis Kenyon would have taken her arm and directed her out.

She shook her head fiercely. Her courage returned as she saw Malcolm stir, heard him moan faintly.

"No, I will help. We will need hot water. Oh, do not pull the shirt from him! Wait, let us soak it in water, and remove it gently, or the wound will open again."

She was at the bed in moments, easing Malcolm's shoulders onto the pillows. He was hot to the touch, full of fever.

A basin was brought hurriedly, then a footman came in with a pitcher of hot water. Valerie dipped a cloth in it, gently soaked the wounded area. Then slowly she pried the cloth away, gently so that it would not cause further bleeding. She forced herself not to remember that this was Malcolm, dear Malcolm. It was someone who needed her skillful aid and strength and courage.

A nightshirt was brought from the immense cupboard. His wounds were bathed, ointment applied. Malcolm seemed easier, his moaning eased. He opened his eyes, gazed blankly at them.

"Malcolm," breathed the earl, bending over him anxiously. "Do you know me? Malcolm!"

"Press on," he moaned, "rally the men. Rally now. We must get through the lines . . . tonight . . . get through the lines . . . oh, God, the darkness . . ."

His eyes closed again, his head turned on the pillows. The earl gently pressed his hand to the hot forehead, then bent and kissed his son's cheek. "Oh, my son, oh, my son," he murmured.

"The countess will come," said the butler. "Oh, sir, she should not see him this way." In his anxiety, he was trying to keep the door shut against her.

"Let her come in for a moment," said Valerie quietly.

"She needs to reassure herself that he is alive." She reached out her hand for the trembling one of the countess as she came in. The other hand was cold and the woman shook as she gazed down at her son. "You see, he sleeps now, maman," she said. "He shall have our good care and soon be well. How good to have him home!"

The countess bent and kissed Malcolm, and tried to speak to him. He did not even moan, his face was contained and quiet, his eyes shut.

"He sleeps, mother," said the earl, and drew her away, leaving Valerie and the servants with Malcolm.

She sat by his bed until the doctor came. The valet quietly unpacked the thin valise that had arrived with Malcolm. She turned her head as he did so, and realized that he had laid out a packet of familiar-looking letters, all from her and the family. The sight brought a rush of tears. He had saved these, of all he had brought back with him. Her letters and his parents'.

The doctor arrived, a brusque good man from the village. He removed the night shirt, and examined the wounds. Valerie forced herself to look also. There was a deep wound in the thigh, almost at the very place where he had been wounded before. The flesh was purplish and ugly. The doctor dug into it, and inserted some powdered medicine which made Malcolm moan and twitch. But it must be done, Valerie told herself.

There was an ugly wound along his waist, and up almost to his shoulder. The doctor examined it, grunted, and said, "This must be watched. Infected." He brushed it with medicine, used his knife to cut away some of the flesh that had turned dead white. Valerie remained, though he urged her away.

The earl returned as the doctor was working over Malcolm. Valerie gave him a faint smile.

"Reggie?" she queried.

"Fed and sleeping in his guest room. We owe him much, my dear Valerie," said the earl. "He shall tell us the entire story when he wakes. I think he literally dragged Malcolm from the troop ship and insisted on bringing him home to us."

Her attention returned to the doctor. He was painting the wounds with strong medicine. Malcolm moaned again, opened his hazel eyes, which looked much darker from the pain and fever. He gazed about blankly, stared up at the doctor.

"Don't . . . cut . . . it off," he said feebly.

"Eh?" said the doctor.

"Don't . . . mustn't lose . . . my leg . . . never get home . . . never get home . . ."

Valerie moved closer to the bed, across from the doctor. Her hand gently caressed his whiskered face. "You *are* home, my dear Malcolm, you *are* home," she said, slowly and distinctly.

His eyes looked at her, she thought he did not see her. But he sighed, and his eyelids closed again. He seemed quieter, so she continued to move her hand slowly over and over his face, gently over his chin and throat. He was so thin and worn, down to the bone, she thought.

The doctor looked at the wound on his forehead, back up into the hair. Ruthlessly, he cut away some of the brown curly locks, so he could get at the wound over the temple. He cleaned it thoroughly, then brushed medicine on it.

Finally he was finished. He washed his bloody hands in the fresh basin of water, dried them, as Ralph and Valerie tenderly pulled a nightshirt over Malcolm's head, and settled him again.

The doctor looked thoughtfully at Valerie. "My lady, you will nurse him? Or shall I send a man to do so?"

Valerie looked at Ralph. "We shall take care of him," she said, decidedly, as the valet nodded eagerly. "Just tell us what to do. Your instructions shall be followed carefully."

"Good, good." He took out some tablets from his case.

"Give him one tonight, and one tomorrow morning. I shall come again in the morning. We must watch the shoulder and thigh wounds. They must not be further infected, or he might lose—well, enough of that. I shall come daily until he begins to recover. Do not fret over the fever unless he becomes too hot. If he is hot, bathe his face and shoulders in cool water, not cold. Someone must stay with him night and day. Be sure the bandages are not knocked off as he stirs about in his sleep. Keep him warm and comfortable, easy in his mind. When he talks, speak quietly to him, and tell him he is home. That seems to soothe him."

They thanked him profoundly, and he left briskly. The earl said, "We shall take turns with him. Valerie, you must rest, my dear. This has been a great shock to you."

She shook her head. "I am so relieved to have him home . . ." Her voice broke a little, she steadied it. "The waiting was worse. Now we can do something for him. Let me stay."

Valerie remained with him until afternoon. When Reggie was up, and able to tell his story, she did leave Malcolm with the faithful valet, and went down to hear his story.

The handsome young ex-officer looked weary yet, but he managed to smile and leap up to greet her when she entered the drawing room.

She went directly to him and took both his hands in hers. "How can we thank you, Reggie? You are the kindest person in the world. I am so eager to hear of what happened, I cannot endure to wait!"

He smiled down at her, pressed her hands, raised one to his lips, and kissed it. "You shall hear all. I am eager to boast of it! Aunt Darlington would be proud of me at last! I have acted with passion and intelligence!"

They all managed to laugh. They seated themselves again. A footman brought in a huge tea, on a rolling tray, and Valerie set herself to serve and listen at the same time. The countess had come down to hear, her color pale, but she seemed more recovered. Servants hovered nearby, but no one had the heart to send them away. They too wished to hear and repeat to others in the household all that had happened.

Reggie helped himself to huge sandwiches and tea with cream and much sugar. He seemed famished. They let him be satisfied first, waiting with contained patience until he would speak.

He sighed, with satisfaction, set down the third sandwich, and began. "Well. I was in Piccadilly when I heard the news. A troop ship of our wounded would be in port—and the port was named to me by a friend."

"Some officers?" asked the earl eagerly, as Reggie paused for a big gulp of hot tea.

Reggie nodded. "Ex-officers, with us in the war. Well, I determined to go down, and see if any friends of mine were aboard. I knew how the hospitals were in port, a chap would lie there for hours, maybe days. If I knew anyone, I'd get him some help quick. So I went back to Aunt Darlington, told her I wanted her biggest carriage, a couple of litters, and some blankets. She loaned me her two biggest grooms, hearty chaps—oh, I say, are they being taken care of?"

Mr. Kenyon said, "Treated royally, I assure you. Bed and food and all the wine they can drink. We cannot thank them enough."

"Good, good. Well, we went off straight-away to the port, found all vast confusion. I looked about, managed to locate a mate on the ship—knew him from a voyage down to the Peninsula—asked him about his troops aboard. He said, 'I say, a friend of yours is aboard, Major Villiers, and bad wounded.' Then I knew it was fate that had drawn me to that ship. I said, 'Got to see him, old chap, got to get him home.'"

He paused to draw breath and drink more tea. Never had he had a more attentive audience.

The butler had his head in the door, a maid was finding an excuse to help with the tea cups, two footmen hovered to help. The earl kept hitching his chair forward to hear better, his hand to his good ear as an aid to hearing. The countess had her gaze fixed so on Reggie's face, that she paid no attention to her plate.

"Took a little arguing and persuasion. They were all for carrying Malcolm off to the hospital. I said he would get much better care and devotion at Arundel. Besides, his father would come up, the Earl of Arundel, I says, and would snort fire and brimstone—you'll forgive me, sir, for what I said—and he would be all over them for not taking proper care of his son and heir. Now the Viscount Grenville, says I. When that seemed to be working, I threw in Aunt Darlington, and the Prime Minister, and His Majesty being personally interested, and they led me down to Malcolm. In a stinking hole—they couldn't help it, the ship was packed with wounded, so you could scarcely walk between the litters. I found him, quiet and feverish, and not knowing anything."

He took another breath and went on.

"Got my two husky chaps up on the deck, then went down again to the cabins. Got Malcolm up on my shoulders, and staggered up on deck, got my chaps and the litter. Then they didn't want me to go ashore. I flashed some papers and a medal I got last year, and said 'King's orders, let me pass,' and they did. Lord, Lord, didn't know I could be so brazen. But I was determined on taking Malcolm out of that hell-hole. Oh, excuse my language!"

He looked so absurdly distressed, that they must reassure him and beg him to continue.

"That's about it. I wouldn't go back to London, might get stopped, out of the way anyway. Made straight for Arundel, holding Malcolm, changed horses every time I could get someone to change at an inn, went through the night, came straight here."

"And we are so immensely grateful, dear Reggie." Valerie had tears in her eyes finally. She could picture Malcolm lying unconscious in the cabins, among rows of badly wounded men. Waiting for carriages to take them painfully to an equally crowded hospital ward. Waiting more hours for treatment. "I do not think I could have endured it, to hear that he had been taken to a hospital, neglected. . . ." Her voice faltered, she put her hands briefly over her face.

The earl got up awkwardly, went to pat her shoulder. "There, there, he's home now, where he must stay. Courage, Valerie, you shall not break down now."

She shook her head. "No, I shall not. He is home, that is all that matters. We shall nurse him back to health." She remained only a little longer, then excused herself, and returned to Malcolm.

Reggie Darlington stayed a few days, proved himself a kind friend by sharing the night watches over Malcolm as the fever raged. Ralph, the valet, was devoted, sitting up night after night, always available in the day. The doctor came each day and renewed the ointments, watched fiercely for signs of greening in the wound. But it did not come. They fed Malcolm beef broth, fresh fruit, everything the doctor suggested, and his strength began slowly to gain.

Finally the fever left, and so did Reggie, excusing himself gracefully as his Aunt Darlington needed him in London. They bade him farewell, and he promised to return, and they must write to him with news. They could not thank him enough for what he had done.

Malcolm's progress seemed unbearably slow to the anxious family and servants. It was a week before he seemed himself, and the fever left him, so that he knew he was home. He kept looking about, in a dazed manner, naming them, and speaking to them as though in a dream.

"Valerie, is that you? I must write to you soon, I have not had the strength to write. . . ."

She would bend over him tenderly. "You are home,

dearest Malcolm. Do not fret yourself, having you here is better than any of your dear letters. Do you not feel my hand in yours?" And she would press the weak fumbling hand firmly, and hold his fingers with hers.

Finally he seemed to know he was home and even could sit up for a meal of sops and fruit juices. He fretted over his wounds, sometimes thought he was back on the Peninsula. "I must start out soon on a mission," he would say to Ralph, who would go running to Valerie.

Then she would reassure Malcolm all over again that he was home with his family, that others carried on the war.

She scarcely had time to read the gazettes and her letters. The earl kept her informed, and Mr. Kenyon kindly read all the war news and told her in detail about the battles, in case Malcolm should ask in his peevish invalid way what was going on. By July he could sit up and was always in his right mind, but became even more difficult to manage, for he was too weak to get out of bed.

Lady Deidre had been informed, of course, by the countess. They were amazed when she wrote, begging to come and "help nurse dear brother Malcolm."

It was the countess who said, with unusual firmness and resolution of mind, "No, of course she shall not come. We have no time for entertaining. Nor would it be suitable for her to be in his sickroom. I shall write and tell her to wait until autumn."

Valerie was glad of that. She had enough on her mind, nursing Malcolm, reading and answering letters from friends. Lady Darlington had written several times, in a gracious manner. Her tart wit and sardonic expressions were a delight to Valerie. Reggie would add a humorous scrawl of his own.

We long to meet you in London. I am assured by Reginald that I shall find you most congenial. He praises your intelligence, your coolness and courage, and also your beauty. Much that men know of it! I have yet to find a man who could find intelligence in a Beauty. They are more like to find weakness that they may exploit! London is mad this season, you would be vastly amused by the devilments. I long to meet you, shall you come to London? My best wishes to your dear husband, Malcolm, I wish him well, and that right shortly.

During the night hours when Valerie stayed up with Malcolm, she kept herself awake by writing. She wrote letters to Mrs. Fitzhugh, who continued to correspond. She informed Valerie of the family, how they longed to see her again, the new governess, who was proper and wise, but not their dear Valerie.

She wrote to Lady Darlington, who wrote back witty letters and also sent the newest books from the publishers and advised her in her reading. Lady Darlington had troubled herself to find the articles and stories that Valerie had written and wrote to praise, suggest, and criticize with much acuity of vision.

"What do you write all the time?" Malcolm asked feebly one night, as the candle burned low on the small desk near his bed.

Valerie started and looked around, then came to him. She bent and pressed her hand to his forehead. It was cool, no more fever in him, and she smiled with pleasure and relief.

"Letters, articles," she said, in answer. "How do you feel? Shall you have a drink of water?"

He nodded and struggled to sit up. She reproved him gently, poured out the water, and slid her hand under his head to lift him slightly. He drank slowly, then lay back, watching her contentedly.

"You are not . . . getting . . . sleep," he said, in the weak tones that seemed but a frail echo of his former hearty voice.

"Yes, I shall. Ralph shall come at midnight and watch

with you." She seated herself beside the bed, in the low rocker. "I am so glad you are recovering. The doctor has been so good, watching over you with such care. The wound in your thigh is healing rapidly now."

"It has been . . . so long. I should be up . . . my regiment needs me." His head turned back and forth fretfully on the pillow. "You cannot imagine it, Valerie. The men dead, the wounded. I never saw anything so horrible as Talavera." He shuddered, and lay quiet, his eyes closed, the sweat breaking out on his brow.

She rinsed a cloth in cool water and laid it on his brow. "And I pray God nightly that the war will soon be over. Wars are so terrible . . ." Her voice broke. "All those lives, wasted."

Malcolm shook his head softly but did not seem to have strength to contradict her. There was a new look about him, of gravity, of maturity, new lines engraved about his nose and mouth, over his forehead.

He slept then, and she sat and watched his face. A new worry nagged at her. Would he be so insane as to return to the battles, after the long struggle to keep him alive? She could not bear it, if he should leave again.

And then she knew, as the even breath of her husband assured her that he slept deeply. She knew that she loved him, that she had worried and wept over him before this because she loved him, and felt tied close to him by deeper bonds even than matrimony. She felt tied by a devotion to him, a love for him, deeper than any she had felt for her father and brother. Gently, lightly, she stroked his big hand, the tanned hand that lay so limply on the blanket.

She loved him, and he had married her on a toss of the dice! She wished so fervently that he had married her for love, not pity. What would become of them? Would he want to discard her for one of a gay frivolous nature such as Lady Deidre? Or would he discover in himself, at last, a longing to settle down with Valerie, to have children, to follow in his father's steps?

With this new knowledge hidden in her heart, Valerie went through the next days and weeks. July turned to August. Malcolm was allowed to sit up for some hours each day. He was fretful and must be entertained. She read to him, wrote letters for him, talked to him. The earl came often and tried to talk to him about the estate. However, Malcolm was fretful about that and professed to know little of such matters.

"But you must get out, Valerie, you are so white and tired," Malcolm finally said to her. "Go out for an hour, then come back, and tell me what you see."

He insisted, and she went out and found pleasure working in the garden once more. The sun felt so good, the birds sang, and there were honeysuckle vines with hummingbirds dipping deeply into their long tempting sweetness. She cut several of the late yellow tea roses, arranged them in a tall blue vase, slim and pretty, of China porcelain, and brought them to Malcolm.

"Where did you go?" he asked instantly, and wanted to hear every step of her path.

"You shall see our Shakespeare garden one day," she told him, and went on to describe it. He watched her face, smiled a little, frowned a little, begged her to talk more about whatever she would.

She formed the habit, then, of going out for an hour or two in the morning and the afternoon, and was the stronger for it. The August sun shone brightly, the flowers seemed to burst forth from their buds.

September came and went. Malcolm was able to sit in a large easy chair near the window, wrapped in blankets, and wave to her in the garden below. She was intensely conscious of his watching, and sometimes held up to him an especially lovely flower, or pointed to the bushes or trees, as they turned from green to red and golden hues.

She brought him herbs and flowers to smell, some for

his vases, some to hold in his hands. She taught him the differences between them, and the uses of some of the herbs. They read together the Shakespeare volumes, and then went on to others, some novels, some plays, and volumes of essays, which Lady Darlington was pleased to send to them.

Finally it was October, and Malcolm was strong enough to stand briefly, to be dressed in "proper clothes," as he said gleefully. He shaved off his whiskers, the head wound was healed, and left but a long red scar near the hair line. He used a cane, and was able to come downstairs one memorable October day, to remain for tea and then dinner in the evening.

It was a celebration. The butler poured out champagne for them all and beamed at everyone, with a most unstately expression on his happy face. The maids fluttered about them, the footmen found excuse to come in every few minutes to hear the laughter and joyful conversation.

"You must all toast my recovery," said Malcolm, impetuously. "Forrester, you will bring us champagne for the toast. And in the pantry, everyone tonight must toast my recovery! And I thank you all for your help!"

The butler beamed, bowed, and murmured that it was a great delight and joy to them all that my lord had recovered. The earl then raised his glass to Malcolm, who grinned at him.

"To my son, my very . . . dear . . . son . . . and his safe return home. Thank God for you, my dear boy!" said the earl, and Valerie felt tears very close as she raised her glass to drink with them.

The earl turned then to her, his glass filled again. "And to your wife, Valerie. For her courage, her patience, her goodness to us all, the strength that helped encourage us while you were gone, Malcolm. To your wonderful and devoted wife, Valerie!"

They all drank to her, the countess beaming and patting her hand with her frail one. She flushed and avoided Malcolm's eyes. He looked very thoughtful, suddenly.

It was a very happy evening. They were all, as the earl put it, "slightly drunken! Very very slightly, for sheer joy and happiness. We must have some of the fine brandy tonight with our coffee. What better occasion . . . except one . . ." And then the earl looked very thoughtful and pleased, in his turn.

Valerie wondered briefly what occasion he referred to, then forgot his words. She would long remember that happy evening. For it was the last one she really enjoyed. The next day Lady Deidre arrived, with her abigail, her trunks, and her valises, prepared for a long stay.

Dancing in, beautiful as ever and as bewitching in sheer black chiffon and silk, Lady Deidre clasped the hands of the countess. "Oh, my dearest, how I have missed you." And then she turned to Malcolm. "Oh . . . Malcolm . . . my dear." And she kissed him on both cheeks, like a sister.

Or not like a sister. Valerie saw the lively blue eyes, the shimmer of effective tears, the brilliance of the smile she had bestowed on Malcolm.

"And you are practically well again," said Lady Deidre, and clasped her hands together, with her blonde hair making her look like a holy angel. "Oh, praise God for it! I have prayed and prayed for you! How I wanted to come and help! But now I am here, and I shall help amuse you in your recovery! You shall all be lively again!"

It sounded like a threat to Valerie. The countess was definitely happy to see Deidre, the earl had to smile at her brightness and charm. And Malcolm—Malcolm spent the next two hours at her side, talking to her, listening to her, in apparent complete delight. He could not take his gaze from her beautiful creamy face, the blonde curls teasing at the white throat, the effective black lace against her chin, the small white hand that touched his arm every now and then in gentle sympathy.

Chapter Eight

Deidre came, lingered, dominated every conversation when they were together. Valerie watched in silence, feeling peeved, cross, finally very concerned. Malcolm seemed to enjoy her so much, he laughed more often at her wit, the stories she told of her friends, and what went on in London.

Deidre took it on herself to read him the gazettes, so they were together each morning for two hours, alone in the drawing room. She read prettily, skipping over the war news hastily, then going on to comment on the gossip pages and the doings in Parliament. She had met many of the men concerned, she always had some personal note that made them alive and real.

Valerie spent more and more time in the gardens, or off in a carriage with the earl. She was not happy, but she kept busy, and so the time went.

A brother officer came home and sent on to Malcolm the personal possessions that he had had to leave behind in Portugal on their hasty sailing. Malcolm opened the trunk and took out the contents with great pleasure.

"My sweaters that you knitted, Valerie! How warm and comfortable they were under my coats, I assure you! It was a miserable cold and wet winter. And even the home of the Portuguese don was sometimes chilly of an evening."

She lifted the sweaters, noted how worn and torn they were. One had an immense rip in it, just over the breast. She swallowed.

"I must make more for you. It will be cold this winter again," she said quietly. "Shall I have these washed?"

"No, throw them out," he said, looking at the rip also, his face rather gray and weary. "They have done their service."

She said nothing, but folded them up to carry them away, thinking she would keep them, hidden in her wardrobe. She wanted to remember that they had kept Malcolm warm and protected for a time.

He threw out his old socks, then dived again into the trunk to bring up a package wrapped in crackly paper. "There, there it is! I bought a Spanish shawl for you, Valerie, the prettiest I could find."

Beaming, he shook it out of the paper and held it up. She caught her breath in pleasure. The shawl was large, of a creamy silk, patterned in deep red roses, green leaves, and a long fringe. She swept it about her shoulders, over her green dress, and it covered her shoulders and arms, down below her waist, with the fringe hanging below her hips.

"How beautiful! It is most lovely, thank you, Malcolm!" She fingered the silk, her face glowing that he had thought of her and bought it for her. "I shall wear it of an evening, the Spanish touch is all the fashion! It would look well over my cream taffeta."

"You look very lovely in it." He stood, seeming to wait, and she glanced at him questioningly. With a shrug, he turned back to the trunk, took out another parcel. He seemed a little embarrassed. "I brought you also a black mantilla, Valerie, but would you mind if I gave it to Deidre? She enjoys presents so much, and it will help take her mind off her grief for Eustace. She misses him so much."

Valerie bit back a tart word. She looked at the lovely

black lace mantilla, imagined it on Deidre's blonde head, and said, gallantly, "Of course you must, Malcolm. And it will look beautiful on her, she is stunning in black."

"She does not wear black because she is beautiful in it!" Malcolm said it sharply, as though Valerie had criticized. "She is genuinely in mourning for Eustace, though you do not seem to believe it!"

"Oh, yes, I believe it," murmured Valerie. Slowly she took off the Spanish shawl, and folded it with shaking hands. Lady Deidre was succeeding in making them further apart. Was this in innocence, or was it a part of a plan? Surely she did not think to win Malcolm as her husband, he was a married man already. But she took her sober thoughts with her back to the bedroom, where she folded away the shawl and Malcolm's discarded sweaters.

She was present when Malcolm gave the mantilla to Lady Deidre at tea that afternoon. Deidre opened the paper with pleasure, cried out happily at the sight. "Oh, I must try it on at once!"

She ran over to the mirror that decorated the top of the mantelpiece, and laid the black lace carefully and coquettishly over her blonde curls. It was stunning, and she turned back to Malcolm for his approval.

"Beautiful," he said with charm, and came to arrange it a little differently. "The Spanish ladies wear it so, with the point down over the forehead, just above the eyes. It makes their eyes shine, just as yours are now, Deidre."

She reached up impulsively and kissed his cheek. "How kind you are to me, Malcolm!" she murmured.

He patted her cheek. "And you appreciate everything so much," he said. There seemed to be some meaning behind his words. He returned to his seat. The earl was scowling over his tea, the countess looked thoughtfully at Deidre still admiring herself in the mirror. Louis Kenyon muttered something under his breath, set down his cup, excused himself, and left the room.

Valerie felt a little sick. She remained, to chat quietly

with the countess, while Deidre perched near Malcolm's chair and talked brightly with him about London, the mantilla setting off the bright gold of her hair.

"I have about half a dozen of these mantillas, from my officer-beaux," Valerie heard Deidre say. "However, I shall cherish this one the most, because it is from you, dearest Malcolm!"

Valerie was shocked. She broke off her sentence, stared at Deidre, who was patting Malcolm's hand confidingly.

"Is it the London fashion, to accept presents from men not of one's family?" Valerie asked sharply. Malcolm glared at her, Deidre looked troubled, then laughed.

"Oh, my dear Valerie, you really must be presented in society, and learn our ways," she said gaily. "You really do not comprehend London at all! It is not like the country! We are more like Parisians! I shall explain it to you. One does not accept a dress, but one can accept gloves, or a mantilla, something for the hair, or jewelry. An intimate garment, no, but something like this, yes, it is quite proper."

"I see," said Valerie coldly. She was furious, and soon left the room. She retired to the study and sat down in the corner with her papers.

Louis Kenyon glanced over at her wrily. "One does not leave the battlefield, if one wishes to win the battle, my dear," he said gently.

She tossed her head defiantly. "I am not in a battle, sir!"

"I'm afraid that you are, Valerie," he told her. "And the enemy is clever and has many weapons you would scorn to use."

She compressed her lips and tried to work on an article. Now that Malcolm was recovered, and Deidre amused him by the hour, she found time hanging heavy on her hands. She went out in the carriage, traveling about the estate when she could, or worked in the greenhouse or the gardens. However, when she must, she retreated to the study and worked on the books there, or composed letters and articles. She found herself too troubled in mind to concentrate on it, but it gave her a pretext to be away from the sight of Deidre hanging on Malcolm's arm, or touching his hand with gay confidence, or whispering little witty things to him.

Malcolm came in presently limping heavily and leaning on the cane which had been his grandfather's. The earl had unearthed it, and given it to him, a fine ebony cane with an ivory handle, made in India.

He glared at Valerie, working quietly in the corner at her desk. "Must you hide yourself away? This is not polite to our guests," he barked.

"Have we guests?" she asked, with mock innocence. "I thought it was only family this evening."

"You know very well that Lady Deidre is our guest!"

"You manage to entertain her very well. I do not know London society, so I bore her," snapped Valerie. Louis Kenyon got up, and discreetly left the room.

"Come now, that is no excuse. You should remain, and learn of manners from her! If you would but talk to her, you would learn much! She has been in the finest society."

"She does not wish to talk to me, but to you," said Valerie, irritably. "She cares not for what women have to say."

"That is a very unjust remark! I am surprised at you, Valerie. I thought you prided yourself on having a cool and intelligent mind!" he jeered.

The earl came in, heard their upraised voices, and frowned at them. He closed the door after him. "Good, good, you are alone. I wished to speak to you both," he said sternly.

Valerie felt immediately like a rude child. She got up and went over to him. "I am sorry, sir, we are quarreling again. I have a quick temper, I fear."

She hated for the earl to be upset, she knew how troubled he had been over Eustace, then the long worry over Malcolm. She patted his shoulder soothingly, and he took her hand in his.

"Malcolm," he said, beckoning to his younger son. "Come here. I would talk seriously to you also. I know you and Valerie strike fire off each other like flint and iron. However, you are married, and she has been a good and devoted wife to you. No one could have been more thoughtful of your mother and me, no one more conscientious a nurse to you."

"Yes, I realize that, father, however . . ." Malcolm began belligerently. "Her manners to our guests . . ."

"That is another thing altogether. I will speak to you on more serious matters." The earl flushed, his bearded cheeks showing red, above the graying hair. "Your valet has confided in me, at my request, that you do not sleep together."

Malcolm stared at his father, his pale invalid's face began to flush. Valerie burst in, her voice high-pitched.

"He has been very ill, papa!" she said. "You cannot expect . . ."

"He is well enough to hop around all day," said the earl sternly. "Now, if I had been him, I would have been in my wife's bed as soon as possible, as soon as I had recovered my senses, wounds or no wounds. Nothing could have kept me from her side! But you, Malcolm, you seem somewhat lax in your marital duties!"

"Valerie has shown no signs of wishing me near. While I was gone, she went off at once to the far ends of the country," said Malcolm sullenly.

"What is in the past, is in the past," said his father. "You are married, you are my only son and heir. Do you ever think of the future, of Arundel, of your family? You must have children, I want my grandchildren at my knees before I depart this earth! No such shilly-shallying around will do!"

Valerie felt one fiery blush. She could not look at Malcolm.

"Valerie does not wish to live up to our marriage vows," said Malcolm bitterly. "She has told me bluntly she wishes a divorce. I do not please her, I am no intellectual! I do not even amuse her, as Reggie Darlington does!"

"Enough of such bickering!" said the earl sternly, forcefully. "It is your part to woo your wife, Malcolm, and I am ashamed of you that I must remind you of it! If I were young, and had such a charming lovely devoted wife, I should not be slow about wooing her!"

He seemed really upset and angry. Malcolm gazed at him thoughtfully, then at Valerie. Valerie cried out,

"Do not look at me! If we do not suit, that is an end of it! I never wanted to marry, I am quite satisfied to teach and write my articles."

"Nonsense, Valerie, there is more to life than such matters," said her father-in-law, more kindly. He patted her nearest shoulder. "I have come to love you as a father. I know you resent Malcolm's lack of interest, his attentions to another woman. But Deidre at least knows she is a woman, and bothers to attract a man, even though he is like a brother to her! You could take lessons from her. She dresses for men, she is flattering in her attentiveness . . ."

"I'll take no lessons from her!" cried Valerie, and ran from the room. She took refuge in her bedroom and burst into tears of rage and shame. Even her dear father-in-law had turned against her! Comparing her to that—that flirt!

She had to force herself to calm down, to dress for dinner. She went down late and was conscious of the redness about her eyes which no powder could hide. She was subdued and quiet at the meal, and excused herself soon after coffee was served in the drawing room. Deidre had worn another low-cut black chiffon gown, with the black mantilla alluringly on her golden head, and diamonds in her cars and at her wrist. Valerie felt a dowd. She was only a country miss, she reminded herself bitterly.

Glenda came to her soon after she went up. "You have a headache, my lady?" she murmured, and soothed her by massaging the muscles at the back of her neck. Valerie put on one of her pretty little nightdresses of cream, with embroidery about the low neck and sleeves. Malcolm had never seen her in these, she thought bitterly. The countess had brought them from London for her. And Malcolm did not even bother to come to her bedroom!

She lay awake for a time, in spite of the darkness, brooding sullenly. She wanted to leave at once. Mrs. Fitzhugh would give her a reference, Lady Darlington might know of another position. Malcolm had been unable to conceal his reluctance to embrace his wife!

She was almost asleep, when the door opened abruptly, and a dark shape came in. She was startled, and leaned up on her elbow sleepily. "Who is it? Glenda? What do you wish?"

"It is I, Malcolm, you husband," said his ironic voice. He came over to the bed. "I know you do not wish me here, but it is beyond us! Father wishes it."

"Oh, the devil!" she cried, with unaccustomed wrath. "Go away! I don't want you here! The best thing is a divorce! I shall get a position . . ."

"You have a position here, my dear wife! You simply don't live up to it, sulking and brooding and glaring all the time! London will polish your manners, my girl!" And he jerked off his robe, and slid into the huge bed beside her.

She tried to slide out the other side. He grabbed her and pulled her back with unexpected strength.

"No, let me go . . . let me go . . ." She struggled against him.

"Ouch . . . don't pull like that," he said, suddenly human again. "My side hurts like the deuce."

Her struggles ceased at once. "Oh, Malcolm, I'm sorry . . . I'll get some salve . . ."

"No, stay here. Come on, Valerie, it isn't so bad, is it? You didn't hate me before I left," he coaxed, drawing her to him.

She went stiff. "I don't want you to . . . to embrace me because your father ordered you to!" she said wildly. "And I don't want your child! You'll just want a divorce . . ."

"Stop such nonsense. We're married. And you'll have to live up to your marriage vows, Valerie," he said, sternly, abruptly more mature-sounding. "You can't hem and haw about, you know."

It was so ridiculous, if she hadn't been so disturbed she would have laughed. He drew her down beside him, his arm about her. His other hand stroked her loosened hair.

"You know, we could be friends, I thought we were friends," said his coaxing voice. "You took care of me so devotedly while I was ill. I would wake at night, and find you bending over me, so pretty and anxious. And you would hold a glass of cool water to my lips, and murmur like an angel. I loved your hand on my head."

She sighed. "Oh, Malcolm, that was different."

"Why? You took every care of me, as a wife should. And those letters of yours—how I waited for them, how angry I was when the ships were late, and I did not hear. They seemed the only foothold on sanity I had at times."

He murmured to her, stroked his hand over her hair and face, and gradually she relaxed against him. He bent over her, and brushed his mouth gently against her cheek, down to her throat, over her shoulder which his hand had bared of the silky nightdress.

It seemed so long since he had touched her in desire. She remembered some of the nights they had spent together, and soon desire was rising in her also. Why couldn't she turn off the thoughts that made her bitter and enjoy what she had?

If she could but forget that he had lost at dice, and forced himself to marry her . . .

If she could but forget the sight of Deidre sitting on the arm of the chair, while he showed her how to fasten the mantilla . . .

If she could but forget his reputation as a rake, his charm, the fact that now he did his *duty* toward her as his wife . . .

She sighed deeply. He raised his head. "Valerie? You do like me, don't you?"

"Of course I do, but . . . but our marriage . . . we should never have married . . ."

"Oh, play another tune!" he advised her coarsely and angrily, and his arms snatched her closer to him.

His kisses crushed against her throat and shoulders. Then his head moved up, and his mouth covered her lips, forcing them open. He thrust his tongue between her lips, and his hands caressed her roughly, no longer gentle. She felt his fingers on her breasts, under the silk, and the nipples rose up and hardened in his fingers.

Something weakened in her and went soft. Her arms went up about his neck. She felt his hair in her fingers, the soft hair she had stroked sometimes when he was feverish and could not rest. Her hands went to his bare shoulders, to the thin bony frame, and it seemed as though her heart turned over in pity, he had been so tough. She could feel the scarcely healed wound in the shoulder, and her touch was easy on him, stroking gently.

He muttered her name against her throat, like a groan. He moved over her, and drew up the nightdress to her thighs. She felt the hardening of his body, the fierceness of his desire as he came to her in need and desire. Not love . . . but perhaps this was enough . . . it had to be enough.

They came together, again, again, and her whole body welcomed his hardness and drive. She opened like a flower to the sun, warmly, wanting, blossoming under his touch, her mouth opened to his, the kisses fierce from long repression. He lingered long on her, and finally drew off, trembling with his emotions.

She was limp also, shivering with the reaction. He drew up the covers over them both, and held her closely to him. He whispered in her ear, "You are so sweet, Valerie, you are so sweet when you give in. God, I dreamed of you at nights, wanting you. Did you want me also? You won't admit it if you did!" And he gave her a playful little slap on her bare thigh.

"Oh, Malcolm . . ."

"Don't talk. We just fight when we talk. Just kiss me," and he pressed his mouth fiercely to hers once more.

She hated herself that she could not resist responding to him. He did not love her, he just desired her. There had always been this intense sexual flame between them. But when he was in his right mind, she thought, he wanted someone like Deidre. Light and amusing, with the gossip of London at her fingertips.

She lay awake long after he had slept beside her and stared into the darkness. Could this be enough? If she had a child, would the marriage last? Or would he grow bored and leave her for London and its pleasures? She could not endure that, to raise his child, to remain behind, nor did she want to go to London, if all London held more Deidres!

Well, she could try to make it work. The earl wanted it so much, he wanted grandchildren, and she adored her father-in-law. She loved Malcolm, but she feared to show him so. Would he mock her, or worse, feel sorry for her?

She could not think straight, she decided. When Malcolm's arm lay heavily, possessively across her body in sleep, when his head lay beside hers on the pillows, and she could turn her head and gaze into his sleeping face, she could not think. She must wait until tomorrow, until another day, to try to decide whether to leave him and live in desolation, but independence. Or to remain, to be humiliated and scorned by such as Deidre.

However, if she had his child . . .

A child of Malcolm. A thrill stirred in her. What if she had his child? He would not discard her then, he was too gallant, too conscious of his duty. Yet if he went off and had his mistresses, as rumor said he had in the past, how could she endure that?

It was a puzzle beyond her solving. She finally turned a little, and felt his arm tighten about her. She stroked her hand lightly on his good shoulder, loving the touch and feel of his hard bare flesh. He was safely home, she thanked God for it. Perhaps if she started a child, he would be reconciled to remaining here with them.

He did seem more content, yet when he was completely well, he might wish to leave. She would not hold him back, yet she would die a little every night if he left her.

What could she do? What did other women do? She did not know.

Malcolm stirred, roused as she moved in bed. "Valerie? Still awake?" he murmured in her ear and kissed the lobe.

"Yes. I'm almost asleep," she said.

"Didn't I get you weary enough to sleep?" There was a teasing note in his voice that warned her. She tried to move away, his arm tightened, he raised up, and bent over her.

"Oh, Malcolm, don't again . . . you'll hurt your leg . . ."

It was no use, his mouth was closed over her mouth, silencing her, and his hands moved hungrily over her. "It's been so long," he said, when he finally left her lips, to roam over her shoulder. "You're so soft and silky. What is that perfume?"

"Lilac," she managed to say before his mouth closed over hers once more.

His hands pressed on her breast, teasingly. "This time is for you, love," he said. She did not know what he meant then. But presently he was moving on her, then stopping, then moving again. She caught her breath, she seemed on fire.

"Oh, what are you . . . oh, Malcolm . . . oh, ohhhhh . . ." She tried to shift under him, to press herself upwards. She wanted something, wanted it badly. He eased himself just out of reach. Then he moved again, sharply, and she cried out, softly, in a strange pleasure.

His fingers teased at her, the fire built up and up. She grabbed at his waist, slid her arms about his back, her fingers dug into his hard spare flesh. She tried to pull up, she wanted it, wanted it, and yet he kept putting her off.

He muttered endearments breathlessly in her ears, kissing the lobe, biting softly at her ears, her nipples, her shoulders. He was all over her, moving, drawing her with him, building up a fire in her that began to burn fiercely bright.

"Ooohhh," she gasped, and something went off inside her, like a series of explosions, soft and violent. She was helpless before it, and Malcolm knew it. He pressed deeply into her, his body so close that it seemed to imprint itself on her very flesh in an image that she could never erase or forget. And all the time, they were bound by lips, arms, thighs, so close, so close.

Then he finished in her, also, and the explosions burst again in her. From violent movement, she collapsed into limp submission, exhausted, yet deliriously happy. Malcolm laughed softly into her ears.

"Enjoy it, darling? That was the best yet, oh, darling! Valerie, you are so adorable! Tell me you enjoyed it!"

"Ooohhh," was all she could say. He kissed her breasts, and slid off, to draw up the covers again, satisfied, nuzzling his face against her as he went to sleep again. And this time she slept also, she could not remain awake.

Chapter Nine

Valerie tried very hard to be satisfied with her life. It was difficult when Deidre remained constantly, ostensibly to comfort Eustace's mother. Actually, thought Valerie, retiring yet again to the study, she was charming Malcolm constantly, appearing to be sweet and gentle, yet her look of hate would flash at Valerie when no one else noticed.

Valerie thought, "Deidre is trying to separate us! She wants Malcolm now! He is the heir, he is Viscount Grenville. And nothing would please her more than to separate us, before I have a child!"

Malcolm still came to her bed, but not every night. And they would quarrel, a spark could set them off, and they did not speak for days. Valerie felt helpless to stop this, they seemed to quarrel so easily. And Deidre was always there, to laugh and egg them on, or say how it was done in polite society, or mock at Valerie under the guise of advising her.

Valerie turned more and more to the earl. She begged for more work to do.

"Come, come, child, you work enough," he said pleased. "If only you could persuade Malcolm to take some interest, I should be immensely happy!"

However, Malcolm took little interest in the estate. When he was bored, he would take out his carriage and ride off, sometimes alone, sometimes with Deidre. He rarely asked Valerie. When the earl reprimanded him, Malcolm said, "Valerie doesn't want to come, she is too busy, aren't you, Valerie?"

And his mockery sounded just like that of Deidre. Valerie would turn away, furiously, and go to the study to work.

"You only play into her hands," warned Louis Kenyon. No one else seemed to notice anything, but that Malcolm and Valerie had had another spat.

"If he prefers her company, he is welcome to it!" flashed Valerie. She took out her articles and books and bent over them.

Mr. Kenyon shook his head and returned to his own work on the accounts.

The earl came in, frowning. He looked thoughtfully at Valerie's flushed, rebellious face. Finally he said,

"I should like to ride out to see one of the tenants. Will you come with me, Valerie? It is not so bad for a November day, the sunshine is quite bright."

"Oh, yes, I'll get my cloak and bonnet." She got up at once.

He sighed. "You will come with me, why not with Malcolm?"

"Three is a crowd, father," she snapped, and then asked, "Do you truly wish me to come, or were you testing me?"

"Of course, I wish you to come." She ran off to get her cloak, hoping he would forget his arguments. However, in the carriage, he continued them gently.

"How lovely the day is," she said happily, as they settled into the open carriage. "Which direction do we go, papa?"

"To the Forsythes," he said. "Her baby is a year today, and it is their first child. I thought we would take them flowers and a gift, here it is."

"How thoughtful you are, papa." She smiled in

pleasure, partly at the thought of seeing the adorable baby.

"I enjoy children," he said gently. "I live for the day when I can hold my first grandchild."

She turned her face from him, and stared at the wintry fields through blurred vision.

"Now, Valerie, what is this that makes you quarrel so with Malcolm? You are not so with me, nor with my wife. We love you dearly. You were good in writing to him, he admits it. You worried over him, nursed him devotedly, but now that he is well you will have nothing to do with him. Do you love only someone distant or ill?"

"You know that is not true," she said, in a choked voice. "He . . . he cares nothing for me. He wishes he were free!"

"I cannot believe that," said the earl firmly, giving a keen look at her profile. "He married you willingly, even eagerly. He had never so much as proposed to anyone before."

"He won me at dice!" blurted out Valerie. The secret had remained too long in her breast, causing a cancer of self-doubt. "Or rather, he lost at dice! They cast dice to see who would have to marry me and take care of me. And Malcolm lost . . . he *lost*!"

"Good heavens!" barked the earl. "Where did you hear such a ridiculous story?"

She turned to him, full face, her lips quivering, her lashes wet with tears. "A . . . a fellow-officer who was there, sir, and witnessed it all! I cannot doubt it. Malcolm scarcely knew me, he just came and told me of Clarence's death, realized I was alone and in a bad position with my cousin's ill behavior. Then he proposed and said he must marry me. I did not know it was a . . . a *debt of honor*, as the gamblers call it!"

The earl stared at her, realized she was serious. "I cannot believe it . . . yet . . . oh, my dear child, do you think Malcolm would have married you for such a reason?"

"Yes, sir. He is a gambler and a man of honor," she choked out. "I should have said no, no, a thousand times, should I have known why he asked me to marry him! And now he wishes also that he had not! Me, a woman of intelligence and able to take care of herself!" And her head went up proudly. "I can make my own living! I shall not depend on him!"

The earl took both her hands, and patted them gently. "There, there, how distressed you are, my child. Do not fret yourself. I shall speak to Malcolm, he shall clear up this ridiculous misunderstanding, and all will be well between you. I am sure that he honors and respects you, no matter for what reason he married you."

"No, tell him nothing!" she said curtly, withdrawing her hands and wiping her eyes with her small white handkerchief. "I am too humiliated by it all. We shall live together decently until I am twenty-one, then I shall leave. That will be in a few more months."

He sighed deeply at her obstinacy. "No, my dear. You shall not. You are married in sacred matrimony, I wish you to remain married to him. You are good for him, you will help settle him down. He needs to learn of the estate, to take up his duties as my only—my only remaining son and heir."

His stern voice broke, and it was her turn to comfort him.

"Forgive me for upsetting you, sir. I had not meant to speak of this. It is between me and Malcolm, and we shall resolve it."

"I hope so," he said, more cheerfully, drawing another meaning from her words. "If you but have a child soon, he will reconcile himself to the marriage, and settle down to be a good husband and father. I know the lad, he but needs responsibility to mature him. Look how his Army tasks helped to make him more grave."

She turned away. He did not understand, nor comprehend how hurt she felt. She did not want to remain where she was a heavy duty and responsibility to a man. No matter how much she loved Malcolm, it would be very bitter to remain under those conditions. He did not see how her woman's heart yearned to be loved and adored. Not just the physical passion that Malcolm felt for her. He could feel that for any attractive woman.

No, she wanted to be loved and wanted and needed for herself. She knew there were marriages of convenience, she had witnessed them, and sometimes they worked out well, when there was affection and respect. But she felt too humiliated at his obvious attentions to Deidre. There was his previous reputation to consider, he was a rake, a gambler.

What if she did have a child, and once the novelty had worn off, Malcolm should run off about his own amusements? She would be left to raise the child, endure the amused comments of persons such as Deidre and her society.

No, no, far better to be away from them all. She could obtain another position such as that with Mrs. Fitzhugh, where she was honored and respected, a governess to young children, helping their minds expand and mature. That would be a noble task, enough for a lifetime of work. And satisfying, far more than to be a bed-partner of a man who grossly neglected her by day.

But she said no more of this to the earl. She enjoyed the visit to his tenants, rocked the baby in her arms, and kissed his petal-soft cheek. She talked of gardens to Mrs. Forsythe, while the earl discussed the spring crops with Mr. Forsythe, and where the cattle should be moved for better grazing.

On the way home, she spoke with the earl brightly about the matters of the estate. They needed more feed for the cattle, they might plant more fields in grain. The apples had done well, the trees should be pruned yet again.

"I wish Malcolm took your interest in this," he said finally, as they drove smartly into the graveled driveway leading up to the castle. "What a satisfaction to know that the next generation shall carry on the work! My father often grew indifferent, I had a great task bringing all up to snuff after I inherited. Eustace was not strong, yet he had an interest in all this. I do hope that Malcolm shall take yet more interest."

She smiled, and patted his hand and said nothing. Was it in her power to change Malcolm, and get him interested in the work? She doubted it very much.

Her doubts were increased when they entered, to find that Malcolm and Deidre had returned from their drive, bringing a half a dozen young people from the village as their guests for luncheon. The servants were flying about, they had had no warning of the little invasion.

Valerie went to change her sober blue gown for something more elegant, a rose silk with lace about the throat, and then descended to arrange the flowers for the table. The gardener had sent in some of the last of the roses and pinks.

Malcolm came to the small room off the pantry where she worked, with an apron over her elegant gown. He was obviously angry.

"Here you are! You refuse to ride with me, yet go off in a minute with my father!" he raged. "Do you hate my company so much?"

About to flare back at him, she bit her tongue. Perhaps this was her opportunity. "Malcolm, your father needs much help on the estate. I wish you had come with us today! You would have been able to help in decisions about the fields."

"I care nothing for the fields! My men are fighting and dying on the Peninsula, and I am unable to join them yet! Have you seen the gazettes from London?"

"No, I have not," she said quietly. "I shall look them over this afternoon after the guests have departed. Is there . . . bad news?"

"Bad enough," he said, and pressed his hand to the scar on his forehead, where a vein throbbed heavily. "Viscount Wellington has had to retreat before the French. They are followed, harassed. No one knows what Wellington is about. All I know is that I should be with my men. I should never have left Portugal, I know it."

Her gaze was troubled, even as she automatically arranged yellow tea roses with small pale pinks in a low blue porcelain bowl, and then taller spikes of the last columbine in a pair of pale cream porcelain vases. She studied them, head to one side, then adjusted the heather-colored columbine against the lavender, and thrust some of the deeper rose just below them.

"Very pretty," said Malcolm, finally, in approval. "You do know how to arrange flowers."

"Thank you," she said, with slight irony. She had been arranging the flowers here ever since she had arrived. Had he not ever seen them before? Perhaps he had not noticed, or did not really care what she did—in the daytime.

They went in to luncheon, Malcolm in a little better mood. He made them all laugh with some stories of the wars, jests about the language of his men as they fought like tigers. They were not the kind of stories he had told Valerie, of the wounds, the slow dying, when some of his Portuguese spies had been hanged from trees by the French. He gave the impression today that the war was all jokes and comradeship. But she remembered vividly some of the other tales he had told to her alone.

She sat quietly in her place at the earl's side, and made some conversation with the squire's son, who was a little more sober and conscientious than his sister and friends. From her experience in the household of the Fitzhughs, she knew what some of his father's duties were, and was able to speak with him about them, about the village, the school which now thrived.

Deidre, in an ethereal gown of gray gauze with touches of black lace at her throat and wrists, held their attention much of the time with her light brilliant chatter about London. She could tell a story, with wit and elegance, which revealed much of her life. She showed them subtly about what circles she moved in London, as the stories unrolled. She had met the Prince Regent at a ball, and as he danced with her he had said. . . . Or when the cabinet members had fought their duel, Lady Jersey had informed her sternly of her feelings on the matter. . . . Or an officer friend of hers, a colonel, had begged her to marry him and go to the Peninsula with him, but she could not, of course, though he gave her gifts of jewelry and laces from Spain.

All this, with the lightest of touches, showing how men fell over her, how popular she was, how sought after. Malcolm listened with pleasure, sometimes sending a significant glance at Valerie which she refused to meet. Was this what he expected of her? She had no wish for light flirtations with officers and men of wealth!

The squire's daughter was all ears, begging humbly for more information. Did one wear black gloves in mourning all the time? Was it proper to ride in the Serpentine with only a groom? At what age could one be presented, and did it take a special invitation of the King or the Prince Regent?

Deidre talked on and on, holding all their attention in her sparkling face, her vivid blue eyes, the palms of her small hands, delicately making a point with a gesture or wave. The countess beamed on her fondly, even the earl found her stories of interest.

"And when were you presented?" the squire's daughter turned eagerly to the silent Valerie. "What happened, when was it?"

Valerie opened her mouth to deny it. Deidre squealed.

"But, of course, she has not been! The Viscountess Grenville has not been presented! How odd! She must be, and before she grows much older! Maman, we must see to it," and she turned eagerly to the countess. "We must take her to London, polish her up, and present her! Oh, what fun!"

Malcolm took her up on it. "Of course, we must go. It would be jolly, wouldn't it, Valerie? You shall be presented at the next season. Maman, you could make the arrangements, could you not? We shall open the town house."

The countess hesitated, then shook her head. "We are still in demi-mourning, Malcolm," she said. "I do not think it would be proper. Besides, we are so contented in the country. I do not think I could endure to return to London so soon."

Deidre's sparkling face lost some of its joy. "But, maman . . . I mean, countess . . . I beg you . . . think of Valerie! She should be presented! It is only right! And how she would enjoy London! There is no place like it. You must consider it, please, for Valerie's sake! She has slaved her fingers to the bone, taking care of Malcolm in his illness, now trotting all about the estate, looking after everyone, working so terribly hard. Does she not deserve a holiday?"

The squire's son turned to Valerie beside him. Clearly, he said, "But, my lady, you have not said how you feel about it! Does the prospect give you much pleasure?"

"I should not care for it at all," she said bluntly, and all the table heard her. Some gasped, some smiled. Malcolm shot her an ugly look, and Deidre pouted.

"I must change her mind for her," said Deidre prettily. "I will talk to her, and tell her of the delights of London society. We have not had a good long talk for such a long time!"

The countess looked very troubled, the earl stern. Malcolm was scowling heavily. The squire's son rather tactfully turned the conversation to another subject, that of the village school, and Deidre lost interest.

Malcolm came to Valerie that evening in her sitting room, where she was going over an article she was preparing for an editor.

"Scribbling again?" he asked. "You did not even remain to speed our guests on their way!"

She sighed. She had a headache, and she pressed her hand to her forehead. "I remained for three hours, and waited for tea to be served before I excused myself, Malcolm," she said, with what patience she could muster.

"And you were so rude about Deidre's suggestion of going to London! Must you be so difficult! It would do maman a world of good to go off to London, she needs to be brought out of herself, and forget her mourning for Eustace."

"I cannot see how that can be accomplished by revisiting the unhappy scenes of his fatal illness and death," she said bluntly. "It cannot help but bring back great sorrow. And your father does not care for London."

"It would not be so long a visit," he coaxed, sitting down on the sofa opposite her rosewood desk, and gazing at her from under his long dark lashes. The hazel eyes gleamed. "I can see you now, radiant in a gown of lilac silk, with an overdress of silver gauze, the belle of the ball. You waltz quite well, you know, and you always follow my steps well in the country dances."

"The waltz is not really proper," she frowned.

"Oh, come now, do not be a country miss! You would enjoy it, all of London. The bookstores, how you would go mad in the crammed bookstores! And the plays, we shall go to any play you desire, even though it is so stuffy it makes me fall asleep!"

He was so charming and coaxing, that she had to laugh. The prospect of bookstores did enthrall her. Lady Darlington continued to keep her well stocked, but to see the actual shelves of books, the new ones and the favourites . . . Her eyes gleamed.

"I should like to see the bookstores, and perhaps to meet Lady Darlington, who has been so kind," she said. "And plays . . . would you truly take me to see a play or two?"

"I will strike a bargain with you," he said, with mock solemnity. "For every ball you attend with me, I shall take you to a play. Agreed?"

"Agreed!" she laughed. "But . . . oh, Malcolm, I truly think your mother does not wish to go."

"It is a long time until spring. We shall talk to her before then. I merely wished your promise not to oppose the scheme," he said, more soberly. "I do think it would do maman good to go to London once more, for the longer she is away, the more she will dread going to our town house where Eustace died. It will hold sad memories for us all. But we must put them behind us and continue to live and enjoy life."

She wondered if that was his thought or Deidre's. She fingered her quill thoughtfully.

"Well, you long to return to work," he said, rising, and coming over to her. He bent over her, lifted a long curl, and put it to his lips. She could feel his warmth behind her. "What are you working on so hard?"

"An article for a magazine, on the education of females," she said.

He growled, then laughed, and bent and kissed her cheek lingeringly. "Do not work too long, come down early for some sherry before dinner," he coaxed. "And wear the rose dress with the gold gauze, it is so becoming on you. And my amethysts? Will you?"

She agreed, and he went away. He could be so charming, twisting her around his fingers when he chose. She took the long curl in her fingers, remembering his touch. Oh, how difficult it was, to be a female!

She drew a fresh sheet of paper toward her, and began to write, slowly, then more swiftly.

> For a female who is faced with the choice of a marriage to someone disagreeable to her, there is no greater satisfaction than the fact that she can say 'no' without being a burden to her relatives. An educated female can obtain a post as a governess, a teacher, even a worker of accounts. I believe that, in the future, more and more ladies will seek out lines of employment. It is best for them to be prepared for this.
>
> I suggest strongly that a well-rounded education for a woman can be her salvation. Rather than to tie herself to a bully of a man, or a weakling, or a drunkard, she may choose to remain free of such entanglements. She may, by virtue of education in mathematics, reading, writing, literature, and languages, outfit herself in such a manner that she may apply for a well-paying post, and manage to keep herself, modestly as befits a lady
> . . .

The ideas flowed. She became absorbed and stopped only when Glenda tapped at the door and entered. "It is time for you to dress for dinner, my lady, had you forgotten?"

Valerie sighed, stood up and stretched herself. "The rose gown with the gold gauze, Glenda," she said and smiled at the maid's concealed surprise. "And the amethysts. If I hurry, I can be down in time for sherry."

She was down before seven o'clock. Deidre was already there, lovely in her favorite sheer chiffon, with diamonds sparkling at her wrists and ears. She was laughing, telling them of some event. She paused to gaze at Valerie as she entered.

"But how charming you look tonight, Valerie!" she said, so sincerely that Valerie might have believed her had she not seen the cold look of the blue eyes. A flicker of the long lashes, and the look was gone. "A good dressmaker in London, and you shall be all the rage! I do beg you to consider going to London in the spring, for the season!"

"That is up to the family, Lady Deidre," said Valerie serenely. "Yes, thank you, Malcolm," she said, as he nodded to the sherry bottle in his hand. He poured out a tall slim glass for her, she accepted it and smiled up at him. Immediately he perched on the arm of her chair, with his own glass in hand.

The earl gazed at them in genial satisfaction. "Perhaps we shall go for a few months," he said. "We will think about it. After all, Valerie should be presented! And she does deserve a holiday. I never thought to have a daughter who would please me so well, eh, Hannah?"

The countess smiled and nodded, but with more reserve. "Valerie has been a great comfort to us," she said. "And Deidre also, of course."

Behind Deidre, Louis Kenyon stood near the table of sherry. He grinned, raised his glass to Valerie in a mute salute. She gave him a slight nod. Maybe this was the tack to try!

Malcolm put his hand on Valerie's ear. "I like those amethysts on you very much, darling," he said. "You shall also have the diamonds, I am having them reset for you in a lighter style. Should be ready for the holidays, eh, Louis? Mother, do you think lilac suits Valerie best, or blue, or rose?"

"With her dark hair and brown eyes, she can wear all the colors, my dear," said the countess, fluttering her hands a little helplessly. "I am amazed that you are at last noticing a lady's dress! You may be willing to outfit her then for her presentation! I really ought to write after Christmas to Lady Darlington and beg for the latest patterns. Valerie should take more interest in clothing."

Deidre sat silently, saying little, her long lashes down over her blue eyes. It was hard to know what she was thinking, but Valerie did notice one small fist clenched on her knee, before the older girl smoothed it out again, so the long slim fingers lay quietly on her lap.

Malcolm came to Valerie's bed again that night, the first time in a week. He came with passion, silence, and a great fiery need for her that seemed to burn them both. When it was over, he lay back and breathed great gulps of air. She was out of breath also, he had practically squeezed all air from her.

However, when she had recovered a little, and his arm stole about her comfortably, she snuggled up to him, her head on his chest. It was sturdier, he was filling out somewhat with the rest, the outdoor riding and walking, the good food.

She laid her hand on his heart, felt the steady rapid beating of it. If it only beat for her, how happy she would be! He did like her, he showed it. Perhaps liking and passion could be enough. If she had a child also, they might make a marriage that would last.

"Valerie," he grumbled, sleepily. "You're sweet, you know it? When you ain't stiff and angry, that is."

She laughed a little mischievously. "And you're sweet also, when you aren't yelling at me, and ordering me about!"

His arm tightened cruelly hard for a moment, then relaxed. "Little devil," he said, and bent to kiss her mouth again, suddenly hard and honey-sweet. His hand slid up and down her arm, in a sleepy caress, then he yawned, and fell asleep.

Chapter Ten

The holidays saw them all more cheerful. The countess consented to put off her black, and went to grey and even cream, and the earl expressed his satisfaction to Valerie.

"Dear Eustace is gone. However, he would never wish for her to weep and mourn forever. We still have Malcolm and you, my dear, and the hope of grandchildren. We must be more cheerful!"

She smiled, though the mention of grandchildren still gave her a pang. Deidre continued to wear her black, but as she went out to dances and village affairs quite freely, no one considered her in mourning.

Valerie had begun to think seriously about gifts for Christmas. She had been secretly knitting a cashmere shawl for her mother-in-law, in a pretty shade of blue, with an elaborate fringe knotted around the edge. When it was completed, she purchased more wool in the village, and began scarves for Malcolm and her father-in-law and for Louis. She had little money and was too proud to ask for any. She used what she had earned from her articles and stories for the wool.

Deidre was a puzzle. She would not care for shawls, she thought they were unfashionable, though comfortable. Valerie finally bought some fine linen, and fashioned three handkerchiefs, with tiny hemming.

She busied herself about the manor also, helping with

the decorations. They had always brought in branches of green, with those also of holly berries and mistletoe. Valerie set them about, carefully, and arranged fresh vases of flowers from the last of those in the gardens. Soon there would be some from the greenhouses as well, in time for Christmas and New Year.

Deidre went out more and more. Malcolm sometimes accompanied her, though the earl frowned. She cannot go alone, thought Valerie, but why cannot the groom take her and bring her home? She has many friends.

Valerie did accompany Malcolm to the village hall, for a grand dance before the holidays. She wore the rose dress with the gold gauze, and was pleased that she knew so many of the company. She was much in demand for standing up in the cotillion and the country dances. No waltzes were played.

"I declare, you are more popular than Deidre," Malcolm told her, when he finally found her again. "I have scarcely seen you this evening! I thought you did not care for such amusements!"

"I do not care to go as an unwelcome third," she flashed. "The other occasions, you went to Deidre's friends, I was not invited! Should I push myself in unwanted?"

"Nonsense," he said, but he had flushed and looked uncomfortable. "Of course, you are always welcome. You show so clearly that you do not care for such matters. . . ."

Deidre came up to them, as Valerie was about to snap a reply. Deidre was with the squire's son. "Do let us change partners," she smiled graciously at them both, with a cold inquiring look to her blue eyes. "I have not had my usual dances with you, Malcolm dear!"

Several older ladies were near enough to hear Deidre's clear ringing voice. Looks were exchanged, curiously, and Valerie felt all were staring at the four of them. She turned abruptly away from Malcolm and Deidre, who was already hanging onto his arm.

The squire's son bowed, smiled, and led Valerie away. "I say," he said in a low tone, "she can be downright rude! And everyone is talking, that they go together to occasions, and leave you at home. Is this the way the London beaux act?"

"I suppose so," she said, with an attempt at a smile. She was stiff with humiliation.

He was kind enough to change the topic again, to the preparations for Christmas, to the children's party at the manor, and so on.

She was more than ready to leave before Deidre could bring herself to say her farewells. She stood in her cloak and bonnet at the entrance for quite half an hour before Deidre reluctantly went for her cloak.

On the ride home in the carriage, Malcolm sat opposite the two girls. Valerie was silent, her hands clenched inside her pretty swansdown muff. Deidre's elegant gloved hands were in a muff of white fur. One might think she was the Viscountess rather than Valerie, thought the miserable girl, staring out at the white-frosted fields.

"Poor Valerie is exhausted," said Deidre, lightly. "She is not accustomed to such late hours. You must sleep later in the mornings, my dear! You will not keep such early hours in the city! Only country people do so."

Valerie stiffened again, and could not bite her answer back. "For those who have no work to do, late hours will answer," she said crisply. "I imagine you often sleep late, Lady Deidre! You seem to have nothing better to do, than to amuse yourself, and run around the countryside! I should be ashamed to behave the guest for such long months, with no tasks or work done, to pay for my lodging!"

"Valerie!" breathed Malcolm. "You forget yourself! Your manners are shocking! Deidre is a guest, she is not to work! No one thinks she should."

One hand went up to Deidre's eyes, her voice came in a muffled broken way. "Ohhh . . . that you should imagine so! I feel myself at home here, not as a guest! You make me see how foolish I am to believe I am welcome . . ."

"Nonsense!" cried the distracted Malcolm, scarcely knowing how to act with her. "You are as dear as my sister! Eustace adored you! If only you had married him when he begged you to do so, you should be really my sister now!"

Deidre burst into real tears, careful, however, not to disturb her careful makeup. Valerie sat stiffly in her corner, as Malcolm leaned forward, comforted her, offered his big handkerchief, and generally behaved as though he would wish to take her in his arms.

Valerie went up to her room at once upon arriving home. She could face no more scenes. She knew she had behaved badly. However, one more word from Deidre, and she would have slapped her face! She was shocked at the violence of her own feelings.

She heard Malcolm come to bed about two hours later, as she tossed and turned, sleeplessly. He did not even come through her room, much less to her bed, but went directly to his own small bed in the dressing room.

The next day, Malcolm scolded Valerie severely for her manner toward Deidre. Valerie took it in silence for a time, then she turned on him.

"I wish you had married Deidre instead of me," she said fiercely. "I wish you two would go off to London and amuse yourselves, and leave me alone! You two are of a kind, frivolous, born only to amuse yourself, a rake, a rake, yes, you are! You think nothing of the labor that goes into this estate, you care nothing for how hard your father must work! Well, I wish you joy of her, and you cannot leave with her too soon to suit me!"

Malcolm stared at her, as though a small kitten had turned on him with claws bared. "Well!" he said, in a long drawn breath. "That is beyond all! How can you say that? It would make a terrible scandal if I should go off to London with . . . besides, I have no wish to do so! Of all the nasty remarks, of the worst-thinking mind I ever heard . . ."

"You are shocking the villagers," she told him hotly, her brown eyes flashing fire. "I was told last night everyone wondered at you and at her! You make your name a laughing-stock! And they feel sorry for me—sorry for me! You are always escorting her about."

"You are jealous!" cried Malcolm, beginning to grin. "Ah, I see it now! You are jealous of all my attentions to her! Confess it, now, Valerie!"

"I am jealous of my reputation," she flashed. "And of your families', both the Arundels and Lady Deidre's. When all the village talks, they will soon say there is no smoke, but fire is about!"

"You're jealous!" he crowed, like a small boy taunting her. He grabbed her shoulders. "Confess it, you are jealous of her! Come on now, be honest!"

She stood stiffly in his hands, unable to deny it. Her face spoke for her. He bent and kissed her mouth, fiercely, then laughed and let her go. "It's all right, Valerie, I shan't be mad at you anymore. You're jealous, I can understand that," he declared sunnily. "We'll get you some fine clothes too, and some diamonds—wait till you see your presents at Christmas! Then you shall not be jealous of her any longer. I have ordered some things for you."

"You may keep them!" she declared furiously, and wrenched herself away from his presence. She turned her back on him, her hands shakily going to a chair back to hold on to it. "Or give them to Deidre! I shall leave you as soon as I am twenty-one, I swear it!"

"I swear you are the worst-tempered female of my acquaintance!" he shot back and dashed from the room.

As though in defiance, Malcolm escorted Deidre out

again that very evening. They did not even tell Valerie where they would go. Valerie, her mouth compressed to keep back fury, went early up to her room. She worked at her desk for a time, then blew out the candles and crept into bed. Malcolm had not even listened to her, he cared not for his reputation.

Probably in London, he had jaunted about as he wished. He had been a gambler there, a rake, quite the young beau. No doubt he longed for a return of those days.

He meant to make a fool of her, she thought savagely. He would carry on his affairs. She wondered how far the one with Deidre had gone—and thought the worst. Deidre would care for nothing, so long as the money, the jewels, the fine dresses flowed in. These were loose times, Valerie had found from reading the London gazettes. All followed the example of the Prince Regent—and his mistresses were freely talked about.

Much later, she heard voices cautiously lowered in the hallway. They went on and on. She wakened from her drowsing, and lifted her head to listen. Was something wrong? Was someone ill? She heard a soft sobbing and rose from the bed, catching up her warm robe.

Cautiously, she opened the door, and peered out into the darkened hallway. It was just light enough, from the candles at the end of the hallway near the stairs, that she could see the two figures standing there, together, very close.

Then she saw them. Malcolm, holding Deidre in his arms, his hand stroking her light blonde hair caressingly. She was sobbing on his shoulder. Valerie could not hear the words.

But she could see them, near Malcolm's bedroom door. He stroked her hair, then lifted her chin, and talked to her softly. She shook her head, the blonde hair spilling over her shoulders. Her hand reached up, she touched his cheek.

And he bent his head and kissed her cheek, then her mouth. They were clinging together.

Valerie came out of her daze, to find herself standing cold and chilled. She shut the door, softly, turning the handle slowly so it would not even click.

She was shivering, long deep shudders, as she stood there in the nightdress and robe, in the cold December night. Malcolm . . . kissing Deidre.

She had imagined their embraces. The reality was much, much worse. Malcolm, his lean strong body half-bent over the slight curved figure of Deidre. His face against hers, his mouth seeking hers. Valerie pressed her fist to her own mouth, that had known his hungry demanding kisses.

She was cold through, not just from the night air. Malcolm. He had taken Deidre as his mistress then. It was reality, not just a fear.

A door closed softly, the voices had ceased. She tensed again. She heard someone moving in the next bedroom, slowly, a murmur of voices. A door closed, the wardrobe, she thought.

Presently, the bed creaked.

Was Deidre there, in his bed? Was she? Right next door to his wife? Valerie longed to throw open that door between their rooms, confront them fiercely, scream aloud of their blatant affair.

But she could not. She would not do it. They were callous and "sophisticated," true Londoners, they would say. It would only hurt Malcolm's parents—and herself.

She crept into bed, curling up into a ball of pain. Her feet were cold, her legs, her whole body. How could she endure this? She could not, yet she must.

The next few days were sheer torture. She went about in a daze. She smiled like a mechanical doll, she nodded, she spoke, she did not know what she said. She knew only that Malcolm continued to drive Deidre about the countryside, they laughed together, talked for long hours.

The weather had turned bitterly cold. She did not ride out, she said it was too cold for her, and remained in her room, reading and writing. She attended to her duties about the manor house with mechanical attention—the flowers from the greenhouse, the herbs to be planted in pots, a dinner planned and the guests arranged at table.

Guests came, she smiled, she spoke, she was quiet. No one seemed to notice anything wrong. Even the countess had a subdued joy those holidays, with the house full, people coming and going, Malcolm, dear Malcolm home from the wars. Deidre had a hard, triumphant look on her face, at dinner she wore the most glamorous of gowns spangled with diamonds, her blonde hair high, a tiara on her curls.

Sometimes Louis Kenyon looked at Valerie and seemed about to speak. Then he would stop himself, and shake his head. The earl was absorbed in his work, there was a party to be planned for the estate children, gifts to go out to the tenants. Valerie had helped choose and wrap them, he sent them out, and attended to seeing them all on the estate.

Valerie completed the decorations of the drawing rooms and dining room with mechanical efficiency. There were green pine boughs on the mantels, red Christmas candles on the tables. She completed her gifts and wrapped them, with no pleasure in her.

Christmas was a hollow family celebration for her. New Year would come and go, and presently she would be twenty-one, and she might slip away, she thought. No one would miss her now.

The countess was ill one day and did not come down to dinner. Deidre boldly slipped into her chair at the long dining table, and smiled at the earl. "I'll just show dear Valerie how to do this," she said sunnily. "She must have the experience one day, you know."

Valerie was too numb to protest Deidre's arrogance in taking the countess's place from her. She seated herself beside the earl as usual, her face contained, her head averted from the end of the table where Deidre sat.

Finally Christmas came, the holidays were merry for them. The earl was beaming, and told Valerie why.

"At last, my dearest wish has been granted, my dear," he said.

Valerie stared at him. Was Deidre to have Malcolm's child? But he was too complacent, not shocked at all.

"Malcolm is selling his commission," explained the earl. "He has agreed to take his place on the estate and learn the work. I know the battles will be fierce in Spain, I told him I could not go through another such experience if he should leave us."

He looked at Valerie hopefully, waiting for her reaction. She could think only that Deidre had persuaded him, that he remained here because he wished to be with Deidre.

"That's fine," she said dully. "I am . . . pleased . . . for you."

He showed his puzzlement, said jovially, "And for yourself as well, my dear! He will be home with you . . ."

Not with me, thought Valerie again, and turned away. Malcolm came into the study presently.

"Did you tell her the news, father?" he asked, looking toward the desk where Valerie sat, her shining brown head bent over her books.

"Yes, I think she is dazed with the shock of it," said the earl kindly. "Tell her again, assure her you mean to remain with us, that you will sell out."

Malcolm was still gazing at Valerie, beginning to frown now. She made herself look up, glanced past him rather than at him.

"I am very happy with your decision, Malcolm," she said, colorlessly. "Your father is most happy."

He came over and sat down beside her. "Truly? I wonder!" he said in a low angry voice. "You spend all your time to yourself, you never join us."

"Why should I? Is not Deidre enough company for you?" she snapped. "She has the time to amuse you . . ."

"That again? Play another tune, my dear! I tell you this, I should rather be with my regiment than listen to your vitriol all the day! And they need me there in the Peninsula, I have read in the gazettes that old Wellington is expecting any day to meet the French. By God, for two pins I would go!" he ended violently.

She sighed and finally put her hand on his. "No, Malcolm, I beg you, do not go. We worried about you so long," she said sincerely. "I truly think we should not be able to endure it, should you depart again for the Peninsula."

His face softened, he raised her hand to his lips. She felt the warm mouth on her hand. "I swear I never will understand you, Valerie," he said, for her ear alone. "Blow hot, blow cold. But you are so nice when you wish to be. Come out with me today, I long for a ride in the carriage. We shall go wherever you say."

She hesitated, he began to frown again. She finally nodded. "I should like to go, Malcolm. We could take the gifts to the Parkers, I do enjoy visiting with them."

He grinned, pulled her up. "Go get your cloak and bonnet then, there's a cold wind. I'll be around with the carriage in fifteen minutes. Papa, where are the gifts for the Parkers?"

The earl had been watching them anxiously from the corners of his eyes, pretending a great search over his desk for some papers. Now he gave a sigh of relief, got up to point out the pile of gifts for the Parkers, and sent a footman out with them to the carriage.

In twenty minutes, they were on their way, laughing in the cold, crisp December day. Valerie's heart felt lighter than it had for days, since she had witnessed that scene outside her bedroom door. The pain of it had lingered, to dig deep into her sensitive heart. Malcolm did not seem to realize what he did to her, how he hurt her. Perhaps this was the way of most men, that they could not be loyal, did not even think of loyalty.

Must she be loyal then, without his loyalty? Must she love without being loved in return, content with the scraps of his attention when he wished to throw them to her? She could not answer. She loved him, but she despised herself for loving a rake and a gambler, a London beau who carried his ways to the country, and made their name a scandal.

The Parkers were frankly surprised to see Malcolm, and welcomed them both heartily. Two of the young children were there, and Valerie took them in turn onto her lap, to tell them stories, and sing a song or two. Malcolm seemed surprised at her, and sat watching her thoughtfully between conversations about the spring plantings and the horses that were due to foal.

They drove home in the dusk, silent, as they passed along the country lanes. Ice crackled on the branches, sometimes snapping with the report of a pistol shot. The fields showed brown under the frost and some patches of snow. A rabbit scurried from its burrow into their path, and out again, just under the hooves of the horses.

"There'll be fine game in the spring, you shall have rabbit stew," said Malcolm. "That'll be one use for my musket!"

He had a tinge of bitterness in his tone. Impulsively she tucked her gloved hand into his arm. "Malcolm, you will not go back, will you? We have worried so much. Your father and mother are quite gray with it. You are their only son, now, and if aught should happen to you . . ." Her breath caught in her throat.

He squeezed her hand between his arm and his warm body. "I gave my word, I have written to sell my commission," he reassured her. "Do not mind if I grumble at times! It is my nature."

She laughed a little and leaned her head briefly on his shoulder. She would miss him, she thought, when she left.

She must leave him. She must. But she would see him settled here first, and so repay them for their kindness to her. No matter whom he married, they would love her. They might remember Valerie with kindness, she wanted that. But she must go one day.

She closed her thoughts to that. It was too painful.

Christmas finally came, and the family gathered with Deidre in the great drawing room to exchange their personal gifts. Other gifts had arrived from friends and distant relatives, and Valerie had been amazed to find herself with a sable coat from a four-times-removed cousin of Malcolm! Also there were gifts of tweed cloth from some Scottish cousins, fine candies from Holland, a cairngorm necklace and bracelet from other Scottish relatives.

"You are quite fine," observed Deidre over her parcels. "What a welcome into the family! So it is to marry wealth." She had been careful to speak in a low tone, so the others did not hear. Valerie did not try to answer that, but she felt some of the pleasure draining from her.

She managed a smile, when Malcolm came over to her, a large box in his hand. "My dear, the diamonds have been reset. I wish you to have them now," he said, rather solemnly. "They have been in the family more than one hundred years. I asked for a light gold setting, to suit your coloring and height."

Valerie was very aware of Deidre's jealous stare as the box was snapped open. It was a large maroon leather box, with a maroon velvet interior. Set carefully on the fabric lay a fine diamond tiara set in gold, a matching necklace, a pair of exquisite bracelets, and five matching diamond rings, with gems of various sizes.

"Oh . . . how beautiful!" she gasped. "They are fine . . . too fine, I should be afraid of losing them. . . ."

"Nonsense," said Malcolm, smiling. He set the tiara on her head, and begged her to choose a diamond ring to wear. Deidre jumped up and came over to try on a bracelet. Valerie would have numbly allowed it.

Malcolm shook his head firmly. "No, Deidre, this is for Valerie," he said. "Eustace gave you quite a few, these are for Valerie."

Valerie's cold heart warmed at his tone. Deidre pouted and looked as though she would beg. "I only wished to try them on," she told Malcolm and went back to her seat, to watch hungrily as a diamond bracelet was slipped on Valerie's wrist, and the necklace about her throat.

Attention went then to the earl, exclaiming over his fine woolen scarf from Valerie. "I shall wear it all the winter!" he said. "How fine and beautifully woven this is!"

Louis Kenyon was equally pleased with his, and the countess graciously put her cashmere scarf about her shoulders at once. When their attention was all distracted, Malcolm came back to Valerie, another small box in his hand.

Before giving it to her, he said, flushed a bit, "I say, you know I have never asked you if you had money enough. I shall set up an allowance for you at once. It never entered my head that you would not ask for money should you require it."

She flushed in turn. "You mean . . . my gifts are mean," she said, in a level tone. "I paid for them with my earnings from my articles!" And she tossed her head, as though to say she did not care.

No one was looking at them. He put his hand on her cheek in a gentle caress. "No, I did not mean that. Your gifts are made by yourself, and the more dear for it. You give of yourself, Valerie. However, you shall have an allowance. Meantime, I . . . I chose this myself, designed it for you. I hope you like it . . . a London jeweler made it up."

He flipped open the small box. Valerie caught her breath. It was nothing like the grand sparkling array of diamonds. It was an exquisite brooch of jade leaves, with several small diamonds on them like dewdrops. And the flower was of purple amethyst petals set in the jade leaves, as naturally as though they had grown there. Small, perfect, a delight.

She reached for it, tears in her eyes. Malcolm had thought of her, designed it for her, planned it for her. Just what she would have loved, should she have had any idea of it. She lifted it from its white velvet bed and held it in her hand; it covered only half her palm. She stared down at it, until the flower brooch dissolved before her gaze in a mist of tears.

"Do you like it?" Malcolm's anxious whisper recalled her.

"Like it? I never, never saw anything so perfect in my life, so beautiful. I . . . I shall . . . ch-cherish it all my days."

He bent over and kissed her forehead gently. "You mean it? I'm glad. You're a gem yourself, Valerie, you know?"

And even when he left her, and went over to Deidre to tease her about her many gifts from as many admirers, Valerie still felt the warmth in her heart and on her forehead. He had thought of her, had given her a gift he had hoped would please her, had kissed her gently like a lover.

It was something she would cherish always, along with the brooch he had designed.

Chapter Eleven

Valerie had looked forward to her January birthday for a long time. It would mean that she would become twenty-one years of age, it would mean that she was free to leave. She thought of it, even thought of taking out a small trunk to begin to pack her personal possessions.

However, Malcolm seemed to have changed a little. He was kind and gentle toward her, he often shared her bed at night. Selling his commission had been a giant step for him to take, but he had done it, and now he had set the past behind him.

He took little interest in the estate, however, and still rode about on horseback on fine days, or in the carriage, taking Deidre about as before. But he did not speak sarcastically to Valerie, she supposed she must be grateful for that.

She had a long letter from Lady Darlington, enclosing some lovely pattern books for new dresses. In the firm black handwriting, only a slight tremor in the lines betrayed her age.

> My dearest Lady Grenville, I long to make your acquaintance. Your mother asked me to send some patterns to you. If you wish to order some gowns, I shall undertake to have my own favorite dressmaker make them up in any color you shall choose. The countess is

anxious that you shall be as well-dressed as any lady in England! She gave me many directions concerning you.

Valerie studied the lines wonderingly, and read them again to make sure she had not misunderstood. Nothing more had been said about going to London for the season. The letter continued:

I hope when you come that I shall see you often. I admire your bright mind and intelligence. I have read your articles and stories with care. I enclose a copy of the latest magazine with a story of yours, in case another copy would be welcome. The girl in your story behaved like a fine lady, I approve of her! However, she does not show herself sufficiently yielding to the will of her husband. I do not think his requests of her unreasonable. However! We shall argue about that comfortably sometime!

She continued with kind words about the style, then news of her godson Reginald Darlington, and others of whom Valerie had heard. She finished with gossip of London, in her usual witty manner, and signed herself, "Your affectionate elderly friend, Seraphine Darlington."

Valerie took the letter to the countess, after some thought. The lady read it over carefully. "Yes, yes, how good she is. She was considered very forward in her day, my dear," said the countess, musingly. "However, her heart was ever good and kind, rough though the edge of her tongue could be! Her husband was ever devoted to her. How sad it was that both her son and daughter did not live to reach maturity. Reginald has been a great comfort to her, he is a real son to her."

Valerie asked presently about the dresses and the pattern book. "I do not mean to go to London for the season, maman," she said, as gently as possible. "I see no need for many more dresses. You have outfitted me in a grand style. I have all I need, truly."

"Hummm," said the countess, her fingers fluttering

through the pages. "Do look at this charming style, Valerie! It would please me if you would request this one, at least! Even though we do not go to London, you shall be fashionably dressed for cotillions here! What about this gown also? Do you not like the charm of it? It would suit you in rose, or a pale cream, would it not?"

Valerie tried firmly to refuse them all, but when Malcolm added his voice to the matter, it was settled. He flipped through the book, pointed to one and another with interest. "There, that one, Valerie, with the charming little ruffle about the hem! That is for you. In lilac, I believe, with the Greek effect about the waist, and those little doings about the sleeves."

Even the countess laughed softly at his masculine description of the fashion, and her eyes lit up from their usual sadness. An order was sent off in a week, for half a dozen gowns of the latest styles, in lilac muslin, blue lace, rose taffeta, green gauze over silk, a deeper lavender crepe de chine, and a pink brocade. There were matching items also, a redingote pelisse, a cloak of blue velvet, bonnets with frivolous feathers and ribbons adorning them, little shoes with wedge-shaped heels of the latest style.

Valerie could not help feeling flutters of pleasure, both at the prospect of having all these pretty new garments and also at the kindness of her relatives in insisting that she must have them. Of course, she reminded herself, practically, they would wish her to dress well, in her position. But they all seemed to take a personal interest in how she looked, how she felt, as though they truly loved her.

She was startled when Malcolm took off suddenly for London. His parents did not seem concerned and put her off when she asked anxiously if it was about his commission.

"He has not regretted resigning, has he?" she asked the earl, in the study, after Malcolm had left in the carriage. "He does not go to his commander?"

"No, no, do not think so," he soothed her, with a twinkle in the brownish hazel eyes so like his son's. "I am sure he does but go on an errand or two."

Deidre was sulky that he had not taken her along. "He knows I longed to go," she declared in the drawing room the first evening. "I have so many friends there! They will think it odd that I did not come! Why did he not invite me to accompany him! He went so quickly, I could have been ready in a day if he had but asked."

Valerie bit her lips to say nothing. The earl frowned, and Louis Kenyon puffed fiercely on his pipe. It was the countess who spoke in her gentle voice.

"My dear Lady Deidre," she said, more coolly than she usually spoke to the girl. "It would not have been in the least proper! When we remove to London as a family, of course you shall accompany us. However, to go only with Malcolm—when he is married! And you a single female! No, no, your mother would never approve. The house has been shut up, besides, and Malcolm shall stay with friends. It would not have done, it would not have done!"

Deidre swallowed, kept her temper back with an effort. She shot Valerie a mean look, as though to say it was all her fault. She spoke meekly enough, "I am sorry, my lady, I did not mean to offend. Wherever are my manners? Of course, it would not do."

"Of course not," said the countess.

"Of course, I might have stayed with my friend, the Countess of Lancaster! She often writes, begging me to come and remain with her."

"I consider the woman rather forward," said the countess, her gaze intent on the little bit of embroidery in her delicate hands. She set in another neat stitch. "However, these are different times. If you shall write to your mother, and secure her permission to visit the Countess of Lancaster, I shall arrange for grooms to take you to London."

Did Deidre turn a shade more pale? Was there apprehension in the blue eyes? She quickly denied any wish to dash off to London.

"Indeed, in this cold weather, it is so much cozier in the country, with the carriages to ride, and a strong stone house to remain in," she said, with a pretty laugh. "I do adore Arundel, do not think I do not! Later on, we shall all go to London, and be comfortable in your beautiful town house."

It was difficult to read the expressions of the countess. Her hands would flutter, her eyes turn vague, she changed the subject to one that seemed irrelevant to what had gone before. Yet Valerie received the strong impression that for once the countess was displeased with Deidre and cool to her that evening.

Malcolm returned two days before Valerie's birthday. He came, tired, yet cheerful, full of the London gossip, a carriage full of parcels which he carried directly up to his room, whispered to his father, exchanged grins with Louis Kenyon. Valerie wondered irritably what was going on.

She had reminded no one of her birthday. It was something she did not want to mention. She had told them she would leave when she was twenty-one, and she felt a little desolate that she had done so. However, it would be better to make the break soon. Malcolm had resigned his commission, he was well again, hopefully he would one day take an interest in the estate, and her task here was done.

She must be out and about her own concerns, making a new place for herself in the world. She wondered what Lady Darlington would say if she made another application to her for a reference as a teacher or governess.

She drew a deep sigh and bent over her books again. She had almost completed another article, about some of the women in Shakespeare's plays. She admired some of them strongly. It was her first attempt at more literary material.

Malcolm came to her bed that night. He teased her that

he had missed her immensely, and had compared the London females with her, most unfavorably for them.

"I saw one girl who reminded me of you, but her eyes were not so big and soulful, her shape was not so slim and rounded." His hands were roaming about her, and she squirmed.

"You are tickling me," she scolded.

He only laughed, and bent over her, to close her mouth with his own, in a strong possessive kiss. "Did you miss me?" he murmured.

"Well . . ."

"Did you?"

"Yes . . . some . . ." she admitted reluctantly.

"Some! You are a mischievous imp! Before I have done, you shall admit that you missed me a great deal!" And he tickled her until she squirmed with helpless laughter, and kissed her until she could scarcely breathe, all the time demanding that she pay a forfeit, and admit she had missed him with all her heart.

"I give up . . . I give up . . . do not tickle me again! Malcolm, I give up . . . I did miss you . . . a great deal . . ."

"Kiss me to show you missed me!" he demanded arrogantly, and held her face in his hands tenderly, looking down into her dark eyes. His own gaze was intent, keen.

She pursed her red mouth, he lowered his head slowly, and her hands went to his head to draw him closer yet. They kissed, long, sweetly, and his body pressed more hotly to hers.

When he moved his long limbs against hers and drew up the modest nightdress to her thighs, she tingled with apprehension and desire. His hands were so big, so sure, so demanding.

When the thought came, "Did he treat Deidre like this?" and she felt the pangs of jealousy, she tried to stiffen against him. Too late, for he could sense yielding in her body, know that she wanted him with sensual need.

He leaned over her, murmured, sweetly, into her ears, teased her, courted her, and finally their bodies met in a long exciting embrace. Her hands went over his bare hard shoulders—he rarely wore his nightshirt when he came to her now. It was only in the way, he said carelessly. Her hands slipped down to his back, to the strong-muscled thighs, she would feel the scars of his battle-torn body, and pity would mingle with desire and need. She would remember the long months, when they did not know whether he lived or died.

Life was so short, so fraught with dangers. If he wanted her tonight, she would give to him, freely, generously, because tomorrow was uncertain. There would be the honey-sweetness of memories, at least, should she leave him. And so she lay with him, and let him do as he pleased with her, unwinding her braided hair, burying his face in it, stroking over her rounded body, taking her with wild hunger when the need grew too great to be contained in him.

When he drew off, sighed, and lay back to take great gulps of air, she moved also, to lie with her head on his shoulder. She lay with eyes shut, savoring the delight of being with him, so close, knowing he was satisfied with her. Knowing that her body had pleased him, her hands had given him pleasure, her mouth had known the keen hunger of his and responded.

She knew when he slept, his arm relaxed a little about her, and his breathing grew regular and deep. She stroked one hand lightly over his shoulders, her fingers tangled a little in the thick brown mat over his chest, down to his waist, in an intimate gesture she had not dared to make when he was awake.

How attractive he was, how masculine, how strong, how charming when he chose! No wonder he was spoiled for attention, no wonder he demanded what he wished, for he had but to ask and the ladies would fall over themselves to give him what he wanted. She sighed a little, lightly, not to waken him. When she left him—if she gathered strength to leave him—he would not be long alone. Who would not want such a man, such a lover, no matter how moody he would become, or cross, or demanding?

In his sleep, Malcolm moved in the bed, turned on his side toward her, his arms automatically going about her, and drawing her to him—for warmth?—for need? He did not waken, and she lay there, brooding for a time, before she slept also.

Her birthday began on a bitterly cold January day. Frost had made delicate patterns on the windows, one could not see out to the white-clad trees, the furry look of the bushes. Valerie put on one of her warmest dresses, a lilac wool with a matching shawl, and shivered on her way down the drafty stairs to the first floor.

She was one of the first into the breakfast room. The earl stood up when she came in—he was always first there—and Louis Kenyon soon came in. She stood at the buffet, debated as usual whether to take ham or kidneys, settled on ham this morning, and a boiled egg. The footman served her coffee, she added thick country cream and sugar, and drew a deep breath.

The earl looked fidgety, pleased though, as well. Mr. Kenyon was his usual calm self, bent over his kidneys and eggs, his muffins and marmalade.

The countess came in, early for her, every silvery-white hair in place about her broad forehead. Instead of going to her place, she paused beside Valerie and bent to her, and kissed her forehead.

"Happy birthday, my dearest Valerie," she said, with a smile.

"Now, you have spoiled the secret," said the earl, displeased, though grinning from ear to ear.

"Oh, I didn't know—you remembered!" cried Valerie, flushing and a little tearful.

"Remembered? Why, Malcolm has had all of us in fidgets . . ." The countess broke off, moved in stately fashion to her chair, and was seated by the footman devotedly. "Dear me, I never can keep a secret," she said mildly.

Malcolm dashed in, rather flushed and guilty-looking. "What, you are all before me? I had hoped . . . never mind . . ."

"She knows," said the earl. "Mother let it out."

"Oh, dash it all," said Malcolm, crestfallen. "About the party this afternoon and all?"

"No, you just let that out," said Louis Kenyon and began to laugh. Presently, they were all laughing and talking at once.

Malcolm had planned a surprise party for her, some twenty guests for afternoon and dinner. Valerie was bewildered, a little frightened at the attention, but pleased and guiltily happy for all that. And she had thought they would not notice her birthday!

Malcolm crammed his breakfast down, earning his mother's look of reproach. He could not wait. "We are going into Mater's sitting room after breakfast, Valerie, the packages are there. Family first, you know!"

"Oh, you should not have bought presents for me," said Valerie, feeling more and more self-reproachful.

"If you don't like them, I shall be angry," said Malcolm, grinning across the table at her, looking five years younger than his age. "I went all the way to London for them, I must have certain items, and Mater piled additional commissions on me!"

"I already had mine planned," said the earl, with great satisfaction, and gave her a wink.

She could scarcely eat or drink, though Malcolm scolded her, and teased her that she was more excited than at Christmas. She was, she admitted.

She was thankful that Deidre had overslept, as she often did. It was the family only that went into the countess's drawing room. There Valerie exclaimed over the pile of gifts, parcels, bundles, boxes, on the tables, the sofa, and even on the floor.

"Do not be overwhelmed, my dear," said the countess, sounding more affectionate than usual. "These are just the dresses we ordered," nodding at the boxes. "You can open them later. I do hope you will wear one of the most charming for the party this afternoon."

"Whatever you like," breathed Valerie. Malcolm pushed her gently into a big chair and handed her the first parcel, a heavy box.

"Open this first," he commanded eagerly. "I want to see if you are pleased with it."

She managed to get it open, felt in the piles of soft paper for the object within. Finally she grasped it, but it was heavy. Malcolm impatiently helped her, lifting out a huge Chinese porcelain vase of softest rose pattern.

"It's called famille rose, I think," he said, eagerly. "Like it? It's for the flowers."

"Oh, Malcolm, it is the most exquisite . . . how beautiful . . ." She stroked the side of the vase, with its lovely oval pattern filled with flowers, the background of rose and white. It felt silky to the touch.

Malcolm took the vase from her, threw the box to the floor, and brought her another. She opened one box after another, as the others watched her, indulgent smiles on their faces at Malcolm's eagerness and her bewildered pleasure.

The countess had given her—besides a dozen lovely gowns for summer and winter, and two cloaks—four bonnets, half a dozen pairs of slippers, a delicate reticule of gold embroidery, a long strand of pearls with earrings and brooch to match.

From the earl, a pair of huge boxes, which contained more than twenty-five books! She lifted out one and another, gazed at the titles, exclaimed over them. "Just what

I wanted, oh, I have longed to read this . . . how did you know . . ."

From Malcolm, the Chinese vase, a box of ivory objects—carved elephants, a delicate house of ivory, a cute pair of puppies, the most beautiful fan she had ever seen. She opened the ivory sticks, and beheld the design on the silk fabric, a Chinese house, a rounded bridge, two lovers in kimonos, cherry blossoms on a tree.

"Wherever did you find. . . ?" she began.

"An import house. Reggie wrote, said you would like the stuff. He took me round when I got to London, they had saved some fine things for me, on his request. He is a good chap!"

She smiled at Malcolm. "And you are so . . . very kind to me," she said, her voice choking. "I shall enjoy these all . . . so very much."

Even Louis Kenyon had thoughtfully ordered something special for her—some thick folios of fine paper for her manuscripts, some new quills, black ink and blue, and a rare book of poetry in an old leather binding.

"I am quite overwhelmed," she finally said. "How can I thank you all? You are so generous, so thoughtful . . ."

"You have given us such pleasure, my dear," said the countess. "You are a dear girl."

The party that afternoon passed in a daze. There were gifts from all the guests, scarves, gloves, perfume. The squire's son had the distinction of the most unique gift. Valerie peered into the box in surprise and wonder.

"Whatever is it?" asked Deidre, strolling up. She sniffed, her face crinkled up. "Dirt!" she said, in disgust.

"No, bulbs," said Valerie, as she drew out one, then gently patted it back. "These are some of your mother's prize lilies, I think!"

"Right you are," grinned the young man. "Shows how much she thinks of you and your gardens! I know she shall be over to scout around and see that they come up properly!"

"I shall plant them at once in the greenhouse! Oh, how happy I am to have them! I have never seen such lovely white lilies as she has."

The dinner table that night was gay and happy. Laughter flowed as lightly as the champagne that Malcolm had ordered. Many wishes were given to Valerie for a happy year, and many more of them. She was dazed, to think they were all so kind to her and wished her well. Deidre watched, a set smile on her face, her jerky movements at times revealing her impatience with all the fuss over Valerie.

But best of all, the following days showed that Malcolm had not ceased to think of her. He invited her to accompany him on his rounds. He had decided to go to all the farms, to acquaint himself with all the tenants, the farm situations, the problems of each.

Valerie went with him gladly, wearing her warm blue velvet cloak, the blue velvet bonnet with bright blue ribbons tied under her chin. At each house, she sat with the woman of the family and the children, while Malcolm and the farmer would discuss the farm. They would go over the crops, the animals, plans for the future.

Going home, she would talk with Malcolm, or more often listen as he mused over the situation aloud. "The chap needs more help, he is getting old, he cannot farm that much land," he said. "If his daughter does marry young Jim, then Jim could take over some of the land. We could build them a cottage on the edge of the lane, down near the river. That would be close enough for her to come up and help her mother. . . ."

Or he would discuss the breeding of the horses. "A chap I know has an Arab, a beauty. I could bring the stallion down for a time, breed him to our mares, and come up with a much stronger line of riding horses. For the farm work, of course, we need the heavy dray horses. . . ."

She listened, and marveled. Malcolm had taken long to

bring himself to the work, but now, as was usual with him, he had thrown himself into it with enthusiasm. Would the feeling last? Would he continue to take a keen interest, to work with his father, to learn the estate business? She fervently hoped so.

Had he changed, really? She knew he still longed for his regiment, read the gazettes in so absorbed a manner that he scarcely knew anyone else was in the room. She caught him gazing absently in the distance, a sad look to his mouth.

However, the earl was gruffly approving of Malcolm's change and gave him even more work to do. He seemed to think all was settled now, that they would give him the grandchildren he longed for, that Valerie would remain, that Malcolm had come to see his destiny on the land the earl loved so.

Valerie kept her thoughts to herself. If Malcolm had truly changed, then she would remain with him, she thought. He seemed to like her immensely, he studied to please her. There were no more jaunts about in the carriage with Deidre, she did not wish to visit the farms, and Valerie was invited constantly to accompany him.

When Deidre wished to visit one of her friends, a maid and grooms accompanied her. All went to balls, even the countess, as a family party, in those wintry months. The great town hall was filled to capacity, and Valerie wore her newest, smartest gowns, as the countess urged her to do. She did not wish to flaunt her tiara, but usually wore the amethysts that Malcolm had given her. She would touch them wistfully, like a talisman, the amethysts that were a token of love and friendship—steadfast love, constant friendship.

If only that could be true, how happy she would be to stay! Malcolm did not love her, but he seemed to respect her and to desire her. That should be enough. And if she gave him a child, then he would be happy, as happy as his father!

That is, if Malcolm had truly settled down, and this was not just a phase he was going through.

If the marriage did not work out, if he reverted to his old ways of gambling, running off to London, then she would leave him and return to teaching. She would not be a meek, abandoned wife when she could turn her talents to writing and teaching. She would keep her pride, she vowed fiercely, if nothing else. So she thought, and the winter days went on, with little sunshine, but happier hearts at Arundel.

✦✦✦✦✦✦✦✦ Chapter Twelve ✦✦✦✦✦✦✦✦

Spring came in, with the flowers in the Shakespeare garden blooming sweetly amid rows of fragrant herbs. Valerie spent much time out there, grubbing happily as she replanted flowers and shrubs from the greenhouse, forming the patterns again of red roses, scarlet carnations, pink columbine; the yellow pansies, tiny purple and yellow heartsease, yellow tea roses. And in another bed, the blues, of larkspur, columbine, and later, the asters.

Deidre had become more and more restless with the coming of spring. Still she stayed, and clung the more to the countess, continually reminding her, "But two years ago, Eustace and I were dancing at the Vauxhall Gardens. Just two years ago, we went together to the plays and laughed so much."

She rarely went to her own home, only on brief absences. She said, prettily, sadly, "I cannot leave maman." And she meant the mother-in-law she would have had, not her own mother.

Valerie endured her presence, not liking her, yet feeling sorry for her, because the pretty mouth drooped, the eyes were sad. What she had missed, by insisting on yet one more season of gaiety before marriage! Eustace might have lived, they might have had a child or even two by this time. She would be Viscountess Grenville instead of Valerie.

She was more friendly to Valerie these days. Sometimes she would come to the drawing room where Valerie sat with the countess over embroidery and talk to her earnestly.

"You manage so very well, Valerie, one would never believe you had not been born a viscountess," she said, one day.

Valerie eyed her cautiously. "Thank you, Lady Deidre," she said, drawing another mauve thread through the fabric.

The countess looked pleased. "She is a lady," she said, her hands fluttered gently over the silks, as she tried to choose. "Shall it be the cream or the yellow? Dear me . . ."

"It only wants a season for you to be accepted," said Deidre, nibbling her forefinger thoughtfully. "I can see how you would become more polished as you plan dinners in London. The *ton* are different from the country folks—oh, nice as they are!" she added hastily. "But the sophistication there, the manners, the intelligent talk— how you would enjoy that!"

Valerie knew then which way she was driving. "I do not long for such," she said drily, her gaze on her embroidery. "I am quite satisfied with country ways. I was brought up in the country. All I would care for in the city would be the plays and the bookstores! And of course, ladies like Lady Darlington . . ."

"Of course! How you would like to meet her! Such a woman, with frank, scathing tongue that makes all fear and respect her," smiled Deidre. "I understand she holds meetings of bluestockings, and all discuss some subject, such as the care of orphan children, the education of females . . ."

Valerie's busy fingers paused, she gazed into space. She would enjoy that!

"And sometimes they invite a speaker to address them," said Deidre, watching her shrewdly. "A famous author, some explorer from South America or the Canadian regions. Eustace invited some of them to come to hear a man . . . oh, dear, what was his name, maman?"

"Was it Frost, or Dost, or Cost?" mused the countess. "I do not recall, dear."

"Well, anyway, it was an immense success. There is a large drawing room in the town house, and we had quite thirty guests to hear him lecture."

"I thought you were not amused by him," said the countess, cocking her head over the color she had chosen and peering at it through her lorgnette. "Dear me, is this the color I wanted?"

"Well, I did not understand him much," said Deidre. "Of course, Valerie would have understanding of such! She is so much more an intellectual! Dear me, all the foreigners you would meet, and you could talk to them, in French and German and Spanish! I recall one evening, I was quite in dismay, for my partners at the home of the Prince Regent were all speaking in foreign tongues, and understood little English!"

She went on at this rate, until Valerie was reluctantly interested in going. She must have been talking to Malcolm also, for one evening he said to them all,

"You know, we really ought to go to London for the end of the season, at least, Mater! Valerie has not been presented to society. Reggie Darlington writes, asking when we come, saying his godmother is most impatient to meet Valerie and to welcome the rest of us. What do you think?"

The earl looked at Valerie, the countess was frowning slightly.

"We are still in demi-mourning," said the countess. "And I confess, I do not look forward to the chore of opening the town house . . . such memories," she sighed deeply.

"Nonsense, my dear," said the earl heartily. "You shall have all the help in the world. Valerie will be much in command, I warrant you! She has taken over much of the work here for you, choosing the menus, arranging the flowers, supervising the servants along with the house-keeper. The town house she could manage with one finger! Should you like to go, my dear?"

"Well, I don't . . . know . . ." Valerie looked from the earl to Malcolm to Deidre, who kept her gaze demurely on her coffee cup.

"It should be jolly, give us a relief from the work," said Malcolm eagerly. "I heard that Peter Pratt and Lord Maitland are in town, returned from the Peninsula. How I should love to talk with them. I cannot figure out what is going on!"

"Valerie?" urged the earl.

"Well, if all wish to go . . ." she said, and finally it was settled.

The housekeeper, the butler, two footmen, and two maids were sent ahead to open the town house which had been closed for almost two years. Then there was much packing of trunks, deciding what clothes to take, letters scurrying back and forth like white leaves in a spring wind of excitement. Lady Darlington wrote hastily, almost incoherently for her.

How happy I shall be to receive you! I have been much housebound by a plaguey stiffness in my bones.

However, do call upon me once you arrive, how happy I shall be! Someone to talk to upon my own interests! Reginald shall come for you. I am informing all my friends that you are most intelligent, my dear Valerie, they are almost as anxious as I am to receive you. We shall have lectures and meetings as soon as you come! My dear friend, Lady Alice Prost, has much praised your recent article on education. When I told her that you were now writing on the works of Shakespeare, she declared that she herself would attend you to the theater to a play that is now going on.

Even Glenda was caught up in the excitement. "Oh, my lady, once we have arrived, I shall study the latest arrangements in hair! You shall be the grandest, most elegant lady at every ball!"

"Good heavens," said Valerie, weakly.

It took three closed carriages and the great barouche to convey them all to London, in a solemn procession, complete with outriders in the Arundel blue and gold. Upon arrival, late in the evening, they were all glad to go to their rooms, to find beds freshly made with sheets smelling of lavender, and the housekeeper bustling about happily, sending trays of food and tea here and there.

After the quiet of Kent, London seemed huge, bustling, covered with grit and grime, loud, brassy, like a great aging mistress demanding attention from her lovers. The streets rang with wheels drawn over its cobblestones, the cries of the vendors. "Sweet lavender! Oranges, sweet, sweet oranges! Buy my fish, buy my good fresh fish!"

The countess, once she had recovered from the journey, went at once to the dressmaker's with Valerie and Deidre and ordered an immense amount of clothing, it seemed to the dazzled girl. Deidre took it all in stride, smiling in amusement as Valerie tried to protest.

"But I have dresses—many dresses," said Valerie weakly.

"Not ball gowns," said Deidre, turning to a green-and-gray gauze confection, her eyes sparkling. "Let me see that style, in a blue gauze . . . yes, blue for me," she demanded imperiously.

Valerie sat and watched as the dressmaker and her assistants scurried about, bringing bolts of fabric and dress patterns, showing bonnets crowned with feathers, pointing to the latest fashions from Paris. Fashions from Paris! And in the Peninsula, the forces of France were arrayed against the forces of Britain in a deadly war! It was so incongruous that she must sit and think about it, rather than concentrate on choosing a fabric for a ball gown.

The countess ended up choosing for her, with a slight sigh. "I do wish you would pay attention, Valerie," she said, in a low tone. "Now, I have chosen the rose silk with the rosebuds caught up on the skirts. Which color do you wish for the gauze?"

"Do I need more than one ball gown?" asked Valerie.

The dressmaker's chief assistant hid a smile. Deidre turned about, looking scornfully at Valerie.

"I have already chosen six gowns," said Deidre. "I am sure they will not be half enough! Forget the country, my dear Valerie!"

Valerie bit her lips. She sat back as the countess and the dressmaker consulted. Deidre was choosing recklessly, as though she might never again have the opportunity of buying a gown, a feverish glitter in her hard blue gaze. This was what she wanted, thought Valerie, the dresses, the attention fluttering about her, the thought of dances and attentive men and being written about in the gazettes.

She went home soberly after the long day of fittings. She found Reggie Darlington there, talking with Malcolm. He jumped up to beam at her, to seize her hands and kiss them devotedly.

"My lady, how wonderful to see you again! My godmother has charged me with messages for you!"

"How good of her. Is she well?" She withdrew her hands gently, conscious of Malcolm's jealous scowl.

"Not so well. The doctor comes and prescribes medicine, which she then throws into the basin! She moves stiffly with a cane and complains she never sleeps. But she reads, Lord, how she reads! And she will come to you if you do not come immediately to her!"

"I shall be happy to come to her. I look forward to meeting her and thanking her for her many kindnesses. Do let us set on a time before I am swept away to another dressmaker's," she begged in a low tone as the others came in.

Reggie nodded his understanding, and named a date two days away. The countess agreed to accompany her. Malcolm said, "But I was going to take you to Vauxhall Gardens that day, Valerie!"

"Take me instead," beamed Deidre, happily. "I adore Vauxhall! Valerie can go another time."

"Very well then," said Malcolm, casting a disagreeable look at Reggie and Valerie.

Valerie thought she was playing into Deidre's hands. She knew the other woman had schemed to come to London. The country was Valerie's territory, thought the girl. The city was Deidre's. Now they were in the area where Deidre was most familiar, and she had the advantage. Would she try again to break up Malcolm's marriage and take him for herself?

Valerie felt a strange pain. But she would sit back and watch, she vowed. She would watch how Malcolm reacted. He was bored in the country, he had said so a hundred times.

She had a reason for wanting to know soon how he felt. If he were drawn back to his old ways, of gambling, dancing all the night, flitting from one woman to another, she wanted to know it *now*. She was twenty-one and could leave him. She could find a position, and work. She would not be humiliated by him!

She went to the home of Lady Darlington and found herself touched, amused, pitying the valiant old lady. Lady Seraphine Darlington was in her seventies, wearing often a blonde wig which was brightly incongruous over her lined and wrinkled face. She had startling violet eyes and must once have been a great beauty, for her form was still slim and rounded, and she gowned herself gorgeously in yellow silks and purple satins.

Her mind was alert, bright, and full of strange facts and fancies. Her thoughts darted like that of a brilliant bird from one treetop of science, to another of explorations, on to gossip of the Royal Family.

She soon gave a grand dinner for some intellectual friends and presided gracefully and regally at the table. Some twenty men and women of the most intellectual circles of England came to her table and lingered until two in the morning, discussing, arguing, in long circles sometimes, thought Valerie. She was fascinated.

Malcolm was not invited! He was furious and sulky.

Lady Darlington had tapped him with her fan. "You are not interested in intellect as your wife is, my dearest boy! Reginald is not invited either, he has a bird-wit! That does not mean you are not charming, and I adore you! But you would be bored, and I shall not endure that! I shall send two footmen for Valerie, whom I already love for her mind. And we shall see her safely home again."

"Should I go then, without Malcolm?" asked Valerie, of the earl. Her father-in-law was the only person in the world who seemed to understand her and love her!

"My dear, it shall be as you please. You would enjoy the company, and Malcolm would yawn! Do as you wish."

She decided to go, then, and Malcolm was furious with her and scarcely spoke for a week. He was more furious when she continued to be invited out to bluestocking functions, a lecture by a well-known novelist, a formal tea to welcome writers of a publishing house.

To her amazement and delight, THEY had heard of HER! They greeted her, several said they had read her articles and stories. A publisher cornered her for quite an hour at one tea and tried to extract a promise from her to write a novel. Their praise was balm to her heart.

Lady Alice Prost sponsored her and went everywhere with her, at the request of her dearest friend, Lady Darlington. Everywhere, Valerie was introduced as Lady Grenville, the writer.

Her days and nights were crammed full. The pretty bedroom-sitting room in the Arundel town house was soon full of books which people had pressed on her, letters of invitation to various events, three manuscripts which their authors begged her to criticize—besides the new ball gowns, boxes of bonnets, new slippers, folios of papers on which Valerie was writing her ideas.

Malcolm had his own bedroom. Once and twice and again, she reflected bitterly that since they had moved to town, he had always slept alone—or at least, without her! He had a huge bedroom on the other side of the sitting-room which was in their suite. Some days she did not see him from breakfast to midnight. They went their separate ways, except when they were specifically invited to an event together.

They did go to balls together. She was especially fond of a new ball gown which she had chosen herself, a lilac silk in a shimmering fabric which showed purple, lilac, lavender according to the way the lights shone on it. Over it was hung from the low shoulders an overdress of golden gauze which reached to her feet. With it she wore new little slippers of golden silk, with delicate little heels. And she wore her amethysts.

She came out early into the sitting room to wait for Malcolm. He had returned late to the town house, and she had heard him arguing with his father when she passed the earl's study late in the afternoon. She knew he had been out with Deidre, and her heart was heavy. He was turning out the way she had feared he would—a rake, a charmer, a chaser of women. She knew he had plenty of encouragement from Deidre, but that did not excuse him, she thought. She sat down a little heavily on a chair and rested her feet on a hassock. She must decide soon, it was nearing the end of May. Then would come June, then presently, she must be gone.

Malcolm came from his bedroom to the sitting room, glanced briefly at her, as though he did not even see the pretty new gown, his jewels.

"Ready?" he said.

"Yes, Malcolm." Slowly she rose. She got dizzy if she stood suddenly. So far no one had noticed. But she could not hide it forever, the fact that she was carrying Malcolm's child.

If he knew, he would resign himself to staying married to her. But if he did not know and she left him, she could cut all the ties, far away from him, bear the child and keep it. Then he could marry Deidre, whom the countess loved as her own daughter, whom Malcolm . . . desired . . . probably.

They went downstairs to the carriage. Deidre was ready, she was always on time for balls, no matter how late she was for anything else. She was bubbling over with happiness, radiant in a new gown of white lace and her diamonds.

"I know this will be a splendid evening," said Deidre, sitting beside Valerie, opposite Malcolm. "I just know it! I could dance and dance and dance! I adore London, it is so exciting!"

"Valerie finds London exciting also," said Malcolm, with something like a sneer in his tone. "She runs around with strangers all the day! Did you ever believe you would feel this way about London, Valerie?"

She gazed out the window. "No," she agreed, quietly. "I did not guess it would be like this."

Malcolm stood up with her at the first dance, then went to Deidre. Reggie Darlington came at once to Valerie and begged the honor of a dance. He was gay, charming, devoted. He introduced her to some of Malcolm's friends, some she had met before, others she had not.

She danced with Lord Maitland, a drawling, amusing fellow. She danced with Peter Pratt, and found him serious, willing to talk briefly about the war. "We missed Malcolm, but he was well out of it," said Peter, shaking his head. "Nasty business. Wellington is trying his old tricks, it will be a long drawn-out affair—but he'll win, you'll see."

She danced with others, all the time aware intensely that Malcolm danced frequently with Deidre. She heard whispers, caught curious looks at herself. She held up her head proudly, pretended not to care, forced a smile on her lips for her partners.

She was popular, she was amazed to find that. She did look well in the lilac and gauze gown, in spite of the fact that Malcolm had not even noticed her. She wondered if he was still furious that she had said "No" last night when he came to her room. Probably so.

She had felt dizzy and ill of late, and she did not want him to guess about her condition—not yet.

Presently, Malcolm came back to her. They were playing a waltz, and some of the more decorous ladies had withdrawn to the side.

"We'll dance this, if you'll spare me the time," Malcolm growled in a low angry tone and snatched her away from the wall.

Valerie tried to shake her head, her body stiffened.

"No, Malcolm, I do not wish to dance the waltz. It ... it makes me dizzy . . . please. . . ."

He pulled her rather roughly with him. "You can dance the waltz, I know it! Don't act the prim proper country girl, it don't suit you!"

He began to whirl her about with the music. At first, she rather enjoyed it, the strength of his arm, the light lilting music that seemed to carry her feet to enchantment. Then she began to get dizzy again. The room, the huge chandeliers, the ladies in their delicate dresses, all swirled before her eyes.

"Malcolm . . ." she begged faintly. "I am . . . dizzy . . . please . . ."

His mouth tight, he paid no attention. He whirled her around and around, until she could only hang on his arm and go with him. The music seemed endless, she was feeling sick as well when it stopped abruptly, and everyone applauded.

She was near a wall. She groped her way to it and leaned against it, her hand to her breast. Malcolm turned away. "I'll find someone who does enjoy dancing," he said, in a parting thrust.

She was so dizzy she could not see. Black spots seemed to prick her eyes, her head swam. Was she going to be sick, right here? How horribly embarrassing! She must stay erect, she could not fall down. . . .

A strong arm went about her waist. Had Malcolm returned? She could not see. She groped for his hand, pleadingly.

"I say, Valerie, are you ill?" It was Reggie's low urgent voice, holding her firmly.

She managed to nod, she felt childishly disappointed that it was not Malcolm. But better not, better not . . .

"Felt dizzy . . ." she managed to say.

"I say, Peter, get a glass of brandy, will you? Lady Grenville is not quite the thing."

A glass was brought and set to her lips. She was shielded by the two tall men as Reggie held her upright, and Peter held the glass to her lips. She managed to swallow, once, twice. The fiery liquid burned right through the fog.

"There, that's . . . all . . . right. . . ," she said.

"I'll get a chair," offered Peter.

"On the veranda. She needs some air. Hot as Hades in here," said Reggie. Between them, they supported her to a chair. She sank down gratefully, struggling against tears. Why were they so kind, and Malcolm so cruel?

Both men remained with her for quite half an hour, attentive, courteous, anxious over her. Malcolm finally returned, sought her out. "Here you are. I wondered where you had got to." His voice was stern, controlled because his two friends were there.

"I should . . . like to return home," she managed to say.

"There's supper," said Malcolm in impatient surprise. "We're just going down to it. Come along, Valerie. This isn't the country."

She could have wept. She did not think she had the strength to stand up, much less eat anything.

"I'll get you a plate and bring it back," Peter offered swiftly. "Reggie, what would you like?"

"A little of everything, I'll get some glasses, and we'll have a party out here," said Reggie cheerfully. "I say, Malcolm, why don't you get Deidre and join us?"

Malcolm hesitated, glared at Valerie, then said, "Deidre has already made up a table for us. Why don't you join us?"

"Nicer out here," said Reggie.

"Very well, then, we shall see you later on." And he turned on his heel and left them.

Valerie felt so humiliated and weary she wanted nothing so much as to run away. But she had not even the strength to get up and walk out. She waited while the two young men brought her food, drinks, and laughter. She wondered what Deidre was doing, decided it did not matter any longer.

The ball lasted till two in the morning. She was utterly exhausted when they finally reached home. She stumbled on the stairs, caught herself with her hand on the railing. Deidre and Malcolm were still in the drawing room, having one more drink.

Glenda, sensing something wrong, came downstairs to meet her and help her up. The older woman's mouth was tight with disapproval. Tenderly she helped her to the bedroom, unfastened the tight-fitting gown, and undressed her.

The nightdress slipped gratefully over her head, its looseness and warmth reassuring.

"My lady? Have you told Mr. Malcolm yet?"

"Told him?" asked Valerie, aching with weariness, stretching out on the bed with the feeling she might never be able to get up again. "What?"

"About—about the child, my lady. I couldn't help noticing . . ."

"No, Glenda!" Her tone was unusually fierce. She roused enough to say, "Tell no one! Swear to tell no one! I have not yet planned what I shall do. I do not want anyone to know about it."

"Oh, my lady," sighed Glenda, shaking her gray head. She drew up the blankets tenderly to Valerie's chin, blew out the candles, and left her.

Valerie could not sleep right away. She was thinking, thinking, her mind racing around like a squirrel in a cage, like a little trapped animal.

She must leave him soon, she thought. He had changed completely. Malcolm cared little for her. For the sake of the child, he might keep her as his wife. But she would not want a son of hers brought up like that! The humiliation of knowing he would go from one woman to another—no, better to leave him completely.

Tears trickled down her cheeks, she wiped them away fiercely. She would not cry. She would be strong and brave. She must leave him soon. She would say she was sick of society, hated this life. It was true, she hated the gossip and the license of the women, the cool looks of men who seemed to strip her to her skin with their calculating gaze. She flinched over and over when she saw some of the men, even those near the Prince Regent. Some of them were the worst of all, with their hard reputations, their gaming, the way they treated women.

And Malcolm was well on his way to becoming one of

them. With Deidre's help, he would be the top of the *ton*, one of the Corinthians, one of the beaux every woman in the fast set would set her bonnet for. She wanted none of that.

She wanted a peaceful life in the country, with her child, her garden, her home. If she could not have that, she would settle on making her own living, taking care of her child, well away from him.

So she resolved fiercely, yet could not set a date for leaving. Perhaps tomorrow, perhaps next week, as soon as she was sure of the fact that he felt nothing for her. . . . Then she would go.

Chapter Thirteen

The weeks in London flew past. The earl was already looking forward to returning to his precious peace and quiet. However, the others, including his wife, seemed quite caught up in the turmoil and partying and reluctant to think of leaving.

June came, with a few dusty roses and a wisp of honeysuckle trailing over a small gazebo in the minute garden. Only this, and a few herbs to remind Valerie of the scents and colors of her own gardens back at Arundel. Should she ever see them again? She and Malcolm continued to draw further and further apart.

He was out half the night, often with Deidre. Valerie steadily refused to be out so late and often returned with the countess at an earlier time. Valerie continued to be popular, to Deidre's expressed amazement.

"I do not understand how they can enjoy your conversation, you are so very clever," said Deidre, with wide-eyed innocence, at dinner one evening. "You are besieged with partners for dancing, even though you usually refuse to do any but the country dances."

"Valerie has a natural grace and rhythm," said her father-in-law placidly. "Like to dance with her myself. Doesn't bother you with stupid chatter, like so many females, when you're trying to place your feet right."

Deidre laughed, her soft musical chuckle. "Oh, you are so witty, papa," she said, then caught herself, her hand to her mouth. "Oh, I continually forget . . . I cannot call you that!" And actual tears came into her blue eyes.

Malcolm reached over to pat her hand comfortingly. "Do not get upset, Deidre, you are practically one of the family, you know."

The earl looked thoughtful but did not echo these sentiments. Louis Kenyon had not accompanied them to London—he had no fondness for the city—and had volunteered to remain this time at Arundel and keep the reins firmly in hand.

"Is all ready for tomorrow afternoon?" inquired the countess of Valerie. "And how many will be here for tea?"

"About thirty, maman. I think all is prepared. Lady Prost and Lady Darlington have volunteered to pour. We have made fresh cakes, and there will be bowls of raspberries and cream. I thought it would make a change from the sandwiches."

"A charming thought," the countess approved.

Deidre made a grimace and looked toward Malcolm. "You are not going to remain for the lecture, are you, Malcolm? He is dreadfully prosy and long-winded!"

"Thought I should come," said Malcolm reluctantly. "After all, Valerie is the hostess."

"We could go driving in your new high-perch phaeton, which Valerie detests so, and then on to tea with Lord Maitland and his sister," she suggested eagerly, her blue eyes bright. "We should like that ever so much more."

Valerie clamped her mouth shut over a bitter remark and kept her gaze on her dessert. Malcolm and Deidre spent more and more time together.

Malcolm glanced toward Valerie. "Valerie, should you mind if we do not come to your intellectual tea?" he asked, with rather a cutting edge to his voice. "I do not think we shall be missed!"

"It would be rather rude not to come," said the countess, a little distressed line between her eyebrows. "I know you are not diverted by such events. Still, I have heard he is most interesting."

"Do as you wish, Malcolm," said Valerie quietly.

He shrugged. "Then Deidre and I shall go out," he said, and Deidre clapped her hands childishly.

"Oh, fun," she said. "I adore London! And everyone is so kind. Here, everyone can do as one wishes, and no one even remarks about it!"

Valerie was bitterly disappointed that Malcolm had made that decision, but she thought she would have died rather than to say so. She had been so proud that she had captured a real prize in the speaker, everyone wanted to hear him, just freshly returned from an expedition on the strange Amazon River in South America.

Because of Valerie's friendship with Lady Alice Prost and Lady Seraphine Darlington, the girl had met many famous people. Lady Prost had told her cousin, the explorer, about Valerie, her many interests, and how serious she was about learning of the world. For this reason, the great man, though he accepted few engagements, had consented to lecture in the Arundel town house.

It was a tremendous event, and Malcolm was slipping away, bored at the very prospect! And wanting to be with Deidre, thought his wife bitterly.

It spoiled some of her enjoyment of the next afternoon, though she smiled and chatted happily enough with her new friends. The countess came and the Earl of Arundel, comfortable in his old tweeds, but curious about "Valerie's new friend."

Everyone seemed amazed to see the man, a great giant of a fellow, with a trim beard, fierce mustaches, and the most brilliant green eyes in a sun-tanned face that Valerie had ever seen. For all his hugeness, he was gentle. He held her hand in his big one, bent over it, murmured his pleasure, almost shyly.

"How kind of you to come to our tea," she said eagerly. "I am so longing to hear of your adventures! Oh, to be a man, and be able to run about the world, and see all you have seen!"

Her eyes flashed with the thought. Mr. Prost stood erect again, gazed down into her animated face, pressed her hand once again. "I am honored by your interest, my lady," he said. "I fear many ladies are either bored or horrified by some of my adventures. I have been to strange places and witnessed such events that one would be forgiven for thinking I had been sleeping and had dreamed it all! For South America is another world from civilized England, and these green and pleasant places have never witnessed such savage rites as go on. Yet everywhere I met with kindness. When there was little food, the naked savages shared what they had with me. When I fell from the canoe into the raging waters, near a crocodile, one of them risked his very life, to dive in and push me back into the boat again!"

Valerie was listening with awed look and excited pulses. He had such a quiet, drawling voice, that one had to strain to hear him. His green eyes burned with a vision of faraway places, his voice throbbed with his emotions, which seemed so much deeper and more true than those of the light London society.

"We are so anxious to hear all you will tell us. May I

help you to some tea first? Or will you have brandy or sherry?"

"Tea, please, if I am to talk coherently," he said, with a charming smile. Lady Alice Prost served him, sent a keen look at her cousin's animated face and at Valerie's pretty one.

Valerie had worn today a lilac muslin, with her amethysts at ears, throat and wrist. On her hand was the huge amethyst which Malcolm had given her, her favorite ring. Her thick brown curls hung charmingly about her white throat, not in the latest style, but beautiful. The large wistful brown eyes gazed straight at the person to whom she spoke, she had no flirtatious arts, but somehow one wished to keep on looking into those great eyes.

The crowd almost filled the drawing room of Arundel House. The countess and the earl held court in one corner, Valerie circled about the room anxiously to make sure all had tea or sherry; the raspberries soon disappeared and were much praised.

After four o'clock, Valerie tapped on a glass lightly to gain their attention. Her cheeks were flushed with the unusual attention on her, as all seated or standing turned to listen to what she said.

"Ladies and gentlemen, I am so happy to welcome you to Arundel on this happy occasion. We are indeed honored to have as our guest the great explorer, freshly returned from his journey to the Amazon River in Brazil. He has spent quite two years exploring the river, and his reports to the Scientific Society will be eagerly awaited; and His Majesty has expressed the debt all of England owes to him for his magnificent efforts on behalf of knowledge.

"I am most happy to present to you today, Mr. Gilbert Prost, explorer, lecturer, writer, scientist, who will speak to us informally on his fascinating journeys."

She turned, quite flushed and breathless from her little effort, and curtsied to Mr. Prost, who came forward to the mantel where she stood. It was then that Valerie saw Malcolm standing awkwardly in the doorway, listening. She caught her breath. He had come! She looked behind him for Deidre but did not see the girl.

"My very dear Lady Grenville, how kind you are to introduce me so graciously. I am indeed honored to be invited to your beautiful home. Ladies and gentlemen, have you ever imagined in your wildest dreams that you were lost in the great green jungle, with vines as thick as your wrist joining tree to tree, shutting out the very sky? And orchids of lilac, mauve, creamy white, hanging in such profusion from the vines that they make a fairyland in which are no fairies such as Shakespeare knew, but fierce little Indian savages naked but for a cloth, holding arrows tipped with a poison which kills in ten minutes."

He held them in the palm of his great tanned hand, speaking vividly and eloquently of his adventures, of what he had seen and heard. He spoke of the quiet of the night torn by the husky cough of fierce jungle animals as the jaguar, which could pounce and kill in a few seconds. The cry of parrots, wild birds, bats flying blindly into the light of the campfire. Hoards of small insects which bit savagely and caused a deadly fever.

Mr. Prost was a skilled speaker, his green eyes burning with devotion to his subject. When he could sense their intense interest by the complete stillness of the room, he went on and on, telling of a journey along a tributary of the Amazon, of the canoe tumbling down great cataracts of white water, of immense prehistoric-appearing crocodiles which gaped their jaws and ate an unfortunate dog which had fallen into the water. Some ladies turned rather green as he spoke of the food they had eaten to stay alive, of the sickness. But they controlled themselves, determined to hear all.

He spoke until nearly six o'clock. Nobody stirred. Even Malcolm, seated on a chair near the doorway, kept his gaze intently on the man's face, seemingly as fascinated as all the rest.

Mr. Prost drew a great breath. He was hoarse and coughed a little, then spoke again.

"Forgive me, I have spoken too long. Your kind attention drew me from story to story. I must stop. You are weary, and so am I. Forgive me, I am full of my work, and find it difficult to stop myself."

He bowed awkwardly to the company, which began to applaud, led finally from their absorbed attention to appreciation of what he had done.

Valerie went quickly to him as he leaned against the mantel. She took one of his hands warmly in both of her small ones, and clasped it. "How can we thank you, Mr. Prost, for sharing with us your marvelous story? We shall look forward to reading your articles and the book you are writing. May you always return safely from your terrifying journeys, full of fresh knowledge of our wonderful world!"

The company had quieted to hear her, then applauded again. Mr. Prost bowed again and again, sometimes to them, sometimes to Valerie. It was an immense success, and the babble of voices that rose as the company reluctantly began to depart told how much all had enjoyed it.

Dinner was late that evening, but it was only family and Deidre, so nobody minded. There was much conversation about the stories Mr. Prost had told.

"If you ask me, it was all a hum," said Malcolm, unexpectedly.

"A *hum!*" Valerie turned on him, aghast. "Can you truly say such a thing, when you heard him. . . ?"

"Never heard anything so fantastic in my life. Had to be made up," said Malcolm, not meeting her eyes. He was rather flushed, his mouth defiant. "Nobody could have such adventures. I think he made them all up. Amazes me how much people will swallow."

"Well, I never . . ." Valerie was shocked and trembling. "You cannot mean such a thing! Why . . . why, he has been decorated by His Royal Highness . . . and . . . and . . ."

"Have you seen his decorations? Has anyone? Never wore any today. Who was with him on the journey? Nobody but some natives who don't even talk English!" Malcolm was warming to his theory. "Yes, he's pulling the wool over everybody's eyes. What a hum!"

"Now, Malcolm . . ." began the earl warningly, seeing Valerie's pink cheeks and the beginning of tears in her great brown eyes. "You have no proof of that. Enjoyed it myself. Could be true."

"Of course, it is true!" Valerie collected herself and turned on Malcolm. "Newspaper men have interviewed him, they had written about him during his journey, he sent letters home."

"Could all be faked."

"A very reputable scientific society sponsored him. They know his work."

"Do they?"

"Dear me, what an amusing conversation," said Deidre with a smile at them both. "What difference does it make? If he amused the company, that is enough!"

Valerie was amazed to find herself trembling with anger. "It makes a great deal of difference! A man of honor, evidently, and a man of great experiences . . ."

"Who managd to kiss your hand at least four times in three hours," sneered Malcolm.

The countess looked at her husband, who looked back. "My dear Valerie," said the countess, "I am sure he had such adventures, and he certainly told them well. May I congratulate you on the manner in which you introduced him, and thanked him? You showed great poise. I was proud of you."

"Thank you, maman," said Valerie, her voice stifled.

"We must do it again soon," said the countess placidly.

"Let me see, there is an author, everyone is talking about her, we must have her to another tea!"

And so she switched the subject, so deftly that no one could object. But Valerie rushed away from dinner to take refuge in her sitting room. She felt she hated Malcolm for his cruel remarks, his cynicism. She thought over retorts she could have made. She could have pointed out the great men who had honored Mr. Prost, how he had been spoken of in the House of Lords, and formally acknowledged for his expedition. A hum! How could Malcolm say such a thing!

She had been so happy with the event of the afternoon, it had gone exceedingly well, even the countess had said so. Lady Alice Prost had congratulated her. Lady Darlington had patted her hands and said she was a fine hostess and a very bright woman. And Mr. Prost had said . . .

Malcolm came in as she was sitting at her writing table trying to collect her whirling mind.

"I came to apologize," he said.

Her dull eyes brightened. "Oh, do you believe that . . ."

"No, I don't," he interrupted. "I think he is a great hoaxer, and I don't want to see him here at Arundel again! But papa said I made you cry, and I should apologize, and so I am . . ."

She drew a deep furious breath. "Save your breath to cool your porridge!" she snapped. "Such apologies won't hold water in a sieve! I wish you had not returned this afternoon! You spoiled everything!"

He stared at her. "Too bad that I am not welcome in my own home!" he flared grimly. "Well, I'll go where I'm welcome!" And he turned on his heels and went out, slamming the door so violently that a piece of ivory fell over on her occasional table.

She got up to set it right, her fingers shaking on the piece. She turned it over in her hands. It was a favorite little figure of a dog that Malcolm had given her, in finest carved ivory. How he gave with one hand, and took away her pleasure with the other! How much must she endure? she asked herself wrathfully.

She returned to the article she had been writing, but found her powers of concentration had fled. She could not think about the condition of orphans in homes for the poor, when her mind kept churning about, arguing against Malcolm, wondering where he had gone, worrying around what he had said about the explorer.

In the gazettes of the next two days, there appeared no less than five articles about the great explorer, Mr. Gilbert Prost, newly returned from the Amazon. It told what Lord So-and-so had said of his work, what Mr. Smith and Mr. Jones thought of his scientific manner, what honors were being heaped on him. Valerie read them all avidly, laid them out for Malcolm to see, only to have him ignore them all.

And he took out Lady Deidre in his high-perch phaeton to tool around Hyde Park for the next three mornings.

The earl shook his head over them both. The countess fluttered, and said timidly to Valerie that perhaps dear Malcolm did not care for scientific matters so very much, and perhaps dear Valerie should take more interest in his new carriage and horses.

So matters stood on Saturday evening, when they were all invited to a great cotillion at the home of Lord Berkley. Deidre had been fussing about what she should wear, had finally decided on the gray and blue gauze over silk, with her diamonds, which set off her fair good looks. The countess wore cream, with her pearls.

Valerie had been troubled about her clothing. She had less and less choice now, as her waist had enlarged to noticeable proportions if she wore a tight dress. And she could not endure corsets about her waist. Glenda suggested a new gown, of simple white, Grecian in design, falling straight from shoulders to hem, which was embroidered in purple Greek key pattern. The shoulders were bare, except for the folds of white material about her throat.

With it, Valerie wore the Arundel diamonds for the first time, the small elegant tiara on her hair, as it was dressed high in curls and roll, with three curls falling to one side of her throat. The diamond necklace circled her throat, Glenda slipped on two diamond bracelets on her wrists, and she wore a diamond ring on each hand.

When she had descended the stairs, and entered the drawing room, she saw Deidre's face as she entered. The look was narrowed, catlike, the blue eyes hard in jealousy, before the creamy face smoothed out into a smile.

"How very grand you are tonight, my dear Valerie," said Deidre. "You will draw all your suitors to you, won't she, Malcolm? Reggie is becoming so very devoted, so is Lord Maitland!"

Malcolm was clad in a fine white satin suit, with tight knee-breeches showing his fine calf, his stock precisely tied in an elaborate fall, an immense ruby stickpin holding it. Another ruby glowed on his hand. He gave a quick look over Valerie, as though critically examining her to find a fault.

"I think you are not finding London such a bore as you said you would," he drawled in a disagreeable tone, which warned Valerie he was in a dangerous mood. He lifted the sherry glass, tossed off the last of it, and set it down. "Ready to go?"

"Yes, of course." She was feeling quite weary from the long days of entertaining and being up some nights until midnight. If only they might all return to the country, to peace, quiet, the Shakespeare garden, Mrs. Parker's grandchildren, all the familiar and the dear. She blinked back tears as Malcolm took her arm to escort her to the carriage.

She wore a white velvet cloak over her finery, and he lifted her skirts carefully for her as she stepped up. Then

Deidre followed her, Valerie noted that Malcolm was even more careful with her gauze gown. Always the three of them, she was rarely alone with Malcolm anymore.

And all the comradeship was gone, quite gone. It was as though all the letters they had written to each other, the way they had worried over Malcolm, the nights spent in his arms, all was gone and forgotten in the stiffness and anger that was left.

At Lord Berkley's, there was a long flight of stairs up to the ballroom. Carriages rolled up, discharged their elegant passengers, linkboys held torches high, grooms hastened to take away horses of the single gentlemen.

Music echoed through the long halls, as they walked on the red carpets back to the ballrooms. Smaller rooms on either side were opened, to show tables set for cards. A long evening, thought Valerie. She hoped she would not grow dizzy. She must be careful and not dance so much.

A maid took their cloaks. They proceeded to the ballroom where Lady and Lord Berkley greeted them kindly. They went on into the room where the polished floors gleamed with fresh waxing, chandeliers shone with a thousand candles, French windows were opened to the balconies to admit fresh air and allow guests to wander outside, even down the steps to the gardens.

Malcolm turned to Valerie. "The first dance, my dear," he said, but his tone was cold. He was always so proper, she thought savagely. If only he would tell her the truth! As though she needed to be told! She knew he did not love her, that he merely endured the marriage.

She slipped into his arms, and they circled the room in a silence. The waltz was playing, a slow sweet melody, not a fast one.

"There is your dear admirer, Reggie Darlington," said Malcolm, at the end of the dance. "He is making in our direction! I can safely leave you to him!"

He waited only until Reggie came up, then stalked

away. Reggie gazed after him in mild surprise. "Didn't even say how-do-you-do," he said. "Up the trees, is he?"

"Always, with me," said Valerie bitterly, then bit her lip. "I beg pardon—I should not have said that. Please forget that."

Reggie looked keenly at her, shook his head, and drew her away from the dance floor. He settled her carefully into a comfortable chair near the window.

"Wanted to talk to you, Valerie. And there's more air here." He sat down beside her, close, but not so near as to cause talk. "My poor darling Aunt Darlington has broke her leg."

"Oh, no!" Valerie gazed at him in horror. "She didn't!"

He nodded. "She did. Doctor says her bones are brittle, it could have happened anyway. But she was out in the evening, missed a step, before anyone could get to her she had fallen flat—groaning and moaning. My blood went cold, I can tell you! Tried to pick her up, worst possible thing, she let out a shriek and went dead faint."

"Oh, how terrible, how terrible! Poor Lady Darlington, I am so sorry! Is she now comfortable? When did it happen?"

"Two nights ago," said Reggie, patting her hand held out in sympathy. "The doctor has patched her up, she lies all day in her drawing room and wails that she has nothing to read, and nobody likes her anymore for no one calls. Sorry for herself, and snapping and growling at us all. Miserable, I can tell you!"

"Oh, if she is allowed visitors, I must call on her as soon as possible!" said Valerie, her own worries temporarily forgotten. "Poor dear soul. Such a good-hearted woman. I shall take her four new books, they are elegant reading, and she may enjoy them."

"Here they are, hiding in the corner, it's a shame to disturb them!" cried Deidre's merry voice. She was hanging onto Malcolm's arm, he was glaring at the pair talking quietly together in the corner.

"Oh, Malcolm, Lady Darlington has broken her leg!" said Valerie, to her husband. "I must call upon her soon. She is so miserable."

"Oh, is that right? Too bad, how did it happen?" But Malcolm did not seem really deeply concerned, thought Valerie, and the scowl did not leave his handsome face.

They soon went away, Lord Maitland appeared and asked for the honor of a round dance. Valerie stood up with him, and then Peter Pratt came, and presently Lady Alice Prost with her distinguished cousin, Mr. Gilbert Prost.

He asked for a dance from Valerie and, to her surprise, he proved very graceful. He apologized for his lack of practice.

"Dear me, sir, how could you practice in the jungle? With a monkey, perhaps? But indeed, you malign yourself, you dance very well."

"You are most gracious, my lady. You know, I do not usually enjoy my sojourns in London. They are but a pause before the next journey. However, this time has been different," he said, significantly, gazing deeply into her eyes.

She gasped a little. "Oh, indeed," she said faintly. "I . . . ah . . . do hope you enjoy your stay. How long do you remain?"

"Until the autumn," he said. "Until I am ready to make another expedition. Lady Grenville, may I call upon you one day? It is rare that one meets a beautiful lady who is so intelligent, and so very knowledgeable about such masculine pursuits as explorations! I should like to talk over my next project with you."

"Beg pardon!" Malcolm was at his shoulder, frowning heavily. "The dance is over, and the next I have with my wife!"

Mr. Prost seemed startled. "Your . . . wife?" he echoed.

"Yes, this is my husband. Malcolm Villiers, Viscount

Grenville," said Valerie quickly, conscious that her cheeks were flushed with color. She had not dreamed that the serious Mr. Prost could so think of her, wish to pursue her.

"I beg pardon. I . . . somehow I had formed the impression that Lady Villiers . . . Lady Grenville . . . I mean . . . I did not realize she was married," said Mr. Prost flatly.

"She certainly is," said Malcolm curtly and put his arm possessively about Valerie's waist and led her away. In a low angry tone, he asked, "And what did you say to encourage him, eh? Letting him think you was single! What's going on?"

"N-nothing, M-Malcolm. I was . . . 'mazed as you . . . I but wished to speak about his . . . indeed, I never dreamed . . ."

He whirled her about without speaking, his mouth grimly set. Valerie's mind was whirling. Mr. Prost had thought her single! He had been interested in her, in her!

She could not help feeling flattered, for the man was intelligent beyond anybody she had ever met. He had gone through such adventures, contributed so much to human knowledge. . . . And he had been interested in *her*, Valerie Gray, no, Valerie Villiers! He must have thought the earl was her father, rather than her father-in-law.

"You shouldn't flirt, you know," said Malcolm, just before the music ended. "You don't know how to do it, and people take you seriously! Won't do, you know! Better discourage Reggie, before he falls head over heels!"

Valerie gasped at him. "Well, I never . . . of all the crass . . . ignoble . . ."

He bowed, and left her to Lord Maitland, who promptly took her into another round. She danced more than she had intended and began to become weary and dizzy once more.

Presently she saw Lady Deidre, and the girl came over to her. "Valerie, you look so white! Is anything wrong?"

The blue eyes were keen, and in the candlelight they seemed softer than usual.

"I don't feel well," Valerie confessed. "I am tired from all the visiting this week. I wonder if Malcolm would consider leaving . . ."

Deidre lifted an imperious hand. Reggie promptly stopped beside her. Deidre gave him her sweet smile. "Reggie, dear Valerie is weary, and white, and quite ill. Would you be a love and take her home quietly? She really should not stay!"

"Malcolm will not like it. . . ." Valerie began weakly. Her head was spinning.

"Malcolm is playing cards, I'll explain to him when he returns to the ballroom," said Deidre kindly. "Go ahead, dear, don't wait. You do look sick!"

She helped get the white cloak, set it about Valerie's shoulders, gave her a little push toward the stairs. "Go ahead, do. I'm afraid you will faint, I really think so! I'll explain to Malcolm!"

Reggie took her home, then returned to his own home. It was late, and Lady Darlington was irritable, he explained, when he was long away from her.

Valerie sent her best sympathetic greetings to the good lady and went wearily up to bed.

Malcolm wakened her about four in the morning, coming into her bedroom, lighting several candles, and sitting on the bed.

"Now you can explain what you're about!" he said, as she sat up against the pillows, blinking at him in sleepy surprise. "What do you mean by leaving the ball with Reggie Darlington! Don't lie about it, everybody saw you, and teased me without mercy!"

He was really angry, a white line about his mouth. "Deidre said she would tell you . . . I did not feel well . . ."

"Don't lie! You wanted to leave with him! You were talking with him as soon as you got there! Valerie, I won't have you making me the laughing-stock of London! What do you want, to provoke a duel between me and Reggie? Have you gone so far?"

She was too sleepy to collect her wits. "Reggie has been a good friend to me! Nothing more! He understands . . ."

"Oh, he understands, does he? What does he understand? That you are ready to take a lover? Have you become so abandoned? Has London gripped you in her toils so quickly? And you did not even want to come to London," he jeered. His fists were clenched, he glared at her so sternly, so coldly, that she could have wept. "A country girl! You begged to remain in the country! I should have left you there . . . you do not know how to behave yourself! My mother is most distressed with you!"

"That is very unfair!" she protested. "I love her dearly, I would not hurt her for the world. I felt ill . . ."

"You were not ill when I talked to you just earlier!"

He got up and walked out, slamming the door in the night stillness. All the household the next day knew they had quarreled. They did not speak to each other, except in the most frigid polite terms. A coldness had settled between them, an ice barrier beyond melting, thought Valerie, deeply unhappy.

Chapter Fourteen

Malcolm strolled into the drawing room. "We are going out in the carriage," he said curtly to Valerie, who was working slowly on an embroidered cushion cover. "Care to come along?"

It was so indifferently given, that invitation, that she glanced up at him, then down again. His eyes were cold, his tone was "take it or leave it."

"I should like to go to visit Lady Darlington," she said, in a muffled tone. "Would you mind taking me there?"

He hesitated. Deidre had followed him into the room. "Oh, not to pay sick calls!" cried Deidre. "It is such a glorious day! We want to tool around the park in the open carriage, and see who is there!"

Malcolm continued to look at Valerie. "Then, thank you, no, I believe Reggie is coming later this morning, and will convey me to Lady Darlington's. I had promised to call."

Malcolm did not wait until she had finished speaking. He turned and left the room, Deidre darting after him, calling, "Wait until I get my cloak and bonnet, Malcolm!"

The countess said, very gently, "Was that wise, my dear Valerie? You could have gone with them."

"I promised to call on Lady Darlington," said Valerie stubbornly, her mouth set.

The white hands of the older lady fluttered over her

embroidery. "Oh, dear. But you grow farther apart, my dear. Do you not see? Deidre leads him where she will."

"He is easily led, then, maman!"

"You could keep him with you, if you chose. He is very fond of you."

"Oh, fond! What is that? He cares nothing for me, what I like, what I wish to do! If he wishes to do what Deidre wants, why should I object! We are two quite different people!"

She bent her head again to the work, and jabbed at it so fiercely that it went through to her hand. She sucked the finger childishly, tears in her eyes. The countess shook her white head sadly, her mouth drooping.

Reggie Darlington arrived in about an hour and was shown in to them. "Good morning! Lovely day! Shall you come with me to Aunt Darlington?"

He was so easy, so charming, that Valerie smiled up at him. "Yes, at once. Let me but get my bonnet and cloak, and I shall come."

He sat down to talk to the countess, who was reserved with him, eying him so dubiously that he was rather puzzled. He had always been welcomed in their home.

In the carriage, he asked, "What's amiss? Have I stumbled somewhere? Your mama was all coldness to me."

She hesitated, then finally admitted the truth. "Malcolm is mad with me because I will go out with you to your Aunt Darlington, yet refuse to go riding in his carriage with him."

"Oh, ho!" He whistled inelegantly, raised his hat to some ladies in the street, then went on. "And what about you, Valerie? Do you hate to see him escorting the beauteous and greedy Lady Deidre about? Are you jealous of her?"

He was so blunt, so kindly, so like her brother used to be, that tears came to her eyes. She blinked them back, in the shade of the broad brim of her bonnet. She smoothed her blue velvet cloak over her knees, settled the blue ribbons of her bonnet, until she thought her voice would be steady.

"I . . . I think I am, yes, I admit I am, Reggie. However, if Malcolm prefers the company of such as Lady Deidre, then we have nothing in common. I shall not . . . shall not remain married to a man who is a rake, a gambler, a woman-chaser. That is what I have to decide. If he . . . loves me enough, I may stay. Though I think he has no fondness for me at all."

Reggie was silent for a time, his attention on his pair of matched blacks. His charming good-humor face was unusually serious.

"You are not . . . really . . . thinking of separating, are you, Valerie?" he finally asked.

"Not just separation," she said firmly. "Divorce. I shall leave him. I can work and earn my own living. I would rather do that, than to live with a man I cannot respect and who does not respect me."

"Didn't know it had gone so far," said Reggie, with a sigh. "Malcolm is a good chap, none better, Valerie. My best friend. He would give his life for me, and I for him. Think it over carefully, my dear. Big decision and all that."

"Thank you, Reggie. You are . . . very understanding."

"If you need help at any point, glad to offer," he said, awkwardly. "Might break it up with Malcolm, my friend, but I want to help you if I can. Never thought more highly of any female, except Aunt Darlington. Truth, you know!"

She sniffed a little, raised her handkerchief to her eyes at his rather unexpected kindness.

"Hey, you ain't going to cry, Valerie? Can't do it, we're out in public!" he said, alarmed, which brought a watery laugh.

Lady Darlington was so unaffectedly glad to see Valerie that it brought further comfort to the girl. "Come in, come in, wish I could get up to receive you, but demn this leg! Broken clean across, and giving me the devil of some pain! Excuse my language, I ain't fit for company, but I crave it! Books? Dear girl, you are too good to me! Sit down, sit down, Reggie, the chair nearer to the light so I can see her face! Take the cloak, yes, and the bonnet, you are going to stay for a time, ain't you?"

The dowager was attired for receiving morning guests, in a formidable wrap of blue satin with blue-dyed feathers all down the front and around her wrinkled neck. Her blonde wig had been removed, and instead she wore a close-fitting high bonnet of white muslin and lace down to her ears. Lines of pain were grooved into her wrinkled face, her hands seemed more clawlike today, and she looked every bit her age.

But her voice went on and on, strongly, as though to deny anything was wrong with her. She demanded the news of the world, where Malcolm was, how the ball at the Berkleys' had gone, who was run off with whom, what news of the Peninsula and the Wellington forces.

They talked and talked all the morning, which went like lightning. Tea was brought on a grand silver tray, with heavy embossed silver and delicate China porcelain of white and gold. Valerie poured and talked and listened, until she had quite forgotten her own troubles.

The dowager was amusing, rather risque, full of more gossip and news of London and society than anyone could imagine for one on a sick-bed. She told a story with wit and charm, and a wry knowledge of human nature that had them laughing and nodding in agreement.

"Now, tell me, what is this about Malcolm and that silly Lady Deidre?" she asked abruptly, when she had finished her tea. Her keen sharp eyes were fixed on Valerie's expressions, she did not miss the shadow that came quickly.

Reggie crossed and uncrossed his legs uneasily. "Now,

Aunt Seraphine, you ain't got the right to cross-question the girl," he began.

She waved him to silence. "I'm talking to Valerie. What do you mean, girl, letting that greedy little girl who drove nice Eustace Villiers to his death . . . letting her take Malcolm in hand? Can't you fight for what you want? Can't you see what she is doing? Letting his family pay for her gowns, and another season! Her mother was just like her, grabbing with both hands, until she finally married that stupid Lord Ramsey who gambled all his fortune away within five years."

Valerie gazed at Lady Darlington's shrewd face in surprise. "I . . . I didn't know that . . . I thought they had . . ."

"Title but no money, and the estate whittled down to the manor house," said Lady Darlington briefly. "Mama Ramsey sent Deidre off to marry money and a title, and she keeps pushing at the girl. Know a second cousin of theirs and hear all about it. Now she lost Eustace, and her mama is mad as fire at her. So little Deidre is after Malcolm. Why do you let her get away with her grabbing? She has no right to those diamonds she flaunts about. Lady Arundel is too soft with her, far too soft! I'm surprised at your father-in-law, he is a shrewd one. Can't he see what the girl is doing?"

Valerie gathered her wits together. "I . . . I cannot discuss, no, I cannot discuss the matter, madam," she said with dignity. "I am waiting to see . . ."

"To see if Lady Deidre can get your husband away from you? Fight for him if you want him, girl! Malcolm used to be a wild one, but I thought he had settled down. Give him a child, see if that works."

Valerie's head raised, her gaze met Lady Darlington's firmly. "If he wishes to run about and gamble and dance all the night, it is his decision," she said firmly. "Within another month, I shall decide whether to stay or to go. I am going to leave him . . . if . . . if he does not settle down. But it must be his own decision. I shall not lead him by the nose. If he is not strong enough, then I do not want him. If he does not love me enough, then I do not want him!"

"Oh, bravely said," said Lady Darlington, soberly. "However, my girl, you don't know what you're talking about! A woman today must remain married to be respectable. What could you do, all by yourself? Your father dead, your brother dead. Who would protect you?"

"I shall make my own living. I can teach, I can write. I shall not starve."

"Dear me," said Lady Darlington. She mused, her finger on her lips. She looked at Reggie, who shrugged helplessly. "Well, you must make me a promise, my dear. If you need help, send word by Reggie, or come at once to me. You shall not go adrift in this wicked London. So come to me, eh?"

"You are very kind, Lady Darlington," said Valerie unsteadily. She could endure tormenting from Deidre, cross words from Malcolm, but kindness unhinged her, she thought. "You are very good to me, but I could not lean on you, should I decide to leave . . ."

"Nonsense! I need a companion. Reggie has been trying to find a companion for me for two years! He runs about, doing my errands, exchanging my books at the library, buying me bonnets! I could use a willing young girl to help me. And to have such an intelligent lady as yourself to speak with, to read books with, to be my companion, I should enjoy above all. Think of it! If all goes adrift, come to me!" And she gave a decided nod of her white bonnet.

Valerie finally left, feeling she had two firm friends in them, Lady Darlington and Reggie. They did not question her, nor tell her crossly to behave herself. They treated her like an adult female with a mind of her own. It was a pleasant change from Malcolm, she thought crossly.

Valerie knew she loved her husband deeply, and no

one could take his place. She had worried over him, stayed awake nights nursing him, lain in his arms, met his passion with her own. No one could take his place with her. No one else could live in her heart. However, if he did not prove steadfast in his regard, nor show any signs of loving her, how could she remain? It would be horribly humiliating for her to bear his child and remain at home, while he ran about with women like Lady Deidre, or even the Cyprians that the women whispered about. Ladies of the night, dressed gaudily in the latest daring fashions from France, with breasts showing over the edges of their low-cut gowns, diamonds and other precious gems from their lovers decorating their ears, fingers and wrists. . . .

No, if Malcolm wanted such as them, she would not remain his wife! She would have to leave him. She would care for her child alone.

She worried about the child. What if she could not care for it? What if she became sick? Then she thought, gratefully, of Lady Darlington. That good woman would protect and shield her, and even perhaps let her secrete herself in the country. Lady Darlington had a country home to the north. She did not want Malcolm or his family to learn of the child. If he married Deidre or someone like her, *she* could provide him a child! Valerie would keep her own.

June was wearing on. The air in London seemed hot and stifling to Valerie. She longed as much as the earl to return to Arundel. However, she must make her decision before they removed to the country. She would wait, watch, and decide soon. She could not afford to wait until the child became obvious. And her waist continued to grow.

Valerie was quite ill one morning. Her maid tended to her carefully, put her back in bed after the bout of vomiting, and brought her hot plain tea.

Valerie sipped it gratefully and lay back in the pillows,

exhausted. There was another ball tonight, one of Malcolm's friends, which promised to be noisy, frivolous, daring, and long drawn-out. The countess did not plan to attend. But Deidre had been so anxious to go, saying, "All the world will be there, Malcolm!" and he had agreed and accepted the invitation for the three of them.

The tired girl wondered how she could manage it. She was really ill this morning, she was weary, she was worried about the child. All this jaunting about could not be good for the baby.

Glenda urged in a low worried voice, "Madam, do let me tell your mother-in-law about this! She should know. You ought to see a doctor soon, you know!"

"I know . . . but not yet. Not yet. Somehow I have a feeling this will come to a head soon, and I can decide." She stopped herself, as the older woman gazed down at her thoughtfully.

"How long do you think to conceal your condition?" asked Glenda. "It will soon be obvious even to your husband!"

Valerie knew she should rebuke her but was too upset to care. She closed her eyes and turned to the pillow. "No, I want to sleep. I don't want to think now."

She slept until late in the afternoon, unusual for her. Glenda came to her when she rang and helped her wash and dress in a loose-fitting straight-hanging gown of pale lilac muslin. The ribbons tied under her breasts, which were already becoming more full.

She went down for tea and was grateful to find the room empty but for the countess and the earl.

"You have been ill, my dear?" questioned the countess anxiously, and her father-in-law stood to draw a comfortable chair closer to the fire for her. There was a chill in the air, it was a gray, rainy London day that even June could produce.

"Just tired, I wanted to sleep late," evaded Valerie.

"I wish we had returned to the country or never left

it," grumbled Lord Arundel, reaching for his pipe. "Oh ... shall you mind the smoke, Valerie?"

"No, go ahead, papa," she said. "I do not mind it. Where ... where did Malcolm go?"

"Ah ... out in the carriage, I believe."

Valerie said no more, she figured Deidre was with him. She stretched out her lilac slippers to the blaze. Her ankles were slightly swollen, she noted. She would be heavier soon, and become unsightly. She wondered if Malcolm would be impatient with her and thought probably so. Her sober gaze rested on the pretty occasional table at her side, she picked up a little jade figurine of a horse and fondled it in her fingers. The cool green jade soothed her, she caressed it absently.

Malcolm and Deidre did not return until late. They dashed in. The others were already seated at the dinner table. Malcolm made their apologies. His cheeks glowed with the outdoor air, his brown-hazel eyes sparkled.

"Such a time! We have been racing in the park! I won three times running! The horses are magnificent. I thought I would tip out Deidre and she screamed and screamed!" He laughed down at the blonde girl, who was mussed, her bonnet askew, her blue eyes shining.

"Very amusing, I am sure," said the earl, an edge to his voice. "I suppose you won or lost immense sums on the outcome of the races?"

"Of course," said Malcolm, on the defensive. "Lord Maitland has a pair of grays, but they could not catch us! He was amazed, and offered at once to buy my blacks, but I said I would not sell."

Malcolm held Deidre's chair, she slipped into it, with an apologetic look at the countess. "Do forgive us, maman," she said softly. "We were having such a glorious time!"

"You will be too weary to attend the ball tonight," said the countess, with a drawl to her tone.

"Oh, no, never!" laughed Deidre. "I shall be dressed

and ready by ten, Malcolm dear! You are wearing your blue, are you not? I shall wear my blue gauze, then, and the sapphires you gave me!"

There was a brief silence. Even the stately footman serving them paused, as though sensing the unease. Valerie stared steadily at her plate, a sickness rising in her. Malcolm had given Deidre sapphires! They were close indeed! And Deidre had such confidence, her blue eyes were angelic, her manner at ease.

The action went on. The footman served the countess, then moved around the table with the fish course. Valerie shook her head at it. She was feeling more sick by the minute. Jealous? She was raging—and hurt.

Deidre chattered on—about the race, about what Lord Maitland had said on losing, about the dance that evening, what an amusing time they would have. Some were coming in costume with masks. If only they had thought, they could have worn masks also.

"We shall dance until morning," said Deidre confidently. "I know Lord Somervan, he will not allow the musicians to cease until all have gone home! We shall be very late tonight, Valerie!" And she laughed, her musical chiming laughter.

Valerie did not answer, she was struggling by then with a small portion of meat. She wished she had dined in her room, alone, with a tray of soup and bread. That she might have managed.

How could she ever get through the night? A dance in a warm, humid room, with five hundred guests jamming the floor, laughter, teasing, significant looks at Malcolm with Deidre. Reggie was not attending, he had told her he had no liking for that crowd. At the end of the meal, instead of going to the drawing room for coffee, Valerie retired to her room. She removed the dress with a sigh, and let Glenda clothe her in a loose wrapper. Then she lay down on the chaise longue in the sitting room. She let her gaze wander about it. How pretty it was, how charming, with the little touches of rose and gold. She enjoyed the golden box of her trinkets, a locket the earl had given her, the little ring of his mother, a ribbon she had worn at a dance the first time in London. Her jewels were locked up in another box in the dressing table. Here were the little inexpensive toys she enjoyed.

On the table near her was a small volume of poetry from Lady Darlington. Beside it a miniature of Malcolm when he was a small boy, given by his mother. The sober face looked out at her with such trusting eyes. Would his son look like that? Beside the miniature she had placed a tiny vase with a single white rose in it, one of the few from their garden. The jade vase set off the white rose beautifully.

She lay back with a sigh, thinking of the ordeal to come. Malcolm would be furious again.

Malcolm came to her room on the stroke of ten. He was elegant in his blue silk suit, a sapphire stick-pin in the immaculate intricate stock.

"What, not ready? The prompt wife not on time?" he asked sarcastically.

"I am not going, Malcolm," she said.

He gazed down at her. "Sick again, I suppose? Sick of my company, sick of my friends?"

"It has been close and rainy all the day," she said evenly, not rising. "I think we shall have a bad storm tonight. I prefer to remain inside."

Malcolm said not another word. Instead, he flung out of the room. This time he closed the door softly. What did that indicate, she wondered.

She heard Deidre's happy laughter, the sounds of the doors, the carriage rolling away. Glenda came to her presently and put her to bed tenderly, as though knowing how upset she was. Malcolm had not even cared enough tonight to argue!

It was probably the end, thought Valerie. She must prepare herself to leave.

She wakened restlessly in the night, several times. Humid air seemed to stifle her. Then later, a sharp crack wakened her, and the drumming of rain on the windows. She raised herself to see that a storm had indeed broken, thunder rolled over the city, lightning flashed again and again.

She listened, but heard nothing. It was past four, Malcolm must have come home and gone to bed without wakening her.

She slept again, not waking until morning. It was still raining, a dull, throbbing, ceaseless torrent that shut out all other sounds. But at least the air had cleared.

Glenda brought her tea in bed, then set out her clothes in an unusual silence. The older maid was not usually chatty, but she always had something to say, of the weather, or the events of the day. Now she was silent, her face serious and lined. Valerie rose cautiously, found she was not sick, and gratefully washed and dressed. The sickness phase was hopefully past, and she could be more normal for a time. Until . . .

"Will you have breakfast in your room, my lady?"

"No, I will go down. Is my lord up yet?"

Glenda shot her a strange look. "No . . . my lady. He is not."

"Oh, I suppose he must have been very late last night," said Valerie and went out and to the stairway. She made her way down cautiously. She was easily overbalanced these days, with the weight of the child growing in her.

She was in the lower hallway when the doorway was flung open. The butler hastened to the door, startled. Valerie stared.

Malcolm and Deidre were staggering in, both still in evening dress, covered with cloaks. Her bonnet was swinging from her hand. Their cheeks were flushed, mud covered their shoes and the hem of Deidre's glorious blue gauze gown. Deidre saw Valerie and began to laugh.

"Oh, dear . . . Malcolm . . . we are discovered! Your

outraged wife is up already! So much for secrecy! Oh dear, too . . . too . . . funny for words. Sh—shame on us! So—so late coming home. Ball too delicious to leave . . . oh, I'm falling . . ."

Valerie stood there stiffly, horrified. Coming home at this hour of the morning! Drunken, both of them, and laughing, stumbling, hanging to each other . . .

Malcolm looked at her stiff face and began to explain. "You shee . . . shee, Valerie . . . it's raining, it's real bad out . . . couldn't come . . . storm . . . stayed and stayed . . . had a glorious time . . . you sh-should ha' come with us . . . fun . . . lots of fun . . ."

The butler and a footman were holding up Deidre, who was inclined to sag between them. Malcolm tried to approach Valerie but stumbled. He looked puzzled.

"Legs . . . won't . . . won't hold up . . . funny . . ." he was saying.

The earl came out from the dining room, his face cold and outraged. "Enough! Go to your rooms! Malcolm, I shall speak to you later! Take him upstairs!"

Deidre was laughing drunkenly as the two servants helped her up the stairs. "Such fun . . . fun . . . fun . . ." she was saying, all the way up.

Malcolm seemed a little sobered but could not manage the steps alone. Another footman supported him up the staircase.

The earl came to where Valerie stood, frozen, against the door of the drawing room. "Come, my dear. We shall deal with this later. Come and have some hot tea." And gently, his arm about her shoulders, his worried gaze on her taut face, he led her to the dining room.

The countess was gazing anxiously at the door as they entered. "Was that not Malcolm's voice? Has he just returned from a morning ride, my dear?"

"No, from the ball of last night," said the earl, furiously. "But we will not speak of it now. I shall give him the edge of my tongue later. He acts like an irresponsible child, not a grown man! What a stupidity!"

Valerie sank into her chair. She shook her head numbly at the plate of eggs offered. The footman bent to pour out her tea. She waited until it had cooled a little, sipped it. Her heart felt as though it had icicles on it and would crack if she moved.

Malcolm, out all night with Deidre! Drunken and laughing, not caring . . . coming home at nine in the morning! For all the world to see—and not caring!

◇◇◇◇◇◇◇◇◇ *Chapter Fifteen* ◇◇◇◇◇◇◇◇◇

The earl scolded his son that evening, and Malcolm flung out of the house and was again gone much of the night. At least Deidre was not with him. She was ill, her maid said, and remained in her room.

The next day cleared somewhat. Sunshine broke through the clouds, and London shone with a newly washed look. Valerie went up to her sitting room after breakfast, to make out the menus. She did much of the house managing at the manor house. The countess seemed grateful to give it over to her.

She was scribbling away at the menus for a dinner the following week, when a light tap came at the door. It did not sound like Malcolm's rap. She called, "Come in, please!"

Lady Deidre opened the door, gazed in, entered, a

charming wistful smile on her face. She closed the door after her, glanced about.

"My dear Valerie, I must come to you. We must have a conversation. You do not mind that I interrupt your work?"

She was probably going to apologize for her behavior . . . then go right on with it, thought Valerie. She laid down the quill with a sigh, stood up, and gestured to a chair near the desk.

"Pray, be seated, Lady Deidre."

Deidre seated herself, with a graceful move of her blue muslin skirts. She looked younger today, sparkling, her blue eyes shining, her skin so creamy and fresh.

"I have been having long conversations with Malcolm," she began surprisingly. "Valerie, we must not continue to hurt him, must we?"

Valerie stared at her warily. This was a new attack.

Deidre continued. "He is miserable. I know he married you on . . . on impulse. He felt sorry for you. But he realizes you are an intellectual female, not like him! You two are no more like that chalk and cheese."

Valerie stiffened. It was what she herself had thought.

"He adores gaming, racing his horses, and you care nothing for those amusements. He loves to be out all the night. His father scolded him for it, but why should Malcolm not amuse himself? He works hard at home in the country. Does he not deserve a vacation?"

Valerie was still silent, waiting. Deidre gave a wary look to her, then continued. She wore a great sapphire on her hand, the one that Malcolm had given to her, along with a bracelet and earrings. That great ring somehow hurt Valerie. The blue sparkle was like Deidre's beautiful eyes.

"And you care nothing for him, he said so himself," continued Deidre earnestly. "He knows you feel contempt for him, it makes him furious! Just because he is different from you! But the situation grows worse and worse. It cannot continue."

"I agree with you there," said Valerie, drily.

"Ah, I am glad," said Deidre, with a little sigh. "You see, dear . . . this is so awkward! He wishes a divorce . . . to marry me. He realizes he made a sad mistake. He is, of course, willing to settle a sum of money on you, so that you may continue in the life you so enjoy. He would set you up in a London town house of your own, so that you might be comfortable. Divorce is not considered respectable. However, in these circumstances, when you and Malcolm are so obviously dissimilar . . . it will be understood and forgiven."

She went on, but all Valerie had heard were the words, "He wishes a divorce." Malcolm wished a divorce and was not man enough to come and ask her himself!

She felt hurt, vaguely, though a little relieved as well. She felt as though she had been suspended over a cliff for a long period of time, and had now dropped to the bottom, hurting herself, but at least the suspension was over.

"So, you do understand, my dear Valerie," Deidre was concluding, her blue eyes so serious, her hand reaching out pleadingly to Valerie. Her slim long fingers . . . with the blue sapphire on them . . .

"I . . . understand," said Valerie, though her mouth was so dry she could scarcely speak.

Deidre stood up, shook out her blue skirts, and smiled. "I am so much more suitable for him, you see, my dear," she said gently. "I understand *him*, we are alike. We are amused by the same things. We love to gamble, and ride, and race, and stay up until dawn. We shall have a marvelous marriage! He will be happy with me."

Valerie stood and showed her to the door.

When the door was shut, Valerie sank down into the nearest chair. Her wild gaze went about the room. She must leave this . . . all this . . . she must go . . . she must leave him. . . . He must not find out about the child now! She could not endure to remain married to him, if he felt this way!

But . . . stay . . . Deidre could be deceitful. Was she telling the truth? Did Malcolm truly wish a divorce? He had not said so! Indeed, he had seemed jealous of Valerie, whenever Reggie Darlington was about, or even the handsome explorer!

She must speak to him. But how could she? How bring up such a delicate topic? She must . . . she must . . .

She went over to the desk, sank down into the chair, and gazed at the papers blankly. The pretty Queen Anne table . . . she would miss that, she thought idiotically. And the jade elephant. And the ivory figurines that Malcolm had given her . . . she had left them at Arundel in the country. And the Shakespeare garden. And her beautiful bedroom, where he had come to her and held her.

Malcolm did not come home for lunch. Valerie went down early for tea, but no one had come down yet. She waited to order, sewing absently on the embroidered cushion. Should she take it with her? She had planned it to match the couch in Malcolm's small bedroom. But he would not want it now, not something she had made for him.

Still she went on, blindly pushing and drawing the needle in and out of the blue velvet cushion, with the gold leopard on it. Gold roses were in the four corners, the whole the insignia of the Arundel family. Malcolm had not even noticed what she was doing!

She heard his voice in the hallway and paused in her work. He would probably go up to his room. Then the footman opened the door to the drawing room, and Malcolm came in, looking weary, dusty, in his riding habit.

"Ah . . . good afternoon, Valerie." He shut the door quietly after himself. "I wanted to talk to you."

Her sensitive nerves caught the tremor in his voice.

"Yes, Malcolm," she said, setting down the work, and folding her hands, so they would not tremble.

Striding to the mantel to lean there, he said abruptly, "Lord Maitland and I are going away for a few days. There's a horse fair near his country seat. Fine horses. Thought I might pick up one or two."

It was so different from what she had thought he would say that she could only stare blankly at his handsome sullen face. He turned from her, and she saw only his broad back, his bent brown head, the muddy riding boots.

"Thought I would get away for a time," he said, as she did not speak. "Want to think things out."

"Malcolm," she said, braving herself. "Perhaps I had best say this. Do you . . . do you wish a divorce?"

He did not turn around, though he seemed to grow rigid. She meant to test him, she wished she could see his face. If Deidre had lied, she would know it in an instant.

"Yes," he said heavily. "I think . . . it might be best."

The shock was like a knife into her heart. She could not move nor speak. Her hands were locked tightly together. He went on speaking to the mantelpiece.

"We ain't at all alike. Everyone says so. You shine when you're with the smart ones, who read your articles . . . that you never even bothered to show to me. They say that you're very intelligent. Too intelligent for a slow-top like me! And I'm a rake, a gambler . . . that's what father says. I thought when we came to London that we'd go about together, I'd take you to plays, you would come with me on my amusements. But it ain't like that. You don't want anything to do with my friends . . . except Reggie Darlington!"

There was a sad bitterness in his tone, a finality that stunned her. He did want a divorce!

He swung about abruptly. "I'm going away for a few days. We'll talk about it when I get back. I want to do the right thing, Valerie."

He waited for her to speak. She could not. He flung himself from the room.

She heard him go out again, numbly. She picked up the

cushion, put in a few stitches, blindly. She must go, she must leave him, she thought. And soon. She could not endure another such conversation, hearing him tell her he wanted a divorce. She could not bear to hear of his arrangements for her . . . a town house, money.

The baby! He might want the baby! She must leave before he learned of it, or he might want to take it from her!

Somehow she got through the evening. Malcolm was absent, Deidre did not seem to mind, her face smooth as cream and complacent.

She slept little that night. She heard Malcolm later in the morning, in his rooms, packing, then leaving. He did not come to say farewell, he just departed.

She waited an hour, then went to find the countess. She found her and the earl in the drawing room, alone, the earl smoking fiercely on his pipe, the countess at her own embroidery. They both looked at her anxiously when she entered.

Her pride was up, however, she did not want to hurt them. They had been kind and good to her.

She remained standing. "I . . . I have come to say farewell to you," she said, faltering a little.

They stared.

"I . . . I must leave. Malcolm wishes a divorce. We have come to the parting of our ways. I . . . I beg your forgiveness for hurting you."

"Good heavens," breathed the countess. "My dear, you must not let a silly squabble cause you . . ."

"No, it is not that," said Valerie, clearing her throat. "Lady Deidre is going to marry Malcolm as soon as he is free. She told me herself, I could have guessed it. She said that they . . . they are much alike, he wishes the divorce to marry her."

The parents of Malcolm stared at her as though she had taken leave of her senses. The face of the countess had turned a pearly white, as though she would faint.

"Nonsense!" bellowed the earl suddenly. "She is a foolish giddy piece! He could not prefer her over you!"

"He does. You have seen it," said Valerie, wincing at the bluntness. "He prefers her company, he loves her. I . . . I hope all will go well with them. However, I must leave, so that the . . . the divorce will go through smoothly for . . . for them."

The countess laid her white hand on her heart. "It is madness!" she breathed. "Deidre . . . she adored Eustace! She cannot love Malcolm . . . he thinks of her as a sister! No, no. You must wait and speak with Malcolm . . . straighten this out."

"I spoke with Malcolm yesterday. I asked if he wished a divorce. He said, yes. He wishes one . . . I cannot remain."

"Now, now, no hasty movements!" the earl said anxiously, gruffly. He came over to her, put his great arm about her. "You are our daughter, you know! Can't get along without you!"

"M-Malcolm can," she said, and put her hands to her face. She could not endure much more of this. "I . . . I have sent a note to Reggie Darlington, he will come for me in an hour. I will pack and be gone . . ."

"You're going to Reggie?" growled the earl furiously. "That young puppy! I'll have a word . . ."

"No, no, he will but take me to his Aunt Darlington!" Valerie hastened to reassure him. "She has already spoken to me about becoming her companion. You know, she has broken her leg. I will read to her, converse with her. When she is better, we can go about together. She may retire to the country this summer," she said bravely, thinking of her child due in November.

"A paid companion!" The earl exchanged eloquent looks with his wife of many years. "This is madness! Wait and talk with Malcolm! You have no need to make your own way in the world! You are married to him! Wait and straighten all this out!"

"I cannot believe this," said the countess, her mouth quivering. "Lady Deidre! She has remained with us, loved me like her own mother . . . and mourned Eustace . . . what madness . . . she cannot mean . . . But Malcolm gave her the sapphires. I cannot believe he is serious about her . . . but such a gift . . ."

"I must go and pack," said Valerie. She gently put the earl's arm from her. She gave them both a quivering smile. "Goodbye . . . thank you for all your goodness to me. I am more grateful than I can tell."

And she fled, afraid she would break down. She went up to her pretty sitting room for the last time. She rang for Glenda, who then began to take out the items Valerie would take with her.

Impassively she obeyed orders, got a footman to bring down two trunks and several valises.

Valerie left her elaborate ballgowns. She would not want them again. She left behind the elegant bonnets, with the silk ribbons. They were not fitting or suitable for a paid companion.

She packed the simple muslins, of white and blue and lilac and rose. She set out the little ivory puppy, which Malcolm had given her, and the jade horse. She would take those. She hesitated over the jewels. Then she finally took only the amethysts. She could not bear to leave them, besides they were not the type to appeal to Deidre. No one would miss them. She would discard all those false vanities, the hair curlers, the delicate satin slippers with high heels, the flirtatious fans, the gauze-covered dance dresses.

However, she must have the amethysts. The love-gift. Her mouth trembled. She had been foolish to hope and dream, but all young things were foolish, she more than most. Her common sense should have told her Malcolm could not love her, not a sedate, serious-minded female who did not care so much for balls or racing.

Oh, it might have been . . . if she had been different, if

she could have matched his light-heartedness and fooling about . . . if she could have endured to remain home while he danced attendance on one woman after another . . . if she could have sunk her pride . . .

"That is all, then, Glenda," she said abruptly. She had heard the carriage, Reggie Darlington had come for her. She gave one last look about the room. The footmen came, picked up her trunks, and carried them down the gracious winding stairs.

She followed, saw Reggie in the hallway. He looked serious, even alarmed. The earl had come out, was talking sternly to him.

"Marriage?" Reggie was saying. "Lord, no! I've asked for the hand of Lady Mary Greenley, but her papa says she is too young, only seventeen, and I must wait another year. Lord, lord, what a coil this is!"

The earl looked rather relieved, kissed Valerie, and bade her, "Be a good girl. You've not heard the last of this! Wait till Malcolm comes home! I shall give him the hiding of his life!"

Valerie shook her head. "No, no, papa . . . don't. It is not Malcolm's fault if he cannot love me. One does not ask to whom one gives a heart." She managed a tremulous smile. "Pray . . . wish him well, for me. I did not ever mean to hurt him."

Reggie escorted her out to the carriage. Behind her came Glenda, formidable in black bonnet and cloak. Valerie gazed at her maid, aghast.

"But Glenda . . . you cannot come . . . a paid companion does not have a maid of her own . . ."

The maid frowned. "In your condition, my lady?" she asked, in a low scolding affectionate tone. "I should never forgive myself if I let ye go alone!"

And firmly she got into the carriage with them. So off they went. The earl gazed after them mournfully, and Valerie's last sight was of his gray head, his sturdy arm waving in farewell.

Lady Darlington welcomed her with enthusiasm and tact. She did not question her. She sent her up to a very pretty sitting room and bedroom of her own, which Valerie was privately convinced must be a guest suite. Glenda looked satisfied, and began briskly unpacking at once. A tray of tea was sent up to them.

"Oh, she is treating me like a friend," murmured Valerie. "Oh, dear, I must explain . . . I do mean to work for my living!"

"And when the baby comes, what then?" demanded Glenda, rather fiercely for such a mild woman.

"I shall keep on working, Glenda!"

Glenda made a rude sound and went on unpacking. She set out tenderly the little ivory puppy, the jade horse, the miniature of Malcolm as a boy.

"Oh, I did not know you had packed this!" cried Valerie, picking up the oval miniature and gazing at it tenderly. "I meant to leave it, to return it to . . . to his mother."

She pressed the little picture to her lips, tenderly, then set it down with a sigh.

"I must send it back," she muttered. Glenda shook her head.

"You'll have your tea and get some rest, my lady. I don't know what will become of you if you don't get off your feet. Look at them, all swollen now."

She fussed over Valerie, persuaded her to lie down for a time and sleep. Presently Valerie, much rested and refreshed, changed to a white muslin gown with blue ribbons, and went down to thank her hostess for her kindness.

She found Lady Darlington holding court in the drawing room, five of her cronies with her. They stared curiously at her, but were too polite to question her. The talk was of a new novel by a very pretty lady of quality. Was it based on her real amours? Or were they made up? A lively topic indeed.

She and Lady Darlington were alone for dinner, and it was served on trays in the drawing room.

"I shall not question you, my dear," said Lady Darlington, leaning back wearily into her cushions. "You are too wrought, and I too weary. Only let me say I am pleased to have your companionship. Reggie is often out, and I am a lonely old woman. I am pleased to have you here. We shall settle the details later."

"You are too good, too kind."

"No tears, or I shall be angry!" said the lady sharply. "Cannot endure weeping. Makes me weep myself. Would you read to me for a time?"

"Gladly, Lady Darlington." Valerie found the daily gazettes, read to her. The articles about the Peninsular War made her think of Malcolm and the worry she had felt while he was there. The articles about the fine horses at a recent race made her think again of Malcolm. There was a squib about a recent ball . . . and again Malcolm came to her mind.

Would there ever come a day when she would not think of him and long that matters might have been different between them?

Reading helped her through the evening, and they both retired early. The next day was much the same. Lady Darlington rose early, read her correspondence. Valerie offered to write letters for her, the offer was promptly accepted. There was tea, with two guests. Over luncheon, Reggie entertained them with the account of some friends he had met at his club, and how they had gambled over the outcome of the Peninsular War. The stock exchange, he said, went up and down according to the way folks thought the war was going. He was amusing, charming, and made them laugh.

In the afternoon, some friends of Lady Darlington called on her once more, remained for tea, gossiped, planned a lecture by an eminent doctor who told of ways to keep old age from creeping up on one. As these ladies were all in the sunny side of fifty and sixty and seventy, they were keenly interested. It all seemed a little vague and dry to Valerie. Seventy seemed so far off. What if she thought of Malcolm all those years, from twenty-one to seventy-one?

She smiled, made herself useful pouring tea, made attentive sounds when spoken to, and let her mind drift on and on . . . about Malcolm. When would he come home? What would he say when he found her gone? Would he be relieved . . . or a little angry? Would she see him again? She could not risk that for long. She must remove to the country and hide from everyone, as the child became more obvious in her.

The thought of Malcolm calmly filing for divorce and planning to marry Deidre . . . that was so painful she could not bear to think of it. Not yet. Not yet.

∞∞∞∞∞∞∞∞ Chapter Sixteen ∞∞∞∞∞∞∞∞

The next day crawled past and the next. Valerie wondered if she could ever endure the loneliness, she was shocked to find how much she missed Malcolm. She had not thought she was with him much. However, they had often met at breakfast, or tea, or attended a ball together.

And now she did not see him, or hear his voice, or worry about him when he was out to all hours of the night. He might be out riding in the rain, and she would stand at the window and gaze out, and wonder where he was. The days and nights seemed blank and empty, in spite of Lady Darlington's real kindness, her many guests, the reading and writing of letters and gazettes.

She tried to work on her articles, but could not. Her mind would not concentrate, she was too unhappy. Also, she had not yet told Lady Darlington about the child. Dared she suggest to an employer that she wished to leave London? All sorts of problems had come up. She had no money, how could she even pay for her maid?

She was sitting at the desk in Lady Darlington's study one morning, writing letters to the guests who were invited to a dinner. The good lady was lying in state in her drawing room, receiving the first of her visitors for the day. When the door opened, Valerie thought it might be the footman, come to bid her to join them and pour tea.

Instead Malcolm came in, grim, haggard, his hair brushed carelessly across his forehead. His boots were immaculate, his blue suit coat fit neatly across his broad shoulders, he was wearing a fine stock in an elaborate fold. Yet somehow he gave the impression of wild-eyed disarray, as though his mind was distracted.

"Valerie!" He shut the door carefully after him and strode across to her. "What is the meaning of this? I returned home at midnight, to find you had fled!"

"Did . . . did you buy any horses?" she asked idiotically.

He stared. "Oh, two, a stallion, and a fine mare for you. You really must learn to ride, you know," he said, then recollected himself. "But you must return home! You cannot marry Reggie! He ain't right for you! What do you mean, running off with him?"

"I didn't. I have taken a post as companion to Lady Darlington," she explained patiently. "Didn't your parents explain anything?"

"Haven't talked much to them. Came right off after you. Mater said you had some bee in your bonnet, and we had better get things straightened out. Whatever did you mean, running off as soon as my back was turned?"

She felt tearful, bewildered all at once. "But Deidre said . . . and you left . . ."

Malcolm was staring down at her, looking rather large and grim, for all his slenderness. "What d'ya want to marry Reggie for? He's as slow-top as I am! If you want to marry an intellectual . . ."

"I never want to marry anyone!" she burst out, untruthfully. "I hate marriage! I shall live as a . . . a free female, and make my own living!"

"You're insane, you're ready for a madhouse," said Malcolm and picked her up out of the chair and began to kiss her fiercely. "Crazy female . . . I should never turn my back . . . you think of the wildest things . . . keep you under my thumb, that's what papa said . . . right about it . . . I'll keep you right there, under my eye . . . never let you go. . . ."

His kisses sent fire through her body, cold for so long. She clung to him weakly, her hands on his hard shoulders, loving the feel of the bone and sinew under his beautiful blue silk coat. He was here, kissing her, ordering her about, and she loved it!

He pressed his mouth slowly to hers, and her eyes closed. She loved the feel of his warm sensuous mouth, the hardness of his arms shut tightly about her, the heat of his body against hers.

"I adore you," he said thickly. "I'm mad about you. I'll never let you go! How could you leave me? I'm furious with you . . . ought to beat you . . . kiss you to death . . ."

"Oh, Malcolm!" she breathed, delighted, so relieved she wanted to cry.

Clasping her close, he drew back enough to look down into her dazed, bemused face, and said, "Look here, Valerie. You come back, return, and I'll see that you have everything you want. It's a solemn promise. Won't have to work, do nothing you don't want. Go to a ball if you want, stay home if you want. Don't have to ride in the phaeton since it scares you . . ."

"It doesn't! You never asked me to ride . . . you always took Deidre . . ." She swallowed on the words, remembering her unhappiness. "Deidre said . . . you didn't want . . . you never wanted . . ."

He led her firmly to the nearby sofa, and drew her down with him. "Got to get this worked out," he said. "Now, start from the beginning. Why did you leave?"

"That's not the beginning, it's the end!"

"Then start where you will. Why have you been so cold and nasty to me? Don't you like me even a little?" He looked so anxious, so unhappy, that her hands cupped his face, and she said,

"Malcolm, I love you so much. Too much to hurt you. If you want Deidre . . . to marry her . . . we'll get a divorce."

"You're mad," he said, with conviction. "I don't love Deidre. Like her like a sister. She's fun to run about with. Drives me bats, begging for jewelry and all. Tears in her eyes, and saying how Eustace would have gotten it for her . . . that's why I got her the sapphires, Valerie, really! Papa said I was foolish, but she went on and on about them."

"Deidre said," she said very slowly, trying to get it clear herself. Malcolm's look was so clear, his hazel eyes so honest and direct. "Deidre said you wanted a divorce . . . to marry her. That you loved each other, and I was not . . . not your sort."

"Wouldn't marry her in a thousand females," said Malcolm, with a frown. "Drive one mad in a short time. Always wanting more things. Wears me out with running around from morning to all night. Too fuzzy in the top if you ask me! Spoiled by her mother, all right. Never could see what Eustace liked in her. Dazzled by her looks, I expect. Though at the last, I think he got tired of her. Thought so from his letters."

Valerie stared at him. Could he mean it? That Deidre bored him? Exhausted him, exasperated him? And Eustace had not been the devoted fiancé he had seemed, that he had begun to see through Deidre?

"Come on, Valerie, stop making excuses. Why did you go? Oh, never mind that," he added hastily. "Just say you'll come back, and it'll all be the same again, and I'll see that you have everything you want. We can live in London all the season if you like, and I'll go to lectures with you, sit through anything! I really didn't mind the explorer chap, thought he was fine except he kept staring at you and kissing your hand! But you can let anyone kiss your hand, just so you don't love 'em. What about it, Valerie?"

His arm was about her waist, she was snugly against his firm shoulder, his voice was coaxing in her ear, his free hand stroked up and down her bare arm. She could not help it, she burst into tears.

"Oh, I say, Valerie, it isn't so bad as that!" he murmured, worriedly, pressing her fingers, kissing her cheek. "Don't cry, it tears me apart, darling! I love you, Valerie. You won't cry any more, will you?"

"I . . . I th-thought . . . you di-didn't want me," she sobbed.

"Not want . . . now, Valerie, you know better than that. Who wrote me all those wonderful letters that kept up my spirits all the time? Who nursed me night and day, for weeks and months, when she was so tired she looked ready to break in two? Who was so sweet in bed, and so lovely. . . ?" he went on whispering sweet things to her, kissing her ear and her wet cheeks.

"I do love you," she confessed at last. "I . . . I didn't think . . . you were so cold . . . and you preferred Deidre . . ."

"Did not—only you were cold to me," he said. "Not

even wanting me in your bed!" He looked down at her reproachfully.

"I . . . I was ill, Malcolm. I mean . . . with the baby . . ."

"Baby?" He looked stunned. "What are you talking about?"

She gulped. "I'm going . . . going to have a baby . . . in November, Malcolm. I was sick at my stomach, and I couldn't let you . . . I mean . . . oh, dear," and she began to cry again.

She caught her breath when he drew her tenderly to him. "You foolish idiot," he said, with great tenderness, holding her carefully. "Not telling me about such a wonderful thing. You're going to have my baby! Oh, Lord, what a marvel! A baby! All our own! My God, I'm insane, I can't believe it! Tell me again!"

She told him again, and he beamed, as though he were already a proud father. A baby, he kept saying over and over.

Then abruptly he was anxious. "Did you say you was sick? Valerie! Have you had a doctor? What if you're too sick? I mean, does mama know? She never said a word—"

"I didn't tell them," she confessed. "I didn't tell anyone. Glenda guessed, she said she thought I should tell you, but I just couldn't . . . not when I thought you and Deidre . . ."

"You mean, you'd ha' kept the baby from me? Valerie!" He looked so hurt that she had to kiss him again.

Someone tapped at the door, rather quietly. At the third tap, Malcolm finally called, "Come in if you must!"

Reggie opened the door and peered around it. When he saw them sitting together very closely on the couch, and Malcolm wiping Valerie's eyes, he looked so relieved and happy that Valerie had to smile through her tears.

"I say, all right now?" he hissed, as though someone

were ill. "Aunt sent me to find out if you was fighting or making up! What shall I say?"

"Tell her we're making up, and I'm taking her right home," said Malcolm with decision.

Malcolm sent for Valerie's cloak and bonnet, told Glenda to pack up and follow them, and took Valerie home. He had the closed barouche, all grand and comfortable, with the crest on the door. Valerie was glad of it, she felt all weepy-eyed, and plain. However, he did not let her go up to her room when they got home.

He had been thinking, and his face was serious. He sent for his parents, and they came to the drawing room.

The countess kissed Valerie, and the earl put his arm about her gently and gave her a hug. "Knew you had to come back," said the earl. "We cannot do without you!"

"She's going to have a baby in November," announced Malcolm, with great satisfaction. "We'll have to take great care of her!"

There was much exclamation and surprise, a joyful phrase from the earl, "Just what I wanted!"

"What I want to know is," said Malcolm, "why Deidre is staying on? She's making trouble, saying all those things to Valerie, and hanging on us. What shall we do about it, mama? Do you wish her to remain?"

"No, indeed not," said the countess, with unusual firmness. "I cannot understand the child, trying to wreck Valerie and Malcolm's marriage! Telling dear Valerie she was going to marry Malcolm herself! I'll send her home to her mother with a note!"

Valerie could not help feeling immense relief. Deidre was sent for and talked to in the countess's private sitting room. She came out with swollen red eyes and a sullen pout to her red mouth. Her clothing was packed in several immense trunks and valises, and any number of hat boxes. A maid was dispatched with her, and two grooms, in two carriages, so that her mother would not have any cause to be angry with their treatment of her daughter.

At the same time, the countess sent a very firm letter to Lady Ramsey, stating that the girl had tried to make trouble in her son's marriage, and she would not be willing to receive Lady Deidre in her home again. She regretted very much the necessity of informing Lady Ramsey that her daughter had behaved in such a foolish and troublesome way and recommended that the good lady arrange a practical marriage for the girl and settle her down.

The earl was frankly pleased to have her gone. He bluntly preferred Valerie and had all along. Once Lady Deidre was out of the house, everything seemed so much more peaceful, the earl declared.

Malcolm had come to the stage of fussing around Valerie, stuffing cushions behind her back, and inquiring whether to send for the doctor. They did send for a doctor, but Valerie decided she would rather have the doctor near Arundel to attend her.

So they decided to go home, to the country. London had lost its blatant attractions for them all.

Her one remaining worry was answered after they had gone home. She had worried that Malcolm might be secretly dissatisfied with the decision to return to the country, that he might long for London and his gaming companions.

They were walking in the garden on a fine July day. Valerie loved to walk there, in her Shakespeare garden, and admire the round plots of roses and phlox, the charming small pansies and heartsease, the purple flags and stately white lilies with yellow hearts. The herbs gave forth their sweet scents, especially in the evening as the air cooled.

Malcolm laid a cloak about her shoulders. "You must not be chilled, my dear," he said tenderly.

"I am fine, thank you, love," she said, happily. He took her hand and put it in his arm, and they strolled along the garden paths as the sun sank slowly, and a deeper blue filled the sky.

"How lovely is the country," said Malcolm. "How much prettier than London! The smoke and the grime grow worse every year."

"Do you not miss the excitement and your friends?" she asked, with seeming casualness.

"No, not much," he said. "Oh, I'd be glad to have a couple of the fellows down. Did you know Lord Maitland is finally going to marry? We are invited to the wedding, but I wrote and said we were going to have more excitement down here in November, with the baby coming! I invited them to come in the New Year, he and his bride. That all right with you?"

"That is lovely," she said contentedly. "I had a letter from Lady Darlington. She has hired a fine companion, an older lady who is a widow, and most intelligent. I am so pleased for her. Her leg is much better. She asked also to come some time when we could receive her."

"Just so you don't ask that explorer chap," said Malcolm, with a laugh. "I think I was more jealous of him than all the others together."

She squeezed his hand softly. "You have no need to be jealous of anyone, Malcolm. I love you dearly."

"You're the best wife I could have ever found," he said, with vast contentment. "Thing is, I can't see why you settled for me! I don't even understand that thing you wrote the other day."

"Yes, you did, after I explained it! I should write it more clearly," she said, frowning a little.

"I'm proud of you. All those things in the magazines. Do you know, the vicar's wife said you was the most intellectual female she has ever met? And a nice woman also!"

He laughed a little, happily, then bent and plucked a fine yellow rose to tuck into her hair. He kissed her as he did so, and smiled into her eyes. "You're prettier all the time," he whispered.

"Oh, and I'm getting so big . . ." she murmured in protest, blushing at his look.

"Father was talking about names the other day. I wondered if we might name him for papa, if it's a boy, and for Louis. He's such a good soul."

"That would be lovely."

"Or if she is a girl," said Malcolm, absorbed in his thoughts. "We might name her for Lady Darlington. I think she would be most pleased. What do you think?"

"I think you are the most considerate man in the world!"

"Oh, I like that, I like that," he said, paused, and kissed her on her cheek, then on her mouth, in one of his slow sensuous warm kisses that thrilled her from her head to her toes.

"Are you happy, darling?" he whispered, when they walked on slowly.

"The happiest woman in the world!"

"I mean to keep you that way," he promised.

She smiled, and leaned her head on his shoulder as they paced the garden slowly. The flowers were fragrant, the air cool and sweet after the warmth of the day. How happy she was! With the man she adored so thoughtful of her, so loving and happy with her. And the baby to come. She would have the best of two worlds, to be a happy wife and mother.

And Malcolm had at last shown interest in her articles and her stories. He approved of her continuing her work and praised her efforts. She would have the joy of continuing her work as an intelligent, educated female. And yet she would have Malcolm, and her family as well.

The fingers of her one hand folded over her other

hand, to caress gently the heart-shaped amethyst ring. The symbol of steadfastness in love, a true symbol now of their marriage. She would work hard—to make sure the meaning would always be true for them.